The Making of Miss M

"I inhaled it."
—Lisa Elser

"A steamy read from page one. Smart, funny and hot! Evie Vane delivers a page turner with real heart."

—Dee Rochelle

"Not just a lively and engaging read but also celebrates unconventional relationships and how they can bring more joy than trying to fit the standard mold of conventional ones."

—Eri Kardos, author of the bestselling *Relationship Agreements* and International Relationship Coach

"Corsets, paddles, and latex catsuits, and yet so relatable. It's an erotic awakening at turns both heartfelt and wickedly funny."

Howard Lovejoy

"If you ever wondered what *50 Shades* would have been like if it had been written by a woman who was actually *experienced in and empowered by* kinky romance, this book will inspire you. Through her witty, entertaining style and commentary, Evie Vane brings much more than you'd expect to this story of Melanie's passionate self-discovery."

—Danarama, Kink University Director and Co-Founder of Two Knotty Boys

"Defies expectations…a welcome departure from the BDSM erotica published in the past decade. Evie Vane's lean, chic, confident writing offers pleasure and inspiration for the reader's own journey for fulfillment in every aspect of life, sexual and otherwise."

—Linda Kim

"Pre-tested on women readers of all persuasions—to the shrieks of laughter, growls of anger, and exclamations of, 'That's exactly how I feel!' Pick any page, you'll know Ms. Vane is Much Woman, and knows the score."

—Keith Korman, author of *Secret Dreams*, *End Time*, *Eden: the Animals' Parable*, and other novels

Also by Evie Vane

BETTER BONDAGE FOR EVERY BODY

THE LITTLE GUIDE TO GETTING TIED UP

The Making of Miss M

A DESPERATE HOUSEWIFE DITCHES
TRADITION FOR KINKY ROMANCE,
PROVOCATIVE THRILLS—
AND SUCCESS ON HER OWN TERMS

by Evie Vane

WANTON PRESS
San Francisco

Wanton Press
PO Box 210739
San Francisco CA 94121

Manufactured in the United States of America

ISBN 978-0-9998276-3-5

This is a work of fiction. Names, characters, places, and incidents are the product of the author's imagination or are used fictitiously, and any resemblance to actual people (living or dead), locales, or events is entirely coincidental.

For all the single mothers

"Live where you fear to live.
Destroy your reputation.
Be notorious."

—RUMI

Contents

The Making of Miss M

Prelude

First Rule of Dominatrix Club

MELANIE MERRIWEATHER contemplated the naked ass draped over her dining room chair, stroking it lightly. Hmm, what to do? A spanking, perhaps—nice and reliable. Maybe a paddling, as a press-on nail going rogue in the crack simply wouldn't do. Really she wanted to whack the guy's butt with a frying pan, the ridiculously expensive one Dan had given her for Christmas. Alas, she had already hurled the pan into the outdoor trash bin, ignoring the bin sticker proclaiming GOES TO LANDFILL! RECYCLE IF POSSIBLE. A soda can had more recycling potential than her marriage to Dan now.

The client scratched his butt cheek. Melanie halted midstroke. "Did I say you could scratch?" Dropping each word like an ice chip into a crystal goblet. *Maybe I should tie his hands,* she thought. *Decisions, decisions.* He would pay for making her think so hard—and not just the $150 an hour.

But aha! He had just provided the perfect reason to punish him. Gotta love small favors. Melanie extracted a bamboo cane from the lineup on the polished mahogany dining table, site of so many lovingly prepared family meals, and swiftly struck his rear end. Tingles dancing along her arm. Yum. A good caning tasted even better than her legendary beef bourguignon.

"No, no you didn't. I'm s-s-sorry, Miss." The words a mumble, beads of sweat glistening along his spine. Melanie immediately opted for a set change away from the dining chairs. First rule of dominatrix club: no sweat, blood, or cum stains on the ivory damask upholstery.

Down came the cane on his derriere again. Then she scooped his shirt off the floor with it, a bored highway worker picking up trash. "Wipe yourself up," she ordered. "And if you stained my chair, you'll regret it. That chair cost more than you make in a week."

The client quickly slid off the chair onto all fours, a hand darting out for the dangling shirt. No unsightly splotches on the chair fabric, whew. But how dare he make her worry about upholstery stains! She skewered his naked back with the heel of her scarlet stiletto. Pushed down into the flabby white flesh until his chest was flat on the floor. His blotchy, sweaty face sinking into the swirls of plush carpeting. The carpeting, thankfully, was stain-resistant.

Near-disaster notwithstanding, pleasure bubbled up inside Melanie. Sure, the client's groveling was pathetic. His paunch, pitiable. But gratitude, maybe even tender affection, had entered the ring of her feelings too. The scene's script was writing itself, but she'd happily take the credit. It was hard enough just balancing on the carpet in stilettos.

"Sorry...what?" Another cane stroke. Another thick red line. Now this was accomplishment. Better than earning compliments on her bake-sale brownies or finding the perfect Jimmy Choos for a new dress. Better even than selling the most raffle tickets for her son Sammy's preschool fundraiser. This was power! She owned the control, no doubt about it. She was not someone you would give a *frying pan* to for Christmas, for fuck's sake. Not if you knew what was good for you. Moisture surged in the soft spot between her legs.

"I'm so sorry...Miss."

"Damn right you're sorry." She made her voice low and mean—sharp, to match the heels and nails. Suppressing the pleasure. "You're a sorry, pathetic, sniveling little boy. But you're not half as sorry as you're going to be when I'm finished with you. Lift your head up." Facial checks were important to read how much he could take. Heaven forbid he had a heart attack—her red latex catsuit was meant for private dominatrix sessions, not the ER.

His eyes darted to meet her gaze. She saw trepidation, excitement. Reverence too. *We have a winner!* Melanie bent over. Nuzzled his damp cheek—the one on his face—enjoying her own growing wetness. He had just made another perfect infraction. Infractions and wetness: sweeter than cake and ice cream.

Back went the cane in its precise spot on the table. Out came a smooth leather paddle. "Did I say"—*thwack*—"you could"—*thwack*—"look me in the eyes?" *Thwack thwack thwack.* Electricity crackled through her veins.

"No, Miss. I'm sorry, Miss." His ass glowed a fiery red now, riddled with lines and a purple blotch that would surely bruise. Legs quivering. Time for a break. *Can't have the clients going away unhappy,* Melanie thought. *Bruised, choked, beaten, sure. Unhappy, no.*

"For God's sake, stop blathering. 'Sorry' isn't good enough. I'm sick of hearing your 'sorry's." Dan had never said he was sorry, the bastard. Not when she cried about that stupid frying pan, her face as crumpled as the pink cashmere scarf blotting her tears. Not when he stood her up for their anniversary dinner, the waiter serving up pity and condescension with the chardonnay. Not when he cheated on her with that *waitress,* the one with breasts like unripe cantaloupes because she had never nursed a child the way Melanie had nursed Sammy—the son she *had borne* him, for fuck's sake. And not when he finally left her, taking that soup-slinging whore with him. Leaving only a terse note on the kitchen table and his dirty laundry still in the hamper.

"But don't you worry..." Melanie refocused on the present, shoving the hurtful memories back into the shadows. This was her moment now. "I'm going to give you some help not talking, and the last words I want to hear out of your mouth are 'thank you' for how nice I'm being, even though you don't deserve it." She ground a spiky stiletto heel into his doughy ass for emphasis.

"Th-thank you, Miss." A worshipful whisper, the sweetest music. Time for his reward. Melanie reached around his head and tucked a ball gag in his mouth, pulling the strap's buckle tight. Took her sweet time selecting a dildo from the brand-new rainbow assortment. Good things come to those who wait.

"Purrrrple silicone, purrrrfect," Melanie purred in her crimson catsuit. She dangled the extra-large dildo in front of his eyes, noting with satisfaction the anticipation and fear. At last she allowed him a glimpse of her Cheshire grin, as she reached for the lube.

Melanie would make him suffer, oh yes. But she would never let him—or anyone else—see the pain and suffering that had led her to this moment.

Part 1

MELANIE MERRIWEATHER

Chapter 1

"Just Let Me Swap This Apron for a Bikini"

(SIX YEARS EARLIER)

MELANIE WANTED to be Homemaker Barbie so bad it hurt. She dreamed of cherubic children tumbling happily around her feet, their color-coordinated designer outfits as sweet as their smiles. Friends pulling up to the mansion in their BMWs, toting Dom Perignon along with their own perfectly attired little angels, ready for a dip in the sparkling turquoise pool. "Just let me swap this apron for a bikini!" she'd call out gaily. Multiple pregnancies would have had no effect on her waistline, of course. And Ken by her side, lean and gorgeous as well—the only thing fat about her dream Ken was his wallet.

(In real life, this is when Melanie would pull out pen and paper to list her goals for the umpteenth time: 1. LOSE 10 POUNDS—GO TO GYM ALREADY!!! 2. MAKE MORE $$$ OR FIND RICH HUSBAND. 3. STOP CHEWING OFF FINGERNAILS. Number three rotated between the fingernails, learning French, and taking pole dancing lessons.)

Then back to conjuring the Melanie Dreamhouse. No gaudy, ornate pink palace bedecked with crystals for her. No, a sprawling modernist marvel with endless glass walls and glossy white lacquered surfaces and designer everything! Kate Spade china, Frette linens, a custom walk-in closet for the best of Prada and Gucci and Christian Louboutin. Agent Provocateur lingerie leaving no room for granny panties in the drawers, because behind every straying Ken is a Barbie who let herself go.

(In real life, this is where Melanie would beat herself up over her own woefully small apartment, furnished with hand-me-downs and thrift-store finds, arranged to hopefully look intentionally eclectic rather than merely cheap. And would lament her outlet-store clothes, crammed in next to the Swiffer in the one tiny closet.)

When Melanie had her Dreamhouse, along with Ken and the passel of beautiful doll babies who loved her more than anything, she would finally know that she was good. That she was actually worth the space she took up on the earth, and not just a sorry excuse. That she *mattered*.

Melanie's modern Dreamhouse could not be more unlike the one she had grown up in, a four-bedroom English Tudor Revival in the tony San Francisco suburb of Hillsborough, where she now sat steeling herself for dinner with her parents and sister. Every Sunday she dutifully trekked down here from her apartment in the city, pretending to enjoy the divine meal her mother had slaved over. Slave compensation for the wives in wealthy Hillsborough: slender diamond tennis bracelets and well-padded IRAs.

Aside from its pretentiously stuffy style, the home in which her parents deftly pretended to still like each other suffered from a faulty foundation: a slab of pretense topped by spiteful one-up-manship. The Melanie Dreamhouse would be pure and transparent in its white gloss and glass, leaving no place for hidden agendas and veiled insults like the ones lurking in her parents' home. And everyone would get pleasantly tipsy on champagne now and then instead of regularly swallowing their resentment with scotch and sauvignon blanc.

"So are you seeing anyone special?" Melanie's mother, Victoria—
never Vic or Vicky—didn't waste time any more than she wasted
compliments. She, Melanie, dad Tom, and sister Harper had just
pulled the tapestry-covered chairs up to the heirloom table, settling
creamy cloth napkins on their laps and reaching for silver platters
and tureens. Melanie marveled, as always, at how much effort her
mother had put into this dinner for just the four of them. It seemed
so wasteful, with all those babies starving in Ethiopia. Or was it
Rwanda? (*Gawd, I'm so ignorant,* Melanie thought. *Must learn more
about worldly affairs.*)

"I'm sure Melanie will tell us when that happens," Tom
said, his nonconfrontational tone so well-practiced, it appeared
effortless. His soothing smile courtesy of Glenlivet French Oak
Reserve. "She's only 26. She has plenty of time to find someone
special." Victoria murmured something placating, but Melanie
knew that would not be the end of it. Her mother would just
regroup and find a new way to attack. Like the robot vacuum
cleaners she had three of.

"It's just so nice to be around other adults and have a grown-up
conversation at the dinner table. You have no idea." Harper gulped
her wine enthusiastically. She always stowed her two kids and
husband at home for these Sunday dinners because, as Harper was
fond of saying, "You have to put on your own oxygen mask before
helping others." Time away from her husband and twin seven-year-
olds apparently comprised her oxygen mask, even though she had a
nanny and worked long hours at her law firm and hardly ever saw
them anyway.

Her sister's choices baffled Melanie. Why have a husband and
kids if you couldn't stand to be with them? *She* would relish the
company of her family. Listen attentively as Ken droned on about
his stressful workday, then give him a nice, relaxing blowjob later.
Would dote on her precious little ones, and hang their crayon
drawings right next to the Lichtensteins and Basquiats, showing
both motherly love and a playful spirit. She would be generous with
affection and praise, stingy with criticism. And above all she would

never, ever nag. Nagging was even less attractive than granny panties.

"How are the twins, Harper?" Victoria asked, tucking an impertinent strand of hair back into place. Salon-perfect dark auburn, ruthlessly free of gray. Victoria always asked about the twins, if only as a formality. Victoria and Tom buried their only grandchildren in gifts instead of smothering them in affection.

"They're fantastic!" Harper loved talking about her boys, if not actually being with them. "Matthew's music teacher thinks he has real potential, although of course Julliard is a long way off. And Robby is a soccer star. You should see the way he just owns the field." Her sister beamed in a surprisingly self-satisfied way, considering she hired other people to teach her sons everything.

"Do they like doing all those activities, though? Don't they ever just get to…you know, play?" Melanie wondered aloud. Not just soccer and violin but swimming and karate too. Plus a Mandarin immersion program at school. Mandarin! Might as well give them flip-flops in a mudslide, because Harper would never waste precious time on a family vacation to China.

Her sister rolled her ice-blue eyes and cocked her head, capped by its no-nonsense platinum helmet hair. "Kids need *struc*-ture, es-*pecial*-ly seven-year-olds"—punctuating the syllables to convey Melanie's mental deficiency. "Structured activities help them feel *safe* enough to explore their *interests*." She blinked and smiled condescendingly. Harper loved feeling superior almost as much as she loved bragging about her kids.

"So is that a no?" Melanie hated to poke, but her heart went out to her nephews, under so much pressure so young. When she had kids, they would do only the activities they wanted to. They would, no doubt, be naturally inclined toward the arts, foreign languages, and keeping their rooms clean.

Harper sighed, dismissing both Melanie and the topic with a quick turn of her head. "Has anyone heard from Alex?" Harper always changed the subject when someone disagreed with her.

Alex, their brother and the oldest of the three, was a big-shot financial adviser in New York, darkly handsome and unabashedly ambitious. This surprised no one, since he was named after Alexander the Great and had received the lion's share of their parents' attention and efforts.

Anything that didn't involve making money, spending money, or having sex held little interest for Alex. His three-bedroom duplex on Manhattan's Upper East Side was professionally decorated and spotless, because he dropped in only to sleep and to entertain clients, fashion models, and exotic dancers. In Alex's book, diving into double D's ran a close second to making money off the Japanese.

When Melanie wasn't envying her brother's exciting lifestyle, she worried that it was keeping him from finding true love. But what business of it was hers how her brother lived? She hardly ever saw him anymore. He had flown the coop as far away from their parents as the continental U.S. allowed.

"I got an email from him." Victoria sounded triumphant, the favored recipient of Alex's precious scant attention. "Which I suppose is what you kids consider the equivalent of a phone call, so that's something. He says he's doing fine and working a lot. That's about it. Communication has never been your brother's strong suit."

Her mother sliced the filet mignon with mushroom sauce and tasted it. Ritualistically. Victoria only ever ate about three bites of everything and then declared herself full. Staying rail thin was as important to her as stuffing everyone else.

"He didn't mention the new girlfriend?" Harper parried with her own triumphant tidbit. "Interesting."

"New girlfriend? No, he didn't say anything." Victoria tried to frown, only a hint of it breaking past the Botox. She rubbed the space between her eyebrows in lieu of being able to scowl.

"They've been dating a month or so," Harper gloated. "She's a PR exec at some fashion label."

"Well, I would be the last to know." Victoria looked reproachfully at everyone and no one in particular. "Does it seem serious?"

Her fork moved in an orderly fashion around the plate as she took bites of everything—potatoes au gratin, sautéed broccoli rabe, and so on, checking for flaws. Melanie wondered why her mother bothered to taste everything, as the food never had flaws. It wasn't allowed to have flaws.

"How should I know?" Harper shrugged. "You know Alex. She could be here today, gone tomorrow."

Yeah, gone back to her coke-dealer boyfriend, Melanie thought. *And the only fashion PR she does is wear Versace to nightclubs.* Alex always dished the real dirt to her alone, trusting her loyalty and sealed lips. "Why does it have to be serious anyway?" She feigned innocence. "What's wrong with just having fun?" She felt obligated to defend her beloved big brother, despite his unbeatable defense of moving 3,000 miles away.

Victoria nailed Melanie with her own version of the mental-defect look. "It's high time he settled down." Oozing exaggerated patience. "He's 32. If he waits much longer to get married and start a family, he'll be as old as a grandparent when his kids are in college!"

Victoria willfully persisted in the delusion that Alex would one day have kids. She counted willing things into happening as a skill, just like cooking a perfect meal.

"Maybe we should invite them both for Thanksgiving." Victoria's indefatigable wheels kicked into motion. "I'm going to brine the turkey this year."

"Mom, it's only September." Harper laughed, the scorn barely perceptible. "If they're still together in two months, you can decide then."

Two weeks is more like it, Melanie thought. *She's flat-chested.* The details she alone knew gave her a private satisfaction; she held them close to her heart as a kind of armor. *She snorts when she laughs.*

Melanie hoped the new girl would last, unlikely as that seemed. This tramp of the month could have been her evil, if skinnier, twin, and she got a thrill out of living vicariously through her. Same hair color, brown sugar. Same eyes, gold-flecked green. But along with their dress sizes, their lifestyles and personalities were worlds apart. Alex's slutty party girl didn't consider a spotless reputation a desirable accessory, while Melanie…well, Melanie spent so much energy on being kind, thoughtful, and courteous that sometimes she felt like she might collapse.

Victoria's half chuckle at Harper's disdainful comment clanged like a warning bell. Melanie knew the drill: first the half chuckle, then the tense smile, then the stormy exit. Her mother's stormy exits were as legendary as her cherries jubilee.

"Well you can tease me all you like." Her mother smiled tensely. "But someone has to think about things like holidays and plan ahead." The smile hung there, incongruous against the rest of her face.

"So, Melanie, how's the gallery?" Her dad could always sense a storm brewing even from his scotch-haze shelter. He'd become highly adept over the years at steering subjects in safer directions, and had a head of gray hair to show for it.

The Van Doren Gallery in San Francisco, owned by the heiress Violet van Doren, sold edgy artwork to people with more money than good taste. Melanie had worked there since graduating college five years ago, doing most of the work while Violet reaped the profits.

"Fine, Dad, same as usual. Thank you for asking," she replied, grateful for the change in course and the positive attention. Tom grinned at her affectionately. Maybe drunkenly.

"I'm so happy you're satisfied with being a glorified receptionist," Victoria inserted unhappily. "Although we could have saved the quarter million in college tuition. You could have just gone to secretary school or something."

"I'm not anything like a secretary, Mom. I help people pick art." Melanie's heart clutched and her throat tightened. *Here we go again. Everyone's favorite person to find fault with.* She reached for a Lenox crystal water glass and looked down at her plate, wishing she could spend the rest of dinner under the table.

Whose idea had college been anyway? Not hers. She had wanted to take time off and travel around Europe. But of course she went, because she was a good suburban girl, and good suburban girls do as they're told.

"Of course you're not a secretary, Melanie. No one said you were." Melanie's dad shifted automatically into placate mode. "And how are things at the law firm, Harper?" Doling out the attention as equally as jelly beans among their childhood Easter baskets.

"Crazy busy." Harper's face lit up. "We're up to our ears on discovery on that toxic-waste case, and a huge potential new client is coming in next week. You know what that could mean if I land him?"

"Partner?" Tom and Melanie chorused together.

"Partner," trilled Harper, only a split second behind. Harper pursued her goals in military-like fashion. Making partner at the law firm was as inevitable as death and taxes.

Great, just one more thing she can rub in my face, Melanie rued. *I'll never be as successful as her.*

"How about a salon day, Melanie? My treat!" Victoria's sudden burst of enthusiasm knocked Melanie back in her chair; she shifted uneasily under the wide beacon of her mother's smile. "We'll go to that fancy place on Maiden Lane. You can get a new haircut, and we'll get our nails done. Maybe there'll even be a makeup person. We can get makeovers. You could be a beautiful new woman in a day!" She blinked innocently, radiating maternal goodwill.

Melanie almost choked on her steak. Ouch. *She feels sorry for me. How will anyone ever want me if my own mother pities me?* But before she could reply, Harper butted in. "Really, Mom. You're so superficial. The reason Melanie doesn't have a boyfriend isn't because of her looks; it's because she has no ambition. Guys don't want a dead weight hanging around their necks anymore—they want someone who's their equal." No particular inflection here, as if she were describing the weather. Smugly.

"Whoa—what?" Melanie cringed at the unprovoked attack. You can't steel yourself for what you don't expect. She laid down her fork, willing the lump of tears back down. *You're so sensitive, Melanie,* Harper would tease her when they were kids. *Are you going to cryyyyyy now, little crybaby?* "I've had plenty of boyfriends."

"Oh, yeah?" Harper challenged. "Name two who lasted more than a year."

"What exactly do you mean by 'dead weight,' Harper?" countered her mother, her voice rising. "Are you saying that women who don't work outside the home are *dead weight?*" Her own résumé included only the domestic arts and staying rail thin.

"Oh, Mom, of course I didn't mean you. You're a different generation." Harper's dismissive tone belied the appeasing words. "But things just don't work like that today. Admit it, you and Dad both think Melanie should be doing something more with her life."

"That's enough." Tom shot Harper a warning glare. Melanie delivered a look of gratitude in return but noticed he didn't contradict her sister. She wanted to defend herself, but confrontation gave her acid reflux.

"I would think that people in any generation would value the sacrifices women make to create a happy, healthy family." Victoria's mouth tightened. "You have no idea how much work—yes, real work—it takes." She stood up and briskly began clearing the serving dishes. Everyone still eating be damned.

Harper sighed. "Nobody is criticizing your choices, Mom."

"You could have fooled me." Victoria's quick retort snapped the discussion shut. "I have a headache and am going to bed early. Goodnight." She stalked into the kitchen with a platter in each hand, taking any hope of a happy end to the evening with her.

The three of them sat there, only the clink of silverware on plates rattling the silence. They finished quickly. Then Tom excused himself, kissing them both. Went into the den to watch CNN, fresh scotch in tow. Harper slid into her Audi. Melanie hauled back up north to San Francisco in her five-year-old Honda Civic, tears streaming down her face the whole 45-minute trip.

Why do they always pick on me when I try so hard to be good? Melanie almost always did what she was told. She kept her nails clean, ate red meat sparingly, held doors for people with strollers. Socked away 3 percent of her paycheck in an IRA, had the oil in her car changed on schedule. Why did everyone treat her like something you'd scrape off your shoe?

RECLINING IN a steamy bath that night amid lavender-scented bubbles, glowing candles the only light, Melanie roughly scrubbed the evening's pain away. Her mother's and sister's bitchy put-downs. Her dad's half-assed subject changes that changed no one's mind about anything. She scoured all the hurt off with a loofah, feeling purified by the scratchy pain. She hoped so much emotional shit wouldn't clog the drain.

Feeling only half restored, she opted for the only other sure route to feeling better. Let her fingers do the walking, pretending they belonged to her Prince Charming. "You're beautiful, you're perfect," the imaginary prince whispered as he softly stroked, working his way into her pink parts. "Your sister is a pushy bitch; you're the sexy one. You're the one I want." The prince fondled her breasts, tweaked her nipples. "Men like real women with curves. You're a real woman." Melanie made him repeat that: "You're a real woman," "You're beautiful," "You're perfect," until her back arched and she let out a long moan of pleasure and relief.

She vowed to redouble her efforts at making Ken, the Dream-house, and the doll babies a reality. Without them, Melanie would always fall short. She would find Ken and prove her worth to the world.

Even if it killed her.

Chapter 2
Why Buy a Tarted-Up Cow When You Can Get a Thoroughbred?

EVERY MORNING, as she blow-dried her hair, carefully applied her makeup, and selected a flattering outfit, Melanie told herself today might be the day Ken would walk through the gallery door and sweep her into a meaningful life. Yeah, pathetic. But she'd gotten used to it.

Every Saturday night, as she transitioned to a smoky eye and a risqué (for her) outfit—Kim Kardashian would come up empty-handed in her closet—for bar hopping with a friend, she reminded her mirror reflection that tonight might be the night she would meet him. The prince among the frogs. She had kissed so many frogs, her tongue was sore.

Self-help books had so far proved unhelpful in her man quest. You must visualize what you want, they say. You must communicate your intentions to the universe, so the universe knows what to send, they said. Melanie had visualized to the point of headaches, had communicated her Ken-doll and Homemaker Barbie goals so loudly, you could hear them in the next galaxy over. Still the universe and everyone in it treated her like a walking doormat.

Tonight's wing woman for club-hopping: Ginger Chipperfield, PR maven extraordinaire for a Silicon Valley start-up. She of the fiery red hair and fearless personality. The target man-meeting spot: Warehouse, in San Francisco's industrial SoMa district, for "a one-night extravaganza of the sexiest performance art anywhere. Join San Francisco's wildest and hottest for drinks, dancing, debaucherous entertainment—and a human menagerie!" So lured the ad's siren song. But Melanie's insecurities were threatening mutiny. Abandon ship!

She rifled through her closet desperately. Frump city. Hipster SoMa already lay outside her usual more conservative stomping grounds, and the performance-art aspect—"aerial acts, body painting, pole dancing like you've never seen!" made it a one-two punch. Too little sexiness in her closet *and* too much fat on her thighs sealed the deal. Surely the promised human menagerie did not include fat cows.

She pulled out her iPhone. "I can't go!" she wailed to Ginger. Wailing at least sounded more grown-up than whining. "I'm so sorry." *I'm so sorry for being a fat loser with nothing to wear.*

Ginger chuckled. "I knew you'd say that. Is it clothes or a crisis of self-confidence?"

"Both. And it's not funny!" Melanie helplessly eyed the clothes strewn over every surface. Like the dressing room at Loehmann's on double-discount day.

"No worries, I'll bring you something to wear. But we're going. You think I can go to this by myself?"

Yes, Ginger *could* go by herself, and she would be hooked up with half a dozen new friends on Facebook the next day. Ginger was a doer, a firecracker, whereas Melanie—well, Melanie couldn't muster up the courage to order a custom coffee at Starbucks.

Thirty minutes later, Ginger arrived toting three outfits:

1. Leopard-print micro miniskirt plus sparkly black top. Read: high-end hooker.

2. Slick black leather skirt plus sheer red blouse with billowy sleeves. Read: high-end French hooker.

3. Black wet-look minidress, shiny as lip gloss, cut for drool-inducing cleavage. Read: high-end French hooker with a whip.

Melanie groaned. "You have *got* to be kidding. I can't wear any of those." A knot the size of a fist clenched in the pit of her stomach. *First rule of fashion: Cows do not dress like streetwalkers.*

"You can and you will," declared Ginger. "Just pretend you're someone else. Someone who wears these kinds of clothes. I do it all the time." She flipped her long, satiny red hair over a slim shoulder. Melanie eyed Ginger's skintight silver minidress, snakeskin slingbacks, and hoop earrings you could fit a wrist through. Why would Ginger pretend to be someone else when she already looked like a supermodel?

"But...but..."

"No 'buts.' Pick one." Ginger crossed her arms and stood firmly on her five-inch heels.

Melanie sighed, noting the irony of being strong-armed by someone with such skinny arms. She opted for outfit No. 1, the leopard skirt combo, the most conservative of the three. Miraculously, it fit—couldn't be something Ginger ever wore herself. A pair of her own three-inch black leather pumps completed the look. No way she could pretend to be someone who wore five-inchers; masquerading as a confident hooker would be demanding enough.

"Now let's do your makeup." Ginger hauled out a big Lucite box packed with lipsticks and eye shadows and professional-grade brushes.

"I already did it," Melanie protested, slightly offended. *I've been reading beauty magazines for 15 years,* she thought. *Can't I even do my own makeup right?*

Ginger smiled. "Looks great—for an office party." She unlocked the box and pulled out a tube of MAC foundation. "But the agenda tonight is scoring men, not scoring points with the boss. Go wash your face, and we'll start over."

Melanie's stomach clutched again. She wished she *could* start over, could go back a week and refuse the invite. Or better yet, go back 26 years and start her life over. Too late now though, with Ginger the force of nature sweeping her along with gale-force persuasion. "Fine, fine," Melanie gave in. She always gave in. "Whatever you say. Let's just do it quickly before I change my mind." She wriggled uncomfortably in the miniskirt on the way to the sink, trying to make it cover more than an inch below her ass. Whatever the entry fee to Warehouse tonight was, this skirt would cost her modesty more.

"Sit here and hold still." Ginger waved Melanie and her scrubbed face over to the chair at the vanity. "This won't hurt a bit." She giggled at her own joke. *Go ahead, amuse yourself at my expense,* Melanie thought. *Everyone does.*

Ginger worked intently for 20 minutes while Melanie fought her inner critic and the urge to fidget. *You can't make a silk purse out of a sow's ear.* She closed her eyes as instructed, sucked in her cheeks and pursed her lips on cue. The brushes felt purposeful in Ginger's hands. Probably wishing they had more to work with.

Ginger snapped the lid on the makeup box shut finally and stepped back. Eyed her handiwork critically, hands on hips, expression unreadable. Dread gripped Melanie's heart. *Here it comes, the moment when Ginger says she's done all she can, but she's not a magician.*

"Well, I've done all I can." Ginger offered a hand mirror. "I'm not gonna…be modest. It's perfect."

Melanie took the mirror doubtfully. Did a double take. She didn't recognize the person gazing out, all doe-eyed and mysterious. Gorgeous.

"Go look in the full-length mirror." Ginger nodded toward the far wall. "To see the whole package. Man, I do *awesome* work. Of course, you had great material to start with."

Melanie rose from the chair unsteadily. The full-length mirror confirmed Ginger's declaration. Gone was her mousy, dishwater-dull self, replaced by someone breezily exotic. Like someone who would lounge on a velvet chaise backstage with Marilyn Manson, sipping absinthe and snorting coke.

"I feel like a different person." An understatement. She felt like her own evil twin.

Ginger reopened the case and started touching up her own makeup. "Who do you want to be?"

"What do you mean? I can't be someone else. That's lying." Melanie couldn't even lie on her taxes, much to the disdain of her accountant.

"Creative license. Who's gonna know?" No wonder Ginger was a PR superstar.

The universe would know. Lying made for bad karma. Then again, the universe apparently had better things to do than make her Homemaker Barbie dreams come true. The universe considered her milquetoast. The universe could kiss her ass.

"Natasha," she said.

"Ah, my dahlink Natasha." Ginger curled an arm around Melanie's waist and wiggled an eyebrow up and down. "You vill quit dis dangerous life of being an international spy and come to live on my yacht with me, yes?"

Melanie giggled. "How big is your yacht?"

"You vill see how big, Natasha. You vill see dat everything about me is veddy, veddy big."

As they broke apart laughing, got their coats and headed out the door, Melanie realized that the ball of anxiety in her stomach had morphed into pleasant shivers of anticipation.

THE QUEUE snaked sinuously down the block in front of Warehouse. Melanie eyed it apprehensively. She had landed among an alien tribe: wild creatures with leather and painted-on latex for skin, stompy boots and studded stilettos for feet. Magnificent plumage too: magenta Mohawks, blue braids, feather boas in every color—on both girls and boys. Some lost-looking souls had missed the memo, distinctly ordinary in little black dresses or button-down shirts, even a few—horror!—khakis. Their presence reassured Melanie while eliciting her disdain. Her alter ego Natasha would never associate with such lackluster losers. People like she used to be.

"Make way, make way." The insistent call came from behind. Melanie quickly flattened herself against the wall. "Everyone make way for Mistress Gardienne!"

"Who's Mistress Gardienne?" Melanie strained on her tiptoes, craning her neck. A six-foot-tall transgender Amazon with a beehive hairdo blocked her view.

"I think we're about to find out." Ginger stepped out onto the sidewalk and nearly got run over by a team of human horses. Four in total: two by two. Leather harnesses over bare skin, faces hidden under leather hoods shaped like horses' heads. Bits in their mouths and tails unfurling from their rear ends. Ginger jumped back just as they trotted by, hauling their precious cargo on a wheeled wooden cart: a stunning china doll of a woman.

The woman nodded regally at the crowd, a serene smile playing over her mouth, black ringlets flowing. Waving queen-style with one hand buttoned up in elbow-length red velvet, the other delicately draped across the waist of her Victorian red silk dress, laced tightly. A dotted veil spilling from the front of her rakishly perched miniature red top hat.

A dog curled up next to her on the cart seat, gently nuzzling her thigh. No, not a dog—a small man, his head a leather dog hood. A studded collar encircling his neck, a leash tethering him to his mistress's wrist. He barked loudly, and Melanie bolted back, banging her shoulder hard on the concrete wall. Geez, didn't they make muzzles in human sizes?

"I think we're not in Kansas anymore. More like Alice in Do-Me Land." Melanie rubbed her shoulder, watching the cart roll on Gardienne cut a striking figure even from behind. Completely in control of her animals, utterly adored by them. Gardienne seemed like the type who not only would order a complicated custom coffee, but would have servants begging to fetch it for her. And strike them with a riding crop if they got it wrong.

"Welcome to San Francisco's seedy underbelly." Ginger grinned. "Ladies' lingerie on the left, up to size 42 regular; human-size pet gear on the right."

It took another 20 minutes to reach the front of the line, but who needed scheduled performances with a reality show this good?

A sleek black limousine pulled up. The uniformed chauffer didn't just open the door; he *lay down in front of it,* right on the street. Making a bridge to the sidewalk. A delicate buttoned white boot peeked out from the limo and then stepped on his back, followed by its owner, a Harajuku-style Little Bo Peep. Parasol twirling.

A beaming pilot in full latex captain's regalia arrived, flanked by five fawning stewardesses in white go-go boots. Pan Am circa 1960s, their latex uniforms gleaming.

Towering drag queens, decked out as diva songstresses and larger-than-life dolls and even one Ursula the Sea Witch, struck dramatic poses for photo ops, leaving trails of glitter and false eyelashes in their wake.

Flashbulbs everywhere. Mostly from amateur cameras, but a few pros too. The press! Melanie hoped her streetwalker getup would not make the Sunday *Chronicle.* Then again, who would recognize her? She barely recognized herself.

Every time anxiety pinched, she reminded herself: *Milquetoast Melanie stayed home tonight. I am Natasha, exotic international jet-setting party girl.* Also, nobody expected her to perform. Nobody expected her to do anything other than watch. Just like at the circus. Any idiot could do that.

They reached the front of the line. A chiseled bodybuilder with a platinum crew cut checked their IDs, muscles rippling under his black T-shirt.

"I like your shirt." He wolfishly took in Melanie's getup. "It would look great thrown across my love seat." His voice was effeminate, startling her, and he winked. Melanie flushed beet red and froze.

"We don't play musical chairs." Ginger to the rescue, weaving an arm through hers.

"Uh, love seats are for sitting," Melanie added. *Ugh, lamest retort ever. C'mon, Natasha, get in the spirit.* "Mostly." She rushed inside to escape her lack of comeback wit.

The cavernous space enveloped them. Red track lights cast an erotic glow through the darkness, reflected in mirrors scattered over walls and propped on posts. A bordello and fun house in one. A fortune-teller in a mermaid tail and pasties motioned them toward her booth; next to her a bare-chested man in a top hat, bow tie, and leather boxer shorts spun an enormous wheel while two girls in corsets cheered. Melanie couldn't make out the wheel's prizes—likely not coffeemakers and cleaning supplies. Maybe a year's supply of human pet food.

Booths lined the lower level's walls, offering body painting and games, selling masks and clothes, some promising hidden delights behind swagged curtains. People draped over a balcony rail above, getting a bird's-eye view of the carnival—no, the bacchanal. Carnivals were for kids.

"Let's get a drink." Ginger's eyes sparkled even more than her silvery dress; excitement crackled off her. Ginger always loved tasting the flavors of the moment. She looked ready to lick these up.

"Good idea." They ambled through the crowd over to the bar. Almost every inch of the bartender's skin sported tattoos—even his face and bald head. *Now that takes guts,* Melanie thought. She could never even get a teeny heart tattooed on her ass.

"Pick your poison." He waved a hand to indicate the choices and looked at them expectantly.

"A Cosmo, please," Melanie requested automatically. "No, wait. Are there any specials?"

"We're doing a Hollywood Starlet." His red goatee jiggled up and down as he spoke. "Vodka and Coke with a crushed cherry, $10."

Gross, mean-spirited, and overpriced, protested Melanie. *Fun and ironic,* enthused Natasha.

"OK, I'll try it."

Ginger chose it too, Melanie noted proudly.

She tried to absorb everything as they wandered around, but the riot of colors and sounds assaulted her senses: the booths, the crazily dressed crowd, several dance floors, each with a different kind of music. Her eyes didn't know where to land.

Help me, Auntie Em! She asked Ginger several times to sit down just to regroup. Her friend in those towering heels was happy to oblige, noting, "High heels are easier to wear when you're on your back."

When the announcement came for the main performances, they both plopped gratefully onto folding chairs. Two beefy guys in black set up a portable stripper pole in the makeshift stage area, marked by four silver posts with black velvet rope hung between. The pole gleamed in the ambient light, in all its phallic glory. *Of course* the "debaucherous entertainment" promised in the ad would include a stripper-pole act. Debauchery and strippers went together like chocolate and peanut butter. *Mmmm, chocolate.* Melanie could have used some comfort food right about now.

"This is gonna be good!" Ginger's face shone with pleasure. Melanie thought of Alex, her brother, on a first-name basis with practically all the exotic dancers in Manhattan. He rated stripping skills higher than domestic skills, and lap-dance skills even higher. Alex pursued multimillion-dollar deals and six-figure bonuses, while chasing girlfriends who could lap dance so he could save money at the strip clubs.

Maybe Alex and Ginger knew something she didn't, but Melanie didn't see the attraction—everything just hanging out, nothing left to the imagination. And so embarrassing for the audience! How were you supposed to maintain any decorum with fake boobs swinging in your face?

But she hid her discomfort, as always. Folded her hands in her lap and arranged a polite expression on her face, always the good girl. Trying to call up Natasha and failing. Adding to her uneasiness, she felt that someone was watching her. Call it instinct. Not so surprising, as the trashy outfit left little to the imagination. Her body was displayed like booth merchandise, so of course someone—*probably some desperate jerk with a fat-chick fetish,* she thought—would want a closer look at the goods.

But every time Melanie surreptitiously turned to investigate, no one stood out as the interested buyer. She shrugged off the thought. *Maybe I'm just being paranoid. Who'd be interested in me anyway with all these hotties around? Why buy a tarted-up cow when you can get a thoroughbred?*

Thankfully, the music started. An Asian girl in a hot-pink bobbed wig danced through the crowd and up to the pole, her ass firm in satiny hot pants the color of cotton candy, small breasts capped off with sparkly pink heart-shaped pasties. She glided past one of the muscular bouncer types, who held the rope open and then stood guard nearby. No overexcited stage hopping on *his* watch—keep your hands to yourself and nobody gets hurt.

"Do they think we're going to rush the stage or something?" Melanie whispered nervously.

"You never know." Ginger raised her eyebrows. "Once I saw… hmm, never mind."

"Tell me." Anything to take her mind off this discomfort. Why had Melanie let Ginger talk her into this? She didn't belong here.

"Shhh," hushed Ginger. "I want to watch." Anticipation glowed on her face, under a thin sheen of sweat.

The hot-pants hottie worked the crowd as much as the pole, teasing as she slid from top to bottom, doing splits up and down the pole's length and hanging on with one hand. At the top she hung by only the crook of her elbow, drawing applause. *That's years of gymnastics right there,* thought Melanie. *Dance too. And probably no ice cream ever.* But the sexy self-confidence, you couldn't learn that or diet your way into it—you had to be born with it. The rest of Melanie's Natasha high quickly deflated. She might be dressed like someone who strutted the streets, but her confidence lay cringing in a corner.

The dancer finished her routine at the very top of the pole, gripping it between her legs as she waved with both hands. Kisses rained down from her hands as she slid down and shimmied off into the crowd, her satin-sheathed ass fading away like a blush.

The burly bouncers moved the pole away as a big silver ring descended from the ceiling. Two girls in shimmering white leotards sprinkled in sparkles popped out from behind a makeshift curtain and hopped on, long and diaphanous scarves trailing from their wrists. As the ring ascended toward the soaring ceiling, an excited murmur ran through the crowd. Working without a safety net. In her hooker outfit among these denizens of wonderland, Melanie could commiserate.

The men in black edged closer under the ring. Like they could really catch the girls if they fell? Please. Brains would be splattered from here to the next dance floor. Falling stars are graceful only in poetry.

I may have no career ambition, thought Melanie, *but at least I don't have to put my life on the line for my job. Safety should count for something, right?* But if safety counted, she'd already own the world.

The two aerialists twirled and dangled and rolled themselves up and down in the scarves, nearing the floor at frightening speeds. Their graceful, daring feats drawing gasps. A top circus act for a top audience of freaks.

Brains intact and showered with applause, the nymphs disappeared back behind the curtain, their smiles radiating to the back row. Who needs safety when you can have the adoration of a crowd?

"Wow, so amazing." Ginger's eyes still gleaming. "Makes me think about a career change."

Makes me think about hiding under a rock. Melanie shuddered, tugging her skirt down futilely as they stood up. "How about another drink?"

"You're doing great, Natasha." Ginger slid an arm around Melanie's waist with girlish ease. "C'mon, you can't tell me that wasn't exciting. Do you think that pole dancer offers private lessons?"

"Let's just get a drink." Maybe another round would help her get her Natasha groove back. Liquid courage and all.

As they inched along through the crowd to the bar—the place

had gotten packed quickly—Melanie's skin prickled with that unmistakable feeling. Someone was definitely watching her. But who? No one stood out as a suspect, although many stood out for other reasons.

All right, she decided, suddenly savoring the unexpected tingles. *Whoever you are, we'll play by your rules.* She tossed her head and stopped scanning for suspects. And just like that, Natasha returned, drawn by desirability. Confidence comes so much easier when you're wanted.

"What's next on the lineup?" Melanie addressed Ginger loudly over the thumping music, as they joined the long line for the bar.

Ginger pulled the folded-up program from her tiny Prada purse. "Mistress Gardienne and her human menagerie."

"Been there, done that." Exaggeratedly blasé. "Already notified the ASPCA about cruelty to animals."

Ginger laughed. "So jaded already, Miss Natasha! Hey, I gotta pee. Will you get me a vodka and cranberry? Not that Coke thing, totally vile. Be right back."

Ginger took off, a whirl of silver under her swinging red hair, for the dauntingly long line for the bathroom. Good thing Melanie had a lifetime of practice waiting patiently.

Soon after, a young woman Melanie didn't recognize trotted up.

"Hi there." She wore a cocktail dress fashioned of acid-green lace; her big, teased hair was courtesy of the 1980s. "I hope you don't think this is weird, but you look totally familiar, and it's killing me that I can't remember where we met."

Never saw you before in my life, Melanie thought instantly. Odd. Was the girl trying to get a better space in the lengthy bar line? But she already held a full drink. Hitting on her? *As if!* No scenarios made sense, so maybe there was no ruse. The gallery where Melanie worked hosted so many art openings; maybe this girl had attended one. Though judging from the bargain-bin dress and the Van Doren Gallery's high-society prices, this girl would have been a mere lookie-loo.

"Maybe at the gallery?" Melanie offered tentatively.

"That must be it." The young woman snapped her fingers. Triumph on her face and...relief? "That one downtown, right?" Melanie nodded. "Remind me of the name again? I go to a lot of openings."

Melanie's Spidey sense tingled again. The girl looked like she attended more lowbrow frat parties than upper-crust art openings. But she didn't look like a terrorist in any case. What harm could it do? "The Van Doren Gallery. On Grant Avenue."

"Yup, that's it! I *knew* you looked familiar." That flash of relief again. "My name's Amy." She stuck out her hand awkwardly.

"Natasha," Melanie replied smoothly. The name rolled easily off her tongue now.

"Nice to meet you, Natasha—I mean, um, nice to *see you again*." Amy smiled awkwardly, cleared her throat, and looked away. "Well, I gotta get back to my friends. See you around, I hope."

"Sure. Have fun." Melanie couldn't shake the feeling of a puzzle piece missing. But whatever—being out of the loop came with the doormat territory. Leave the questions to those pushy investigative journalists, with their afterthought outfits and outmoded hair. Pushiness might earn you a discount at the shopping outlets, but it didn't earn most men's affections.

Curiouser and curiouser, she thought, as the girl disappeared into the throng. *Par for the course tonight.*

She eyed the people dancing to pass the time. Their glittery and goth costumes and states of undress, rolls of fat and jiggly asses and beer bellies on full display. Jeez, how did even the jelly bellies have confidence? Dancing like no one's watching *and* letting it all hang out. Melanie could only ever manage a few petrified aerobics moves on the dance floor.

God, what a stiff I am. Phoning it in my whole life. How had confidence found even these corpulent wonders and eluded her? Twenty-six years on this planet and all she had to show for it was a china teacup collection and a well-used vibrator.

She sighed. Well, at least channeling Natasha had given her a taste from the fountain of confidence. Her usual lame self wouldn't

even be here. Her usual lame self would be perched at an upscale bar, legs crossed demurely, mentally undressing the suit-clad lawyers and finance guys. Wondering if their tongues would work as hard on her girl parts as they did bragging about big, manly deals.

For once she was in with the cool crowd. Tomorrow she'd be back to wearing the Please Tread on Me flag, so why couldn't she let the freak flag fly for one night?

"Whew." Ginger returned just as Melanie reached the bar. "Remind me to wear an adult diaper next time."

"Or you could get a slave boy to tote a pee jar around for you."

"That's the spirit!" Ginger smirked.

"Speaking of which," said Melanie, forking over $9 for a Cosmo in a plastic cup, "have you seen any guy prospects here?"

"Nope, I've been too distracted by the floor show. Let's do some reconnaissance."

"You read my mind. But I can't even tell who's straight and who's gay." Melanie frowned. Barking up the wrong tree wasted time and energy, not to mention being even further demoralizing.

"Just flash a tit and see if they bite," Ginger suggested, straight-faced.

"Here they actually might!" Melanie cracked a smile, but her stomach knotted again.

As they wandered around scoping out potential hookups, Melanie quickly realized that a viable opportunity was less likely than a cheap drink at the bar. None of the potentials had any potential. She saw men in chaps, asses hanging out (gay?); men in chains (silly); men in leather pants toting whips and floggers (scary *and* silly). Men in everything but something that would turn on a nice girl from the suburbs with the mind of a harlot. Where was a sex fiend in a three-piece suit when you needed one?

Melanie loved that San Francisco embraced such diverse identities and sexualities, but the frustration nearly overwhelmed her. She wanted bedroom action so bad, she could taste it. Here she was all packaged like a gift and ready to be shipped off into pleasure central, but the customers' tastes didn't match the merchandise.

Another night, another failure, she lamented, peeling off the miniskirt back at home, alone again. She stared dejectedly at the mirror while flossing her teeth, wondering yet again why no matter how hard she tried, no matter what she wore or where she went, Ken eluded her. *I'm going to die alone, surrounded by nine cats and my knitting. No one will even know I'm gone until the cats start howling from hunger.*

Slipping under the rose-pink comforter, she thought again about the uselessness of visualizing and setting intentions. Where had all her visualizing about naked Ken in this very bed gotten her? Hot and bothered and alone, that's where. As usual. Thank goodness at least for the Hitachi Magic Wand Massager. A poor substitute for a hot-blooded lover, but better than trying to fall asleep horny.

She pretended the massager was Ken's manhood, rolling it back and forth and in circles around her soft mound. *God, you're so big,* she intoned silently. *You're such a man. You're all I need.*

When she finally moaned with the pleasure of release, she tossed the vibrator onto the floor. She didn't like to sleep with the evidence of her Ken-finding failure.

THAT NIGHT Melanie dreamed she was a go-go dancer in a cage at a seedy club, bumping and grinding in front of an appreciative crowd. Men leering, girls flashing their breasts, glittery nipples sparkling. Sexiness coursing through Melanie's body, driven by the music's pounding beat. Her inferiority complexes had taken the night off. She was a queen—no, a goddess. She stroked the bars lasciviously and tossed her beautifully highlighted hair and caressed her impossibly slender, firm body in come-hither fashion. The audience eating it up.

She had worn hot pants and a sequined bra, but suddenly she realized she was in fact wearing nothing at all. Hands began poking through the bars, pawing her stark-naked limbs. Someone barked, and she saw sharp canine teeth flash. She edged back, but the cage left no room to withdraw. The groping hands becoming more insistent, the faces more leering, and then the bars started to dissolve, like sugar in hot tea. Melanie bolted awake, her body quivering.

Sex goddess, ha. Goddess of the losers was more like it. Would she ever figure out how to let her inner dirty slut run wild? Or would she be doomed to a life of channeling Ken through her vibrator?

No. The word rose with a surprising steeliness through Melanie's half-awake mind. *You have only one life to live. Learn how to live it—or die trying.*

She hoped it wouldn't come to that.

Chapter 3

You Gotta Be in It to Win It

Melanie lazed in the sheets, savoring the Sunday-morning bliss: no alarm clocks, no Spanx, no frantic last-minute eyebrow tweezing or chipped-nail-polish fixing. No need to suck her stomach in or worry about seeds in her teeth. No answering to her boss or the demanding gallery clients or anyone. Just herself and her self-help books and romance novels, the only decision-making being which teacup in her extensive collection would get the Darjeeling today. Tea for two would've been better, of course, but she was an art gallery associate, not a magician.

Running a leg lazily up and down the soft queen-size sheet—plenty of room in this bed for when Prince Charming came along—Melanie surveyed her bedroom yet again with pride. Feminine but not too girly; change out a few lilac pillows and some accessories and even the manliest man would feel right at home. And comfy.

Good sleep was so important to good health, and more important, to avoiding ugly undereye bags.

In fact, Melanie's whole one-bedroom flat oozed comfort and consideration. You'd never know that most of it had come from Craiglist. Soothing colors, all creams and sages and pale blues with kisses of pink. Her Mom had sniffed in distaste upon visiting that one time, wondering aloud at Melanie's mental health for turning down her offer to pay for "nice" furnishings. But Melanie had clutched at a shred of self-esteem.

It might not be much, but it was all hers.

"Cheap is as cheap does," her mom had remarked pointedly, raising an eyebrow. "Still, I suppose it is *your* flat." Appearing cheap was as taboo to Victoria as appearing her age. Only your doctor will know if you haggle over the price of Botox, but low-quality furniture is a major broadcast to every visitor.

Being on the upper of the house's two floors, the flat had a view of nearby Dolores Park and no one stomping around above. Excellent feng shui and excellent man-meeting potential, a win-win. Dolores Park drew guys walking their dogs like Ben & Jerry's drew the freeloaders on complimentary scoop day.

Melanie rose slowly, still relishing the lovely ease of Sunday morning. Tucked the sheets and fluffy duvet back in place, piled the mound of throw pillows back on. Who cared if no one else would likely see it today? She liked to be prepared. Opportunity was chance meeting preparedness, she had read. No sense giving opportunity a reason to go knocking on someone else's door.

She stooped to pick some lint off the carpet on the way to the kitchen and retied her long ivory satin robe, bought "gently used" on eBay. What to have for breakfast? Good health and the dream of thin thighs urged low-fat yogurt and fruit, but the bacon called louder. Bacon calories didn't count on Sundays, right? *Of course they do, you moron. And you know bacon is a poor substitute for what you're really craving.*

Sure, all those diet books said unhealthy eating never filled the hole the way you wanted—the hole being literal for Melanie, who could count on two hands the number of times she'd been laid. She knew that unhealthy eating was a coping mechanism and a poor substitute for love, but it was all she had.

Staring down the bacon in its unopened package, she reached for her cell phone instead. Ten a.m. in San Francisco meant 1 p.m. in New York, which on a Sunday meant her brother, Alex, would just be waking up. Or getting a morning blowjob from the stripper du jour.

"Hi, Alex, I hope I'm not interrupting anything." Melanie's first words tumbled out anxiously.

"Mel! No, not at all. Hang on a sec." Muffled voices filtered through, one female and sounding annoyed.

"Just tell her it's your sister." Melanie shoved the bacon in the vegetable drawer under a big bunch of wilting spinach, then closed the fridge door firmly and reached for the teakettle.

"Nah, I like to keep 'em guessing." Alex sounded like he was moving to a different room. "They're more compliant when they're insecure." The woman's interrogations receded. "So what's up?"

"Oh, nothing. The same, as usual. Just making breakfast. Tell me not to have the bacon, OK?"

Alex laughed. "You're a big girl, Mel. You can make your own breakfast decisions."

"Please, Alex. Will you please just tell me?" She filled the kettle with filtered water and wiped up a few spilled drops.

He laughed again. "Fine, fine. Don't eat the bacon. Is that all you wanted, some dieting resolve?"

No, I want to be a size-two Homemaker Barbie with a gorgeous million-aire husband and adoring children, she wanted to say. But what good would it do? Alex could work magic only with money and attracting loose women.

"I went to Mom and Dad's last Sunday. Mom and Harper spent the whole time insulting me, Dad drank nonstop, then Mom stormed out with a headache."

"The usual, in other words. Why do you even go to those, Mel? You know how it's going to end up ahead of time. Why subject yourself to the abuse?"

Because they insist I go. Because I can't say no, Melanie thought.

"It's not that bad," she said aloud. "By the way, your new girl came up in conversation. Mom wants to invite her for Thanksgiving."

"Ha! That crazy coke whore is already history. I have someone new. She doesn't speak much English, but we find other ways to communicate."

"I bet you do." Melanie felt a twinge of sadness about the quick departure of her evil twin. No more living vicariously through her wild abandon. But what did she expect of her brother? Alex held on to cufflinks longer than girlfriends.

"Listen, Mel, don't let the bastards get you down. You know you're like a lamb to the slaughterhouse at those family dinners. You really need to detach yourself. You can't base your self-worth on the opinions of unfulfilled people." The indistinct woman's voice returned, more loudly this time. Alex covered the receiver and shouted something. The voice stopped.

"Anyway, as I was saying," he continued blithely, "you're a big girl. It's time to take ownership of your life. Listen, I gotta run. Take care of yourself, OK?"

Easy for you to say, Alexander the Great, Melanie sniped silently, pulling out the yogurt and fruit. *We can't all make millions sucking back beers in strip joints with foreigners.*

She glumly peeled back the single-serve container's foil. *Besides, I've been taking ownership of my life! The world just keeps taking it back.*

HEALTHY BREAKFAST downed, Darjeeling drained, and dishes washed, Melanie pondered reading material for the park. Always a balancing act, reading in public: It had to be something enjoyable, but it also had to not make her look like a desperate man-hungry loser. That nixed the bodice-ripper romances and self-help books she devoured in private. She settled on a bestselling thriller—it had guy appeal, sex appeal, and an entertaining plot. An entertaining plot would be key in case the park action fell flat.

She did love those romance novels, though. How could you not relish a story where everything was guaranteed to wrap up neatly in the end? With undying love or a multimillion-dollar business for the heroine and all evildoers groveling. The heroines always landed on their Jimmy Choo–clad feet tripping up the aisle in a frothy wedding dress toward the beaming boy next door. The "boy" next door to Melanie was a 70-year-old ex-Marine who swept his steps every morning precisely at 8 a.m.

Why did the heroines always pick the "nice" boy, though? Melanie wondered. *So boring—and, from her very limited experience, lacking in the sack.* Dark mystery men got such a bad rap as marriage potential, but they had sexiness in spades. Damn the assumption that sexy mystery men made bad husbands! Maybe they just hadn't met the right woman to make them change their ways. Every shoe has a mate, right? All she had to do was find the polished leather Gucci motorcycle boot to match her kitten heel.

And when she landed him, she would keep him enthralled. Homemaker Barbie would be a cook in the kitchen and a maid in the living room and a whore in the bedroom. Along with never being a nag, the criminal offense of ungrateful wives everywhere, she would never be seen looking less than fabulous. She would get up at 5 a.m. if necessary to brush her teeth and swipe mascara on before he awoke. Maybe she'd even wake him with a blowjob, as urged in *50 Ways to Drive Your Man Wild.* Put her long-wear lipstick to a real test.

Melanie's eye fell on the "vintage" (thrift-store) cocktail glasses in the rolling silver bar cart next to the bookcase. *Just like the 1950s,* she mused dreamily. *When women were allowed to just be women.* No career nonsense, no expectations at all aside from cooking, cleaning, and sexual servicing. Surely that would appeal to a man somewhere. Surely not every man wanted a bulldozing harridan like her sister. In fact, why would any man want a bulldozing harridan at all? Melanie suspected that her sister had bullied her husband into proposing marriage.

She glided out the door and down the stairs with visions of aprons and waffle makers dancing through her head, action-packed thriller in her secondhand Michael Kors bag. Maybe today, in the park, she would meet *him,* the dark, mysterious, and of course rich man worthy of her undying devotion. You gotta be in it to win it.

THE SUN embraced all and sundry with its glorious radiance outside. The sun didn't care that some of the parkgoers were homeless, or some couldn't tie their shoes yet, or some weren't even human. It certainly didn't care that Melanie hadn't shaved her legs or waxed her eyebrows that morning, and for a split second she considered just trying to enjoy the moment instead of scoping for guys. But no, she couldn't afford to waste time enjoying herself. The clock was ticking; every day brought her closer to wrinkles, cellulite, and sagging. You couldn't be a trophy wife with trashed body parts.

She automatically scanned the dozens of people, skimming over the families, the kids, and the girl posses gathered on benches and blankets, trying to home in on the single guys walking dogs or reading or lying on the grass. Staking out the right territory was critical; you had to make any encounters look accidental, which took a lot of planning.

Melanie chose an unoccupied bench near the play area. The kids' laughter rang over the sand and slides and through the swings.

"Tag, you're it!"

"Mooooom, I'm hungry!"

"Mommmmmmmy, I have to go potty!"

Wistfulness pinched Melanie, as it always did at the playground. When would she have a family of her own? When would she have a baby, a sweet and innocent little darling who needed her more than anything and thought she was Superwoman? At age 26, her mother had already had Alex and was pregnant with Harper, and her dad had been a rising star at his company. At age 26, Melanie had a teacup collection, a dead-end job, and a closet full of discount clothes she wished were two sizes smaller.

Someday, she self-soothed. *Someday I'll have everything I've ever dreamed of. Quitters never win.* Maybe even today that someday would start, although she glimpsed no immediate prospects for a soul mate. That's OK, she could wait. If exercising patience actually burned calories, she'd be a size two.

Several minutes passed. Melanie grew so absorbed in the plot of the action thriller that she didn't notice the handsome young guy until he spoke.

"Mind if I sit?" He gestured toward the empty spot next to her, winding a leash around his wrist. A tail-wagging Golden Retriever dutifully trotted over.

"Of course." An automatic response; her attention still lingered on the page.

"Of course you mind if I sit?" The guy smiled. Teasing her?

"No, I mean…" Melanie frowned briefly, glancing up, but then he seemed so good-natured and cute, all sandy hair and faded jeans and blue eyes bright with good humor. About her age. She shut the book. Action thrillers always took a backseat to real action.

"Please." She graciously waved at the bench like a *Price Is Right* model, while continuing to check him out, searching for clues about his status. Income level was so tough to suss out in San Francisco, where dot-com millionaires donned raggedy jeans and rode skateboards. Baffling. Why have all that money and dress like a homeless person?

Cute Guy's jeans and plain white T-shirt offered no information except that they looked clean. He had a nice build too—lean muscles, not gym muscles, and he had several inches on her in height. Guys should always be taller, unless they were exceedingly rich. Then they could be fat dwarves.

She also liked his affectionate manner with the dog, watching him rub its back and scratch behind its ears. Long and strong fingers. *I wonder if those fingers are good at anything else,* she mulled, her mind inadvertently detouring into the gutter. *Oh, quit getting ahead of yourself! Find out the important stuff first.*

"Are you really into that book, or is it just a ruse?" A guy who took the initiative. Melanie really liked that—being in charge made her queasy.

"Excuse me?" Buying time to think of the best answer.

"Lots of people read because they want to look busy. Or unavailable. Like in restaurants. The people by themselves are always reading or on their phones." He said this nonjudgmentally, just an observation. He had a trustworthy vibe.

"I'm really into it." She paused. "*And* it's a ruse." She tilted her chin down, gazing at him from beneath her eyelashes.

Cute Guy laughed and stuck out his hand. "My name's Scott. Scott Forsythe."

Melanie shook it firmly, the way her dad had taught her. No limp fishes. His skin radiated warmth, the chemistry between them zinging through her hand. The grasp lingered, until finally, reluctantly, she withdrew her hand. "I'm Melanie." No more Natasha. All her exotic alter ego had earned her last night was a solo ticket to vibratorville.

"Well, King Lear here is kind of my ruse, even though he's a great pal. Aren't you, boy?" Scott ruffled the dog's head affectionately. "I got him when I moved here."

"Oh? Where did you move from?" Maybe she could get some worthwhile details. Chemistry meant little without money to back it up; love doesn't pay the rent on a modernist glass house with walk-in closets.

"Seattle. Two months ago." The sun hit his eyes, revealing flecks of green in the sea of blue. Melanie wound a strand of hair around her finger coquettishly. Angled her body almost imperceptibly toward him.

Seattle, hmm, could be promising. Lots of megacompanies there—Microsoft, Amazon, Starbucks. Maybe he had struck it rich and retired early.

"And what brought you out here?" She tilted her head inquisitively, opening her eyes just a bit wider—a casual gesture she had practiced often. "Did you move here for work?"

She could picture it already, relating the fabulous story of their fortuitous park meeting, flashing the enormous rock on her ring finger. *I was just reading, and he wandered by with his dog, total seren-dipity! Can you believe I almost didn't even go to the park that day, since Sunday is a workout day? I know—crazy!* Melanie didn't consider the workout part a lie, because sometimes she stretched while watching TV.

She could also picture those long legs of his intertwined with hers, his sky-blue eyes traveling down her naked body with utmost appreciation, even if she didn't appreciate her body much herself. His lips were so full; what would they feel like against the softest parts of her? *Get a grip, Melanie! Keep the inner slut in check—at least until you find out whether he's got money.*

"No, the move didn't happen because of work, strictly speaking." His voice jolted Melanie out of her spread-eagle reverie. "I work"—he pointed to a popular café across the street—"um, right there."

"Oh." Melanie's interest deflated like a pinpricked balloon. Someone her age who slung java and bussed tables? Check, please.

"I know, I know." His mouth twisting into a wry half smile. "It doesn't look good."

"No, I didn't mean…" Melanie began. But she couldn't finish, because she *did* mean. Still, she didn't like to hurt anyone's feel-ings, even a loser wasting valuable bench real estate. She knew all too well how awful hurt feelings could be.

"You don't have to explain. I get it. Look, I had a longtime girlfriend back in Seattle." The brightness in Scott's eyes dimmed noticeably. "She left me for her grad-school professor. When that happened, I decided to make a new start doing what I really wanted."

"Working in a café?" Melanie couldn't resist. Anger actually prickled her. Those long legs, those mesmerizing eyes, and the most clichéd unambitious job of all? *Arrest him, officer; this is positively criminal.*

"No, being a writer." He looked pained and yet eager. Mela-nie's heart involuntarily skipped a beat. "And if I'm sitting in front of a computer all day at a desk job, it's too hard to sit in front of a computer all night writing."

"Uh-huh." What else could Melanie say? Everyone in California had a novel or a screenplay or a great piece of art in the works, or was inventing the next Facebook, which would make them rich as soon as the company went public. Cold, hard cash in hand was worth 10 ideas in the bush.

Like you're so special? Her inner critic chided. *You don't have cold, hard cash* or *a big creative idea. You just want to latch on to someone else. You're the biggest loser of all.* She tossed her head, trying to shake off the thought. She *did* have big ideas. They just involved someone else footing the bills.

"I'm not saying it's going to be a bestseller, but it's pretty interesting." Scott seemed as oblivious to her inner turmoil as he was clueless about ambition.

"Hmm." Melanie couldn't be bothered to prolong the conversation with someone so inconsiderately unsuccessful. "I'm sure it is." She picked up her book again. "Good luck with it. And it was really nice meeting you, but would you mind excusing me? I really want to find out how this ends."

Scott gazed at her steadily for a moment. "Sure." He rose from the bench. "It was nice talking with you." He hovered for a second and then unwound the dog's leash. "If you ever want to read with a coffee, come over to the café. My treat. I'm there most weekday afternoons until dinnertime."

"I'll do that." Melanie smiled automatically but barely looked up. She had already wasted enough time on him. But oh, those eyes. If only he could back them up with something more than a pie-in-the-sky dream. One dreamer was all any relationship could handle.

MELANIE READ in the park for another half hour, but no other prospects appeared. Instead of wasting any more time just enjoying things, she decided on a calorie-burning walk and some window-shopping. Maybe she'd find something thoughtful to give her mom at the next family dinner, something to smooth things over. *Not that I did anything wrong,* she reminded herself. Somehow she always ending up apologizing, even when it wasn't her fault.

Really, her bulldozing sister Harper should be the gift bringer; Harper had started all that dead-weight talk that caused Victoria's storm-out. But Harper's bringing an apology gift was about as likely as Melanie's falling for a cafe worker.

Melanie sighed. Gift, no gift; apology, no apology. It would make no difference in the end. Her mother might have the iron will of Mistress Gardienne Hunt, but she gave her family none of the loving attention that Gardienne lavished on her human animals. Her mother would never throw Melanie a bone until she was settled into a marriage as unhappy as her own.

WAITING FOR sleep to overtake her that night, Melanie replayed the park scene in her head. Had she been too hasty writing Scott off? Intelligent, affectionate with the dog, good-looking…and those eyes. She could go swimming in their blue depths. Her hand shot out for the vibrator. Imagining his lithe body on top of hers, pressing her into the bed with his forceful thrusts. Imagining his long fingers tangled in her hair, his full lips teasing kisses from her tongue. Her imagination gifted him with a magic tongue and the man package of a porn star, total sexual perfection unencumbered by reality.

Her quick and powerful orgasm spoke to their chemistry.

But where would the accomplishment be in getting a nice guy with no money? Anyone could have that. Landing a gorgeous and rich husband was the only kind of real accomplishment Melanie could look forward to in life. She wasn't cutthroat enough for corporate, wasn't smart or creative or motivated enough to start a business, wasn't beautiful enough to make a fortune on her looks. No, Melanie's success would only ever be measured by the size of her house and her husband's paycheck.

Looks and money aside, Melanie really only got hot for

take-charge men of few words and strong actions. Polite, friendly, chatty men left her feeling high and dry, not soaking wet between the legs. Her dream lover would literally sweep her off her feet into the bedroom, ravishing her and leaving her in a melty heap among the rumpled bed linens—not mop under her feet in a café and collect wadded-up napkins.

Although she would never in a million years say the words out loud, Melanie even harbored a very dark secret fantasy that the first sexual encounter with her dream man would be almost like a possession. He would ravage her, not politely pave the way with small talk. She would be powerless against the brute force of his dominating masculine strength. The thought made her feel really guilty. And really wet.

After her dream man had thoroughly invaded her, ignoring any pleas and protests, and they had lain skin to skin with limbs entwined, he would shower her with affection, brushing her hair, massaging her back with scented oil…then he would take her out to dinner. Someplace lavish, someplace special, a place where he could show her off as the greatest jewel any man could have, and no one but he could possess.

Yes, totally unfeminist and un–politically correct—and unfeasible. In her imagination, her clothes ended up intact afterward although he had torn them off; her va-jay-jay never ached even though he had pounded into her mercilessly; her wrists and hips remained unbruised even though he had held her down with force—but there you had it. People were entitled to their fantasies, right? Life without fantasies would be worse than nights with no vibrators.

Melanie *had to* figure out how to make them a reality.

Chapter 4
As If Anything Else Mattered

FIVE YEARS working at the Van Doren Gallery, and Melanie still loved it. The clean, spare space, its hardwood floors polished to a shine. The white walls without a speck or smudge; the air hinting at citrus and money. And most of all, the photographs and paintings, hung and lit to perfection. The current gritty black-and-whites called to her, luring her into their motel scenes: streetwalkers drawing cigarette smoke through dark lips, limbs splayed like broken-down dolls', expressions empty yet promising everything. She pitied those girls, admired them, envied them. Hopelessness had freed them.

And let's not forget Violet van Doren, the owner, also worthy of admiration and envy. Flamboyant, youthful despite her age—Melanie guessed late 40s, though who could tell with the best Botox, fillers and laser facials money could buy? And hair colorists;

raven strands sprouted eternal on Violet's reverse bob, no grays ever. Being an heiress had its perks.

Violet didn't trouble herself with the day-to-day realities of running her hobby business; that was Melanie's job. And Melanie ran the gallery well, despite the meager compensation. She considered Violet's jet-setting, gala-hopping stories a bonus and had gleaned many important bits of wisdom in her five years of working there. Massages in Bali are dirt cheap. Dukes got first dibs at a buffet, ahead of earls and barons. The rocks in Sedona really are magic, but not as magic as a good facialist.

"One must do *something*," Violet would intone dramatically, sighing and batting her lash extensions, whenever anyone asked why she even bothered to own a break-even art business. Melanie knew how much Violet did even without the gallery, but maybe she needed this fabricated link to the common man. Maybe rarefied air could grow stifling even for hothouse orchids.

Melanie breathed wisps of that rarified air through the gallery's posh clientele but never managed total immersion. Violet had perfected the art of keeping people in their place while affecting democratic goodwill, like a wealthy matron gifting the maid with passé designer castoffs.

Actually, Melanie would have gladly accepted Violet's castoffs—last season's designer clothes; dumped playboy lovers with many cars and few responsibilities—but Violet's subtle code of condescension didn't allow for such obvious pork-dishing. You can't keep up the façade of equality when your leftovers are someone else's treasure.

"Melanie, would you be a dear and make me a mint tea?" Violet would demand in the form of a question. "I know it's not your job, but I just got my nails done."

"Melanie, can you stay just a teensy bit late this Saturday? Misha might drop in to see the Zander photos, and I have to work that boring old fundraising gala for the diabetes people."

"Melanie, would you hold down the fort while I'm at New York Fashion Week? Such a zoo, but Karl is insisting I go. It might mean a few extra hours for you, but you're the only one I can trust."

Sometimes Violet actually stayed in San Francisco and the spirit moved her to come into the gallery, but never before noon.

"Alarm clocks are unnatural," she would say. "You're so lucky you can use one without going batty! Sooooo wish I had that talent."

Melanie ate up Violet's entertaining stories, accepted the left-handed compliments with grace, and ignored the glorified-servant treatment. Being a doormat was practically a job requirement here.

Having a rich inner life came in handy too. With Violet rarely gracing the gallery with her presence, and much of the art itself being sold at evening events, Melanie endured long stretches alone. She considered the loneliness an investment, hopefully paying off in rich and handsome Dream Ken's walking through the door one day. The Van Doren Gallery had no poor clients, only clients with a poor ability to pick art out without help.

I should be learning French. Or getting an advanced online degree, she sometimes mentally beat herself up on particularly slow days, right before getting sucked online into Piperlime's clothes or gossip sites. *Oh, my God, someone at the Vatican got caught downloading porn? How stupid can you be?* Clearly the papal perverts hadn't heard about all the ways to hide your computer's IP address, which Melanie researched so she could stream porn at work. Amateurs.

Not every day, mind you. She saved porn for the days when time moved so slowly that she felt ancient by lunchtime, days when the clock taunted her mercilessly: *Tick tock, tick tock. Waiting and wanting, waiting and wanting. Wasting your life as usual. You'll be old and wrinkled before you know it.* Porn made her feel alive and connected again, even if all the connections were being made by other people. On a video set.

Melanie always remembered to use a VPN service. She always remembered to erase her browsing history. Violet might well laugh off porn at work—rumor had it she'd once appeared in an X-rated Japanese flick, just for kicks—but the filthy slut who lived inside Melanie was no one's business but her own. And her future husband's.

When Melanie wasn't furtively clicking through PornHub at the sleek, glossy white desk discreetly tucked into the back corner, she might surreptitiously read a book under cover of an art magazine. Of course those self-help standbys—promising *30 Days to the Best You!* or *7 Simple Steps to Happiness*—and the bodice-ripper romances. Too bad bodice-ripping hadn't made it out of the 19th century; pillaging pirates made her toes tingle.

On this cloudy and gray Monday morning, she had *Forbidden Fire* discreetly hidden behind *Art and Architecture* magazine, propped on the desk. On the shelf behind, *Be Happy Now!* hid underneath *Nylon* magazine. Melanie perched gracefully on the white leather seat as she read, trying to ignore the tingling in her nether regions as the stable master indiscreetly rammed himself into the baron's daughter in a pile of hay.

And then…a quiet swish as the door opened. The room's energy shifted as she glanced up. She quickly shoved the magazine and book on the shelf and smoothed her hair. Sat up straighter and crossed her legs, hoping the dampness between them would not show through her ivory skirt.

Maybe it was his purposeful stride. Maybe it was how he began assessing the photographs right away, not waiting for assistance and not cowed by their gritty sexiness. Decisively evaluating each for no more than five seconds before moving on. With Violet in Fiji, it fell to Melanie to ignore him for a good five minutes, but how could she ignore someone so powerfully attractive? It would have been like trying to ignore a guitarist during a concert solo.

His body commanded noticing: toned rear end and legs underneath well-tailored (maybe Armani) pants; not even a hint of a spare tire under the perfectly coordinated shirt. He stood six feet tall in his (maybe Bruno Magli) Oxfords, polished to a shine. Melanie quickly calculated the cost of his outfit even before noticing his face. Sold.

And then, when he finally turned to look at her, to acknowledge *her* presence, his face almost knocked her off the chair. Not pretty-boy handsome or even metrosexual handsome, but unapologetically masculine and undeniably seductive. Black eyes that bore through her. Sensuous lips and a full head of dark brown hair. Maybe late 30s? But it didn't matter; the only numbers that mattered now were the price tags on his clothes and how many more minutes she could last before creaming her undies.

His ebony eyes had a bemused expression as he took her in. *Ack, do I have salad in my teeth?* was Melanie's first thought. *Lint in my hair? Oh God, please not a wet spot on my skirt.* She glanced down as she stood up but saw nothing incriminating. Fought the urge to run to the bathroom mirror and tried to play it cool instead. As with the porn, no one else needed to know about her inner chaos.

Melanie knew she should say something, but all the options suddenly seemed to have a double meaning ("Do you see anything you like?") or were just plain inane ("How are you today?"). "Feel free to…" stuck in her throat. She plopped back down behind the desk as if it could offer protection. Swallowed hard as the feelings of inadequacy threatened to choke her.

He seemed to be sizing her up as he strode over, rifling through the files in her mind as if they lay in his own personal drawer. His eyes swept over her, lingering on her breasts in the silk plum-colored camisole, then on her bare legs under the desk. Melanie blushed and tried not to fidget; she hadn't shaved her legs since yesterday. *Why didn't you shave, stupid? But the stubble is barely noticeable! Get it together, Melanie. Don't blow this.*

"Hello." He spoke first, looking directly into her eyes.

"Hello. May I help you?" *Geez, what are you, a shop girl at the Gap?*

"You may." His deep voice calmed her, as did his mirthful expression—as if her obvious discomfort amused rather than annoyed him. "I'm looking for something for my living room."

Did your wife decorate the room? No wedding band on your ring finger, though. Does your girlfriend read fashion magazines there? Oh, geez, Melanie! Quit acting like an idiot.

"Of course. Do you have anything in particular in mind?" Melanie regained her composure as her five years of experience finally took over. With her salary tied to commissions, she couldn't afford to mess up. Lost income was a bigger failure than unshaved legs.

They chatted easily as she walked him through the possibilities. His art knowledge far exceeded that of many other clients; he also managed to drop references to emerging financial markets, rare French wines, and Swiss ski slopes. Melanie merely nodded at those; gossip sites and PornHub didn't cover India's economy.

She strove for intelligent, articulate phrasing. Even consciously waited three seconds before responding, which a self-help book claimed made you appear poised and collected when your internal self is babbling.

And thank goodness she had those years of experience to rely on, because he stood unnervingly close, as if he already knew her. No regard for personal space. Melanie fought the urge to pull away as the animal magnetism drew her in.

As they finalized the sale at the desk, he walked behind the desk and pulled the *Be Happy Now!* book out from its hiding place.

"Are you unhappy?" His tone sounded playful.

"No, of course not," Melanie's answer came automatically, as a mortifying blush crept up her neck. Who was he to be plundering her hiding place without asking?

"Then why are you reading a book on how to be happy?" Still lighthearted, but his expression had grown intent.

Melanie carefully counted to three before answering. "Because there's always room for improvement."

He laughed. "That's a very good answer." And Melanie's heart suddenly danced with giddiness. As if she had won something unexpected. Forget about the sale; his approval felt like the prize.

After signing the receipt, Dan Hightower (according to his American Express Black Card) handed the pen back to her instead of setting it down on the desk. Their fingers grasped the pen together longer than necessary. Melanie cradled the pen in her hand as she watched him walk out the door, feeling the charge still running through it. The heat spread through her hand and up her arm and down through her body to the soft spot between her legs.

Outside, people continued on their errands to nowhere, as if the world hadn't suddenly tilted sideways. As if anything else mattered.

"Hellllooooo, Earth to Melanie!" Melanie's best friend, Deena Flint, waved a hand in front of her face over drinks at the bar she owned, Backslash, after work that night. Deena practically lived at Backslash, on a safe corner in San Francisco's sometimes dangerous Mission District. To offset the faded red leather seats, pool table, and standard wooden tables, the bar offered top-notch cocktails and artisan beers. Clean and quality enough a place not to scare away the young Financial District suits, but divey enough to let them pretend they hadn't sold out.

"Sorry." Melanie smiled sheepishly. "I'm a little distracted tonight." She sipped her crisp pink Cosmo, her guy-scoping radar blissfully turned off for once. Backslash didn't generally draw suitable husband prospects. The male clientele fell into two categories: hipster artists with no money and young finance guys just out of college, who spent their overly generous paychecks on video game systems and enormous flat-screens, not on gifts for girlfriends.

Yes, Deena kept urging her to give up Cosmos—what was she, a *Sex and the City* wannabe? "Try a beer for once," she'd propose. But Melanie always demurred. Beer, so déclassé. A delicious cocktail overrode a tasteless image in a bar with no potential husbands.

"A little distracted? Ya think?" Deena nursed her sparkling water. No alcohol passed her scarlet-red lips anymore, although you wouldn't guess it from her party-girl appearance: tattooed arms and long, inky hair with a single blue streak, copious black eyeliner, clothing a cross between Hell's Angels doll and steampunk vixen. Today a ribbed black tank topped off a long army-green ruched skirt and slim leather boots. "I was just asking if you had plans for this weekend."

Deena had saved Melanie in the third grade from a bullying tormentor, turning him pale and shaking with a single whispered threat, and the two had been best friends ever since. Deena knew Melanie better than anyone. And, miracle of miracles, still liked her.

"Plans? For the weekend?" Melanie echoed her friend. Daydreams of Dan Hightower were driving her to distraction. Holding hands in the park, eating dinner by candlelight, making out languorously on the couch, him leading—no, dragging—her into bed...

"Yes, you know, the weekend? The thing that happens when work is over on Friday? The two days when you get to do whatever you want?" Deena teased, twisting a strand of her unruly hair around an unmanicured finger. No one noticed a manicure when you flew by on a motorcycle at 80 miles an hour.

"Whatever I want?" Melanie parroted blankly. She thought of her fantasy ravaging. What she wanted was unspeakable.

"I give up." Deena sat back with a smile, letting her eyes wander around the bar. "Whoever he is, you've got it bad. Are you going to tell me about it, or you going to deny there's anything to tell?"

"There's nothing to tell." Melanie blurted the response too quickly. "Really." Her mouth turned up in a secretive smile. Dan Hightower had undressed her with his eyes. He had stood close enough for the scent of his expensive shampoo to tickle her nose. Those sparks traveling along the pen. Fantasy fuel for a week! Forget holding hands in the park and dining by candlelight; better that he pin her arms down and dine on her juicy parts in the glow of a red neon motel light.

Just then a guy sauntered over to their booth, leaning over the table and resting his forearms on it as if he, not Deena, owned the place. Too close. Clean-cut and decent-looking, with a milk-fed Midwestern air, but sloppy despite the professional getup: loosened tie, top two buttons of the dress shirt undone. Face flushed and shiny under a layer of sweat. Eyes glazed with beer and arrogance—and horniness? Melanie instinctively scooted farther into the booth. Better to avoid engaging. Horny frat types were good for only two things: providing entertainment and buying drinks. And she already had both.

Deena inclined her head toward the intruder, stretching one lean inked arm diagonally across the table. A warning or an invitation—impossible to tell if you didn't catch the eyes narrowing.

"Hellllllo, laaaadies," Milk-Fed Man slurred.

"Hello." Deena's body tensed slightly, casually alert. She always treated scum nicely until the minute she had to kick their ass. "Having a good time?"

"Suuuure, sure." Milk-Fed Man grinned, angling in. "It's happy hour, isn't it? I'm certainly happy to see two such...lovely ladies sitting alone."

Even if Deena didn't have a longtime boyfriend already, a gorgeous bass player in a locally successful band, she'd never give a guy like this the time of day. Her Mensa-high IQ couldn't stand lowbrow come-ons.

"My friends and I were wondering if you could settle a bet for us," Milk-Fed Man continued, oblivious to the lukewarm reception.

Melanie and Deena sighed in unison. Always with the bets. Guys should spend less time betting and more time thinking up respectful ways to meet women.

"Oh? What's that?" Deena's dark blue eyes grew dangerously stormy, not that the guy noticed. Every pickup line in the world had found its way to her ears already, whether she served drinks from behind the bar or stood in line at the grocery store. Everything from "Want some fries to go with that shake?" to "Does God know one of his angels is out past curfew?" to marriage proposals, albeit drunken ones from guys who had likely stashed their wedding ring in the glove compartment before bellying up to the bar.

"Well, we were talking about women and toward the end of a date..." His eyes glided back and forth between Deena's breasts and Melanie's. "And of course I was saying that no always means no, if you know what I mean, but my some of my friends were saying that no sometimes means, 'Yes, if I like the way you do it.' Who's right?"

Milk-Fed Man beamed as if he had just said something very clever. Swayed slightly, his center of gravity shifting precariously. Melanie inched away from him, closer to the wall. *Please just go away,* she mentally willed him. *Just go back to your stupid friends and leave us alone.* But the words stuck in her throat, as usual. Doormats don't confront people; they just lie there and take it.

Deena waited 10 seconds before answering, shifting her gaze between his eyes and the tattooed snake coiled on her skin, ready to strike. "I think," she said finally, with cyanide-laced sweetness, "that if a woman lasts to the end of a date with you, you should consider yourself very, very lucky."

She swung her legs out of the booth and stood up to her full six feet in the heeled boots, setting her face slightly higher than his. "I also think," she continued, hands on hips, "that you should get your drunk and leering sorry-ass self the fuck out of my bar pronto. Feel free to take your friends with you."

It took a moment for her words to penetrate the guy's beery haze, but when understanding dawned, the self-satisfied grin slid off and his mouth tightened. He muttered something under his breath and slunk back to his friends. Grabbed his jacket, said something to them, and huffed out the door in a cloud of indignation.

"Good riddance, don't you think?" Deena directed her attention back to Melanie, still curled into the booth's farthest corner. Deena smiled, all the tension visibly draining from her muscles. Even the inked snake seemed to recede, its venom no longer needed. "You can come out now, Melanie."

Melanie gawped at her best friend. Such blatant rudeness lay far outside her skill set. If Deena hadn't been there, she would have just squirmed uncomfortably until she could make a beeline for the ladies' room. *How does she do it? Where does she get the guts?*

One time Melanie and Deena had been visiting New Orleans. The French Quarter streets electric with chaos and music and tourists clutching booze-laden Planter's Punches and Hurricanes. A guy had danced right up to them in the full beam of a streetlamp, pulled Melanie into a dramatic dip, and kissed her smack on the lips. "You're beautiful! I love this city!" he had shouted after releasing her, arms wide as if embracing the world, before skipping back to his friends.

Melanie had frozen, dumfounded, but Deena had bounded after

the guy. Brought him down to the ground in one swift foot sweep and straddled his torso, pinning his arms against his body between her long legs. He seemed too surprised to fight back. "That's assault, asshole. You're lucky we're not going to call the police," she had yelled. "You should learn to treat women more nicely." As his posse and Melanie watched in shock, she landed a spray of spit on the guy's stunned face. Hopped up and walked steadily back to Melanie without turning around. He wouldn't chase her; he'd had enough embarrassment for one day.

Melanie *knew* Deena had been right on that New Orleans street. She *knew* guys shouldn't be allowed to kiss random unconsenting women, and *of course* they should be punished if they do. But she also knew, although the words would never find a voice, that she had felt flattered that he had chosen her. And turned on. The kiss had been innocent and joyful, yet stolen. So wrong, and yet so right.

But here at Backslash, the picture had crystalline clarity: lecherous asshole gets shown the door. She was so grateful that Deena had shown Milk-Fed Man no mercy in her bar, because Melanie could only cower. And the jerk had interrupted her daydreaming about the sexy Mr. Hightower.

Why couldn't men just be sincere and genuine? How hard could it be to just be respectful? To say, "Hi, I saw you from over there and wanted to get to know you better. My name is..."? Men and their silly little games of bets and stupid pickup lines. Games almost no one ever won, yet the idiots kept playing.

"Now where were we?" Deena rubbed at a water mark on the booth's wooden table. "Oh, right. You were telling me how there's nothing to tell about the mystery man who's put your head in the clouds."

"There isn't." Melanie forced herself to focus on her friend and not thoughts of Mr. Hightower. Dan. "Honestly. Some guy just came into the gallery." Some guy she was already envisioning in bed, at the breakfast table, at school plays filming their adorable offspring...but she couldn't tell even Deena, her best friend. The universe might urge you to visualize possibilities, but you don't mess around with a potential jinx.

Something extraordinary could be afoot with Dan. Would it be snatched back if she weren't careful? Would she be punished if she presumed anything?

"But if there *were* something going on," Melanie continued, "you know I'd tell you. I tell you more than I tell my own sister." Melanie didn't share anything important with Harper anymore. Why give the enemy artillery?

"Well, you know how I feel about your sister." Deena's mouth scrunched up in distaste. "Your secrets would be safer with a gossip columnist." She gestured in surrender. "But all right. We'll talk about it when you're ready. I'm guessing there's some silly superstition at work here." An affectionate smile.

"You know me too well." Melanie didn't take an ounce of offense. Deena had saved her from that bully in the third grade, had rushed to her defense during The Case of the Stolen Kiss in New Orleans. Deena's black-belt skills and tattoos and Harley Davidson Sportster masked a kind and loving heart, especially for the underdog. Deena used her powers only for good—a very fortunate thing for someone like Melanie.

BUZZING PLEASANTLY from the cocktails with Deena and with visions of Dan rolling behind every thought like a cinematic backdrop, Melanie undressed for bed later that night. Stared at her naked body in the mirror, trying to love it. Why did those few extra pounds make her feel so ashamed? She kneaded the flesh on her thighs, wishing she could break it off like clay and resculpt her body into something more desirable, something that didn't blare out her weaknesses to the whole world. Wishing someone else would truly see her and adore her, would tease her into ecstasy with kisses and caresses. Her own fingers and vibrator filled in as a poor substitute, but what else could she do?

Melanie imagined Dan's dark eyes gazing lustfully at her full bare breasts, and her nipples got perky; she pinched them lightly with her fingertips, pretending they were his mouth, and they stiffened even more. She thought of his hand holding the pen for those few precious sections and imagined both of his hands holding her with the same attention, one fondling her rear end, the other...

She climbed into the bed, hiding under the sheet. Caressed her breasts and her stomach and her thighs lightly at first and then more firmly, thinking of Dan's strong-looking hands. And then, finally, she let her fingers swirl down into that warm, wet place that seemed suddenly greedy and insistent, grateful for the attention and demanding more. She dipped her fingers inside herself, imagining first his tongue and then his fingers and then his manhood penetrating her relentlessly, and as she stroked herself faster and faster and brought herself to climax after only a few short minutes, gasping softly, she imagined him holding her and looking down at her so tenderly, pleased and satisfied. As if her surrender to him were a cherished gift.

When the alarm clock jolted Melanie back to reality eight hours later, her nakedness seemed shameful in the morning sun. She glanced around furtively, even though of course she was alone. Peeled away the bedding, stood up, and hastily donned a silky robe. Headed off into bathroom for a hot, purifying shower to wash away the night's guilty pleasure, planning what to wear to work that day. Something extra flattering...just in case.

Chapter 5
Breathing Is Overrated

THE DAYS dragged across the calendar with agonizing slowness. Melanie couldn't concentrate on even the simplest things. She read the same paragraph over and over in *Be Happy Now!* Her attention drifted off embarrassingly during conversations. She dropped things and kept bumping into things. Thank goodness Violet was still in Fiji, so she didn't wonder whether Melanie had early-onset dementia.

And when each day finally sputtered to its inevitable conclusion, she hid back at home, relieved to be away from the witnesses to her disgraceful daze. No club-hopping with her spitfire friend Ginger or drinks with best friend Deena, no book groups or dinners out. Her focus turned inward instead, where she allowed herself to conjure thoughts of the delicious Dan Hightower during indecent bouts of self-pleasuring. Two times a day now, morning and night. The dirty little whore who hid behind Melanie's perfectly proper façade refused to be ignored. Ignorance is not bliss for greedy little trollops.

Am I losing my mind? she wondered after almost a week. *I don't even know him.* He might be married—no ring, though. He might be gay—but his eyes on her skirt said otherwise. He might have been a tourist—but then why have the photo he bought shipped locally? He might just not be attracted to her—but oh, that sizzle shooting across the pen between their fingers. Maybe he was just playing it cool to gain the upper hand. A masterful plan if so, as Melanie's own hands were now too busy touching herself to care about power games.

Should she could call him? Believable excuses abounded: "Just checking on how the photo looks. Are you pleased with it?" "Hi there, just wanted to confirm the billing address." But they all seemed fake and manipulative. If he wanted to call her, he would, right? He had her business card; no need to dig for her contact info. He knew exactly where to find her. Maybe he was waiting for her to make the first move? But only sluts in heat and desperate women made the first move with a man. Argh, not knowing what to do was driving her mad. *Someone please tell me what to do!* Melanie silently begged the universe.

Against her better judgment, she called her mother.

"Hi, Mom." Melanie spoke tentatively, warily, like a new zookeeper entering the lion's den. On this slow Thursday afternoon, the gallery was so quiet you could hear the art talk. Victoria would just be returning from tennis. Winning would equal a wonderful mood. Losing? Run for your life.

"Melanie, what a pleasant surprise!" Victoria gushed. "I just trounced Caroline Connor 6-4, 6-4. Nice to know I've still got it." Tennis-trouncing ranked right up there with having a nicer house and looking younger than other women the same age. How else would you know if you were winning at life?

"That's great, Mom." Melanie cheered her mom's good mood more than the win. "Hey, listen, I was wondering…"

"What's wrong? Do you need something?" Along with needing to win, Victoria needed to be needed. How else would you know if you were valuable?

"No, no, nothing's wrong at all. Everything's the same." *Except for everything's having changed when Dan walked through the gallery door.*

"Oh, OK." Clearly disappointed that nothing was wrong. "What's up then?"

"I was just wondering, when you and Dad met, did he pursue you or did you pursue him?"

"*Me* pursue *him*? Ha!" Her mom gave a little snort. "In my day the girls did not pursue boys, unless they were the girls no one married. You know what I mean. Why would we do the pursuing? If a boy didn't have the courage to ask you on a date, he wasn't worth dating. And your father was not lacking in either self-confidence or courage—although he did have to compete for my attention, let me tell you."

Melanie glanced up eagerly as the gallery door opened. Could it be...? Nope. Just the mail carrier, unaware of how disappointing he was. Who the hell needed mail at a time like this? She needed Dan to come and ship this horrible funk away.

"Hmm..." Melanie glumly refocused on her inadequacy in being pursuable. "So he just saw you and asked you out right away?"

"Well, we met a dance, so we were technically already out. Your father came over and asked me to dance—we went to the same high school, remember—and the rest is history. He sat with me every day at lunch for the rest of the school year. He just assumed I wanted him to, and I did. Our relationship grew from there, all by itself."

Melanie sighed wistfully. "Dating was so much easier back then. Everything's different today. It's so much harder to know how to act. The right way to handle things."

"Girls today make it harder than it has to be," came Victoria's pointed reply. "How different can it be? Dating is dating. Romance has been around since...well, you know, since...caveman times." Specific facts aren't necessary when you know you're right.

Melanie heard the refrigerator door open; her mom would be pouring a big glass of filtered ice water with a fresh lemon slice. Her drink of choice. Ice water to stimulate the metabolism and burn extra calories; vitamin C to help skin cells renew. As if the $7,000-a-year tennis exercise and $100-an-ounce vitamin C face cream weren't enough.

"Am I correct in assuming this is not a hypothetical conversation, Melanie?"

Dammit. Of course her mother would realize. She might overlook her children's need for warm, motherly affection, but she was a homing missile on their romantic relationships.

"Umm..."

"Right. Well, let me tell you this. If he doesn't make the first move, he's probably not someone you want to be with. So much nonsense these days about 'sensitive' men. They're just little boys if you ask me, not real men. Real men are brave enough to ask the women out. It's the natural order of things. If a guy can't even muster up the courage to ask a girl out, how is he supposed to be successful? In business *or* in life?"

So outdated, and yet so logical. Melanie's heart fell, because it meant Dan simply wasn't interested. She couldn't imagine any shortage of bravery or strength in that masculine body and charismatic demeanor.

Melanie sighed unhappily. "Thanks for the insight, Mom. I've got to get back to work now." She gazed at the empty gallery and noisily moved around in the white leather desk chair.

A pause. "Oooh, did you read that article on juice fasting I emailed you, by the way?" Her mother's tone rang cheerily with false goodwill. "So great for skin and hair, not to mention weight loss!"

Here we go again. "Not yet, but I will." *When hell freezes over.*

"Rebecca Wilson lost six pounds in a month, and she is practically glowing!" Victoria continued blithely. "I'm planning to try it myself if my current system ever stops working."

"So glad to hear it, Mom. Listen, I'd really love to talk more but I'm really, uhhh..." She couldn't say "busy" when the only agenda items involved opening the mail and surreptitiously scanning PornHub.

"That's fine, you get back to work. Maybe someday you'll have your own gallery and you can underpay other people to work while you hop around the world. Wouldn't that be nice?"

Melanie took a deep breath. *It's just her way. She doesn't realize how hurtful she's being. Let it go.* "Sure, Mom. Who wouldn't love that? Really gotta go now, though."

As the phone line disconnected, Melanie stared blankly into the empty, open room. So quiet she could hear her heart beating. She felt so powerless. She couldn't whip a better job out of thin air. She couldn't make her mother stop insulting her under the guise of helpfulness. She couldn't make Dan want to call her, and she couldn't call him.

She made a cup of tea, extra cream and sugar, and clicked on to PornHub. Nothing to do but wait.

FRIDAY MORNING saw Melanie perched at the desk again, as she had every weekday for the past five years. Mrs. Simfendorfer on the phone, prattling on about her latest party. Everyone must come to her because her hundred extra pounds made going out too bothersome, and yet she acted as if her guests should bow down in gratitude for the invitations. With her mansion and obscene disposable window's income, they often did. Social free-loaders couldn't afford egos.

"Yes, Mrs. Simfendorfer. Of course you need new artwork for the entryway! Of course you can't have people think you're not *au courant*. We're showing some very edgy work right now. Why don't I send you some photos?" Melanie twirled a pen and rolled her eyes. Listened to the muffled reply. She could picture the old bat sifting through her closet full of beaded muumuus on hangers as well-cushioned as her rear end.

"I'm so sorry; can you repeat that, Mrs. Simfendorfer?" Melanie hid her annoyance with solicitousness. She'd rather be daydreaming about Dan than playing yes-man to a woman who loved to say no.

("No, not the spicy beef lettuce cups; Asian fusion is *so* last year." "Roses?! No, no, much too pedestrian." "No, plus-ones are not allowed.") But Melanie's salary depended on commissions, and commissions depended on babying clients, even if those clients were fat, selfish widows without an ounce of compassion for a lowly gallery associate's miserable, distracted state of mind.

"Mrfffle you listening? I said, mrble blff..." More rustling and muffling. Maybe Mrs. Simfendorfer was bending over to look at shoes, and the fleshy rolls on her throat were strangling her vocal cords.

Just then the phone's second line lit up, its red blip blinking insistently, irritatingly. Great. Another spoiled client interrupting her train of thought about how to handle the Dan situation. She considered yanking the phone cord out of the wall. *We are experiencing technical difficulties. Please stand by until I get my head together.*

She should have called in sick, but her conscience didn't allow for lies. *But I am sick! Sick of dealing with selfish, demanding clients. Sick of waiting. Sick of having nothing to show for my life.*

"Mrs. Simfendorfer, again I'm so sorry, but may I put you on hold for just one minute? There's another call coming in, and I'm the only one here today." *Actually, I'm the only one here most days, because we can't all be gallivanting socialites with more money than God.*

"No, I won't hold. Just call me back when you can provide your full attention," came the curt reply.

"Of course. Thank you so much, Mrs. Simfendorfer. Again, I apologize. I'll call you right back."

Melanie clicked off and angrily pressed the button next to the blinking light.

"Van Doren Gallery." Her tone just short of snippy. "How may I help you?"

"Hello, Melanie."

The air went out of the room as Melanie shot into hyperfocus. Her body froze even as her pulse began to pound. She had longed for this moment all week, but now that it had come, she felt caught unprepared.

"Hello," she whispered. Excited. Afraid.

Silence stretched between them, every second too slow. For the life of her, Melanie could not think of one single interesting thing to say.

"Don't you want to ask me how I'm enjoying my new purchase?" Dan Hightower prompted, finally.

"Oh, yes, of course!" Melanie grabbed the lifeline gratefully. "How are you liking it?"

"I'm liking it very much." His tone gently teasing, since he had fed her the line. "A number of guests have complimented it already."

"Oh, good!" Embarrassingly overenthusiastic. *Settle down, girl. Stop acting like a besotted teen.* "Do you...do you entertain a lot?"

Dan laughed. "I do my fair share. Perhaps you would be interested in being on the receiving end sometime?"

Melanie carefully counted to three before answering, stifling the "Yes, yes, yes!" threatening to burst out. No need to telegraph her desperation.

"When did you have in mind?" She carefully modulated her tone.

"How about tonight?" he tossed out, unhesitatingly.

"Tonight!" Melanie echoed, dumbstruck. All this time waiting and now he wanted to go out with zero advance notice? *As if I have nothing better to do than drop everything for him? I should refuse on principle. Does it seem too desperate if I say yes? Are my legs even shaved?*

Not to mention if they ended up at her flat—what if she hadn't remembered to hide the vibrator? And the undies she wore were not even silk, just plain old cotton. All the questions and complications rained down on her like an assault. She felt paralyzed, unable to answer.

"Just say yes, Melanie." His voice caressed her, erasing her indecision. Everything fell into place: so simple, just a date. *Of course* she would go out with him that night. How could she refuse?

"Yes," she said. The assault of questions beat a hasty retreat, replaced by a delicious lightheadedness.

"Good. What time do you finish work?"

"Six o'clock."

65

"Then I'll pick you up there at 6. We'll go for a drink some-where and then dinner. Do you like sushi?"

"Yes, but...wait..." The complications marched back in. *I should run home and take a shower, change into something better, clean the apartment...*

"What." A statement, not a question. The tone of his voice making mincemeat of her protest. *Resistance is useless.* Dan would direct everything, and Melanie would go along. Anything else would be like paddling upstream without an oar.

"Nothing," she said. "See you at 6."

Melanie glanced at the time as they hung up: 11:15 a.m. Six hours and 45 minutes until he arrived. She snapped into action. Made a lunchtime mani-pedi and bikini wax appointment at the salon down the street, and planned a trip to the drugstore after for a shaving razor and gel. Toothpaste and floss were stashed in the desk, thank goodness. Undies spotless at least? Check. All the important bases covered, she settled back to the computer to brush up on current events headlines. Wars and crashing economies might be useful for making small talk.

Some things still fell under her control, after all.

DAN ARRIVED at an irritating 6:20 p.m. Melanie valued prompt-ness—for general courtesy but also to show the other person you cared. Not to mention that in the 20 minutes since six o'clock, she had worked herself into a nervous frenzy wondering whether he would even show up.

"Hello, Melanie." Just a breezy greeting as Dan walked through the door, unencumbered by apology or excuse. Also no five o'clock shadow or other late-day fustiness; maybe *he* had gone home to freshen up. *No fair!* Apparently orders to the rank and file didn't apply to the general.

"Hi." Melanie gazed at him shyly. Her hands fluttering like birds from her hair to her skirt, smoothing them both compulsively.

Should she kiss him on the cheek? Shake his hand? She settled for a little half wave. "Let me just get my bag and lock up."

"Take your time." His unruffled demeanor calmed her instantly, even as his appraising eye made her skin tingle. "That's a nice outfit."

"Thank you." Melanie gave the now automatic response after all her self-help training. It was always easier to take verbal abuse than compliments. She had more practice in it.

Luckily, Melanie dressed every day for man-meeting possibilities. A-line skirt two inches above the knee, suggestive but not slutty, and hiding her fleshy, untoned thighs. Silky top cut to show the curve of her breasts. Heels an inch and a half high, comfy but flattering to the calves. She would have suffered in three-inchers, but discomfort led to stress wrinkles.

And Dan was just like she remembered, thank goodness, exuding power and gorgeous masculinity. Crisp Calvin Klein suit and fresh white shirt, a few buttons open, no tie. And the best accessory of all: his eyes taking her in with obvious approval.

Melanie felt those dark eyes burning into her as she shut down the computer and fetched her jacket, straightened a few things on the desk unnecessarily, buying time to calm herself. It felt like he was feeding energy into her, charging her body. If the power companies could tap into that voltage, there'd never be an energy shortage again.

When she went to put her jacket on, he deftly stepped in and took it from her, holding it open from behind. His lips barely brushing her neck. Melanie felt the current travel straight down to her private parts. He smelled so amazing; she wanted to drink him in then and there. Throw her clothes off and let him drag her down to the floor into a pile of surrender. *Keep it together, Melanie. It's too soon to be throwing yourself at him. At least wait until dessert.*

Dan smiled...*knowingly?* The thought unnervingly struck Melanie that he could hear her inner turmoil. *Impossible. No one's a mind reader...right?*

"Well, that's it." Struggling to keep her voice steady, to tamp down the lust. "I'm ready."

"Good. Shall we?" He motioned for her to go first. She quickly punched in the code for the gallery's alarm and turned off the lights.

"Did you find parking OK?" She glanced down the street toward the busy parking garage. Parking downtown tended to be even harder than having a peaceful family dinner.

"Yes." Dan looking amused. "Right here." Nodding at a black Lexus double-parked in front of the gallery, blinkers on.

"Oh, but…you could get a big ticket for that." Melanie's brow furrowed. Not to mention the discourteousness of it; the two-way street could fit only two cars at a time.

"Maybe." He guided her lightly by the elbow through two parked cars, suavely opening the door and closing it as she settled in. *Nice. Beats my poor old Honda Civic any day. It even* smells *refined.* The leather seat delightfully caressed her rear end as the city din faded outside the car's protective bubble. Melanie heard her too-fast breath, the only sound in the hushed interior.

"Sweet car," she remarked, not thinking, as he got in and turned the key in the ignition. *Stupid thing to say. State the obvious much?*

"Yes, it's a fun ride." Dan glanced at her sideways, eyes dipping to her legs. "I do like my fun rides."

The blush traveled all the way to Melanie's scalp. *What am I supposed to say to that? One, two, three.* "So we're going to an amusement park?"

He laughed and glanced at her face this time. Ignoring the car behind honking furiously. "So witty. I like that in a girl."

Melanie twinkled with pride.

"Actually," he continued, "we're going to Bacchus for a drink before dinner. Have you ever been there?"

Oh, sure, I drop $15 on a single glass at four-star wine bars all the time. Who needs money to eat? On about $40,000 a year, all her extra income went to important investments: good haircuts and self-help books.

"I hear it's lovely," she murmured.

"As are you." He kept his eyes on the road. "And dinner will be at du Ciel." The Lexus hurtled down the bus lane, then shot through a yellow light, cutting off another driver. Between his aggressive driving, the blatant compliments, and the delight of dining at not one but two pricey places, Melanie could barely breathe. *Maybe breathing is overrated.*

"Do you always drive like this?" Melanie strove for nonchalance.

"Like what?" He sounded surprised.

"You know…uh, fast and loose."

He let out a small, slightly maniacal laugh. "I wouldn't call myself fast and loose, Melanie. This is the safest way to drive."

"Really?" *A driver's ed instructor would beg to differ.* "How so?"

"Slowpokes cause accidents," he declared. "They don't pay attention; they're just moseying around the streets with their head in the clouds. I pay attention. People who pay attention don't cause accidents."

Goosebumps prickled Melanie's arms. Did paying attention extend to female body parts too? Did it mean noting every sigh of pleasure as his tongue swirled around the tucked-away depths between her legs? She shivered with anticipation. The salacious slut hidden deep inside her could turn even small talk into a pornographic screenplay.

"Whatever you say," Melanie murmured. *Whatever you want,* she thought.

Just a few minutes later the Bacchus valet hurried to open her door. Melanie toyed with the idea of "accidentally" flashing Dan her panties but decided against it: The panties were too plain Jane, the move too déclassé. Plenty of time for spreading her legs later.

As she took the arm Dan offered and let him guide her, Melanie felt that same sense as at the wild Warehouse club with Ginger: like she was falling into a mysterious underground world. Like she was a human girl daring to swim with the mermaids.

ON THE surface the date appeared quite ordinary. He ordered wine for them, a pricey malbec. Appetizers too: Kobe beef skewers and sizzling pork dumplings. They chatted casually, facing each other over a polished dark wood table set with a single candle encased in glass. But underneath it all, in the places where longing lived and desires dominated, Melanie reveled in the extraordinariness. Every time he looked her in the eyes, so deeply, so intimately, her body yearned for him. Every time he lightly touched her hand or arm, a wave of pleasure washed over her. Their table became an island; Melanie, a thrilled castaway.

The details of Dan's life seemed ordinary enough too. Grew up in Santa Barbara; came to San Francisco in the late 1990s to ride the dot-com-boom wave. An only child. Parents had owned a small hotel and then retired to a 30-acre ranch in Colorado. No, they and Dan weren't particularly close, but not estranged either. A UCLA dropout, because college was a hoax—only a piece of paper to show for the $100,000-plus debt, a terrible investment. Now a successful venture capitalist in Silicon Valley. Just hearing the phrase "venture capitalist" made Melanie wet. Everyone knew that venture capitalists in Silicon Valley raked it in.

He lived in wealthy Woodside, less than an hour south of San Francisco, by himself in a big house with a pool. Nope, never married. No kids. Traveled to Europe often to see clients. Melanie's chair almost grew slippery as she imagined the sales-girls at Chanel in Paris fawning over her, courtesy of Dan's credit card. Resting her shopping-weary Yves San Laurent-clad feet in Café de Flore, sipping real *chocolate chaud,* nibbling a decadent cream-filled pastry or glazed fruit tart. Everyone would wonder who the thin and impossibly glamorous American woman was—all calories vaporized in the thin air of her fantasy. No one would dare treat her badly when she was thin, rich, and wearing Chanel.

Yes, everything about the date would have seemed ordinary to a casual observer in Bacchus, the food and the wine and the conversation, the light touching of hands, the eye-gazing. But Melanie's body slowly and surely floated to increasingly higher planes, Dan's voice and gestures inviting her there as clearly as if hand-engraved on linen card stock.

His thumb rubbed the wineglass stem, telegraphing what he would do to her nipples. His tongue savored a bite of beef as he would savor a taste of her inner thigh. He wiped his mouth on the napkin as if he had just drunk from the honeyed pool south of her waist.

"I'm sorry; you were saying...?" Melanie tried to focus. How could she stay on the conversational track with such a hot potential romp pending on the sidelines?

"I was asking you about where you grew up." Dan seemed genuinely interested in her, not just making small talk to get into her pants—er, her skirt, which by now she would have happily thrown off anyway.

"Hillsborough. But it's too boring to talk about." He didn't need to know all the dullness of her suburban childhood. How she had yearned for a dark, mysterious prince to rescue her from the soul-crushing mundanity and the never feeling good enough. How the year she got straight A's, her mother had "rewarded" her by sending her to fat camp.

Melanie told him instead about her family. How her brother, Alex, never seemed to work too hard for anything and yet got every-thing. How her sister, Harper, worked hard for what she had but didn't seem to enjoy any of it. How her parents had been married more than 30 years, marking each year with a proud celebration like marathoners high-fiving each other after every hilly mile.

Miraculously, Dan seemed intrigued by the everyday details of Melanie's boring, unaccomplished life. So she told him about how she loved Sunday mornings the best, when the world fell away into the void of Nothing to Do. About how Saturday nights out with friends were fun too—bars and art openings and movies and the occasional poetry slam, with their in-your-face energy. *Not that you'd ever get me slamming at the mike,* she silently added. *Getting slammed in the sack would sure be nice, though.*

"And you go to a club called Warehouse too, I believe." Dan winked, punctuating the statement. "With a pretty redhead."

Melanie blinked. How did he know about her recent walk on the wild side with Ginger? "Warehouse? How did you...?"

"Do you have a whole stockpile of names you rotate when you go out...Natasha?" Dan seemed to relish her confusion. He looked meaningfully at Melanie's tasteful silk blouse. "And outfits? Do you have two separate closets, one for the good girl and one for the bad girl?"

Melanie stared at him, baffled. "But…" Then it hit her. That nosy girl in the drinks line! She must have been his spy, charged with finding out Melanie's name and where she worked on behalf of Dan. Melanie had not spoken the name Natasha to anyone else that night except Ginger.

So someone *had* been watching her during the pole dancing show. She *knew* it! And the person was now sitting directly across from her. Setting her heart—and other parts—aflutter.

But hmm, sending a fact-finding scout…flattering or creepy? No, that asshole in Deena's bar with the leering pick-up lines—*that* had been creepy. Dan's move made her feel incredibly, deliciously desired. She wished she had the guts to lunge across the table and kiss him then and there. Forget beef skewers; she wanted him to skewer her mouth with his tongue.

Instead, Melanie just looked at Dan helplessly.

"It appears you have some explaining to do, Miss Natasha." Dan folded his arms in a mock-stern fashion, raising an eyebrow.

"Well…" she began. She needed more time to think! How could she explain the fake name and the hookeresque outfit? Men married nice girls, and nice girls didn't slut it up at kinky parties.

Their server returned just then, thank goodness. Cleared the appetizer plates and asked them if they cared for anything else. *Yes, I would care very much for a way out of this shameful mess,* Melanie begged silently.

"It's just that…" she began again when the server had left. No way around it; honesty was the only possible course. As always. Melanie sighed, willing the redness to drain from her face. "My life is pretty conventional." She cast her eyes down at the table, wishing it would open up and reveal a hidden passageway right back to her warm, safe bed.

Dan nodded, watching her intently. "Go on."

"It was Ginger's idea to go—my friend with the red hair. I wouldn't have picked something like that on my own, not the club or the outfit. I don't usually run with the human menagerie pack! Ginger thought a different persona would help. It seemed like play-acting, not lying."

"And did it help?" Dan's expression didn't give away his thoughts.

Melanie remembered how wild and exotic she had felt that night. So free, not caring every second what everyone thought. Completely different from her usual self. Being Natasha had been like being on vacation.

"Oh, yes." Her eyes shone at the memory—and at the possible future with Dan that the night had brought her. "It helped." *It may have dropped the brass ring right in my lap.*

Dan nodded again, slowly, appearing to ponder her answer. "So you enjoyed yourself." A statement, not a question.

"Yes, very much." *But please don't judge me badly,* she begged with her eyes. *Please don't think I'm a slut or a pervert. Please don't decide I'm not good enough for you.*

The seconds before Dan responded crawled around the clock. His eyes moved around her face, unreadable. "It's good to do things outside your comfort zone," he declared, finally. Smiling his approval. He reached for her hand and held it firmly, and Melanie felt as if dark, threatening clouds had parted and the sun had broken through to warm her from head to toe. "It's how we grow."

The sunlight of his approval washed away the shadowy corners of her fears and doubt. If his hand had not been holding hers, tethering her to the earth, Melanie would have floated away on a puff of joy. She could barely breathe, and forced herself to take small sips of air. Passing out would have meant missing all the lovely sensations flooding her body and mind.

The room shrank then, until just the two of them and the table and the candle remained; other people's chitchatting and clinking silverware receded into the background, like a wave slipping back into the sea. Melanie could read the desire in Dan's eyes as clearly as if he had spoken it. Her body responded by tingling from her scalp to her perfectly manicured toes. It was all she could do not to lunge across the table and kiss him right there. Too bad the first move was never hers to make.

Melanie's voice disappeared then, realizing it was no longer needed. Dan's approbation hovered in the silence like the comforting scent of bread baking, and Melanie basked in it like a starving person at a feast. It nourished her more than any real food ever could. *If I had this every day, I'd be thin in no time,* she thought.

She sat there just looking at him, at his face and his neck and his torso and his arms, and his fingers, of course, still clasping her hand. Watching those fingers work every inch of her hand, stroking the crevices and rubbing the palm and gently tugging on the fingertips. If Melanie died right now, the bliss would light up her features for eternity.

Damn the server interrupting to ask them again if they would like anything else. Melanie couldn't help but think, *Oh, yes, I want it all, right here and now.* But Dan merely requested the check. At least one of them could keep a clear head.

"Can I ask you something?" Her voice returning in the car, even as her body still floated. How would she make it through an entire dinner with him now when just wine and appetizers had sent her into such a tizzy?

"You may." The Lexus purring to life at his touch.

"Why?" Almost a whisper.

"Why what?" His gaze focused not on her now but through the windshield, the car smoothly weaving in and out between lanes, leaving the slowpokes behind.

"Why did you notice me that night at Warehouse? Why did you send that girl to find out who I was?" *Because of the slutty outfit? Because you want to have a threesome with me and Ginger? Because I looked desperate and lonely?*

He smiled, eyes still on the road. "You mean aside from the fact that you're hot?"

"I'm not hot," she demurred automatically.

"Are you questioning my taste?" His forehead creased.

"Of course not!"

"Then you're hot. We're agreed." He glanced at her sideways and nodded just once, as if hammering the point in. No further discussion necessary.

They drove in silence for several minutes, Melanie stifling gasps and trying not to think of car crashes. Dan apparently valued small talk as much as he valued defensive driving.

The softly lit sign for du Ciel restaurant appeared out her window at last. "OK…well, aside from"—she gulped—"my being hot, why did you choose me?" *Am I special, or is this just how you meet girls? Spying? Tracking them down at kinky clubs like a predator in the wild?* The image of a leopard grazing on a gazelle's tender flesh flashed in her mind.

"Aside from your being hot," he reiterated, expertly sliding the car into du Ciel's valet space and turning off the ignition, "there's just something about you."

"Oh." *Could you be any vaguer?* "What, exactly, if you don't mind me asking?" Sounding a lot braver than she felt.

Dan ignored the valet standing in the street, holding his door open. His full attention on Melanie. "An innocence," he declared finally. "And yet a fitting-in too. Like you were waiting to be corrupted." He nodded again, then swung his legs out and dropped the keys in the valet's waiting palm. Why wait for a response when there's no room for debate?

What a strange answer! What does that even mean, "corrupted"? And does that mean he's corrupt? Isn't being corrupt bad? Melanie's head spun with confusion, but Dan already stood at her door. She fit her hand into his, and she rose close to him. He closed the door behind her, leaving the unsettling answer swirling inside the car. She watched the valet drive it away and decided to let it go. For now. No sense ruining a $200 meal.

As du Ciel absorbed them into its gracious hush, all plush white leather banquettes and upholstered walls and soft, romantic lighting, Melanie took Dan's arm flirtatiously. As if she were afraid of turning a heel in the thick carpeting. *I could get used to this,* she mused, following the model-attractive hostess to a corner table. *It sure beats eating Lean Cuisine in front of Netflix.*

Melanie glowed under Dan's desirous gaze and attentiveness. He fed her perfectly sized bites of food so exquisite, her eyes slid shut. He dipped a thumb in the wine and rubbed it along her lips, just grazing her tongue. He held her hand between courses, tracing its outlines in the candlelight, every caress stoking her own fire. Anticipation settled Melanie's body into a delicious haze, as sweetly torturous as the flourless chocolate cake she allowed herself only two bites of. Already she was almost too fat to be naked.

Too soon the impeccably dressed server whisked the last plates away, and Melanie found herself back in the Lexus speeding away from du Ciel. Head buzzing with wine and questions. *Will he want to come up? How far should I let him go? It's already so late.* Swallowing a yawn. *If we stay up any later, it's going to be hard waking up in the morning.* Oh, who was she kidding? Just going back to reality after this luxurious bubble would be a rude awakening.

Just a few blocks from her house, Dan pulled over along the side of the park.

"Open your door," he instructed, matter-of-factly.

"But..." *What the heck?* "This isn't where I live," she protested. "It's a few blocks up." Why wouldn't he take her all the way home? Had she done something wrong? Anxiety stabbed her in the gut.

"Open your door, swing your legs out, stand next to the car, and close the door." Dan didn't look angry. On the contrary, the look in his eyes—slightly unfocused, lids lowered—showed his desire. Excitement surged between Melanie's thighs. She did as he instructed.

He left her standing there for what seemed like a long time, but who could tell time anymore? The confusion and anticipation were growing hand in hand, the late-night chill hardening her nipples through the thin silk of her blouse as she stood outside the car. Down the street a young woman walked a dog. *Poor girl,* she thought, *with your boring chores.*

When Dan got out and came around to her side, Melanie could barely think straight.

Silently he slid his arm around her back and leaned her carefully but firmly against the door. Pulled his arm back and reached for her hair, winding his fingers through and tugging, forcing her to tilt her head to the side. Her face a question mark in the streetlamp's dim light.

He eyed her up and down as if deciding which treat to choose from a dessert cart. Settled on her neck, nuzzling slowly at first and then kissing it with abandon, from her ears down to the boundary of her blouse. Melanie's eyelids lowered as she struggled to keep her legs from turning to liquid.

His hands ran up and down the sides of her body, teasingly avoiding the parts she wanted him to touch most. She tried to arch into him, but a firm hand pushed her back against the car. She tried to caress him, but he circled his fingers around her wrist and pinned her arm next to her body. His prisoner, his prey. His cherished object. A long, low, desire-drenched moan escaped her lips.

His mouth found hers, and Melanie suddenly realized how starved she had been her whole life to be kissed properly. He alternately teased her lips with his tongue and probed inside her mouth, and bit her lips oh so softly—he even licked her teeth and sucked on her tongue. Not so much kissing as invading, first gently and then growing more insistent. Taking possession. What could Melanie do but surrender?

She stopped trying to touch him and get closer to him, instead just sinking into the car's cold metal door and his kisses and trying to keep up her end. Letting him take complete control. *Of course* the control was his. He had taken it the moment he walked through the gallery door. No, even earlier—the moment he sent his spy over at Warehouse. Dan had made it clear from the start who the director was; Melanie could only play along and hope she had a starring role.

But why were his hands deliberately avoiding the places that most craved his touch? Her thoughts had no shape anymore, just *Please please please*. The wanton wench in her silently begged him to take her right then and there, to pound into her standing up next to the car. Who cared what Dog Walker Girl down the street would think? Dog Walker Girl was a mouse beneath the baseboards of Dan's stage.

When she could take it no longer, when the unbearable delicious yearning threatened to spill out into words—an invitation, a plea, begging—Dan released her and stepped back. Took in her messed-up hair and smudged eye makeup. Took in her skirt, askew now, and her blouse, its fragile silk crushed under his grasp. Took in her legs, barely able to hold her up anymore, and her eyes, filled with longing. He nodded slowly and smiled, as if to say, *My work here is done.*

"You really are something." His tone glowed in admiration. And for once Melanie felt no need to demur. Pleasing him thrilled her. Besides, contradicting would have been insubordination.

He opened the door. "Time to go."

Protesting had no place here, although every fiber of Melanie's being was doing just that. Those precious few minutes were all the director had allotted her for that scene. Who was she to suggest an alternate ending? She shot him a hungry look but slipped obediently into the car.

The two blocks to her house disappeared in an eye blink. Girlishly, she leaned over and kissed him softly, chastely, on the cheek. "Thank you for a wonderful evening." It came out as a whisper.

"My pleasure." He clearly meant it. And Melanie sailed out of the car and up the steps to her front door, buoyed by his approval.

Once inside, she peeled off her clothes, inhaling the lingering scent of him. Draped them lovingly over a chair. And as she lay between the sheets, not daring to touch herself—how could she erase the traces of his hands?—so many feelings danced around inside her, colliding and bouncing around unchecked. Blissful, painful desire. Satisfaction at pleasing him. Anxiety that she hadn't done enough. Pride over his compliments. And over everything else, anticipation. A man like that would show her what she'd been missing. A man like that would use her body properly.

Dan had awakened her body and claimed her heart in one swift stroke. Raised her hackles with his presumptions. And gave her goose bumps with the spying episode. *Was that girl in the club the only time?* Melanie wondered. *Or has he sent spies to the gallery too? Is he spying on me now?* She pulled the sheets up higher, realizing she had no idea how far Dan would go to get what he wanted. And how badly she wanted to find out.

Her skin prickled, warning of danger, even as her soft mound grew even softer. Her wet parts even wetter.

Melanie would go wherever this ride would take her. Wherever *he* would take her.

No turning back now.

Chapter 6

No Use Crying Over
Spilled Passion

Stupid chores.

Melanie ticked off the day's tasks in her head, irritated: Buy a wedding gift for her cousin Grace. Clean the fridge. Take old clothes to Goodwill. Reorganize the junk drawer. Ugh. Chores belonged to the mundane masses. Precious princesses adored by a venture-capital king did not do chores.

I bet he's rich enough to have a housekeeper, she thought. *Maybe even a personal assistant.* She pictured herself being kind yet firm with the help as Mrs. Dan Hightower, a duchess in a historical romance novel transplanted to modern-day California: "Please retrieve Mr. Hightower's tuxedo from the dry cleaner before Friday night's gala, Consuela." "Mrs. Kvetchner is gluten-free, and her husband is a vegan, so please ensure appropriate menu choices at Sunday's banquet, Hervé." "Shakala, how many times must I tell you that silk must be hand-washed?"

Melanie lolled around in bed, luxuriating in the fantasy. Violet would be a peer and no longer her boss; some other poor girl would fetch them both tea while they chatted about which island to grace with their presence. Invitations to balls and mansions and yacht parties would overflow, their creamy hand-engraved envelopes spilling out onto the entryway's polished parquet floor. Each invitation judged and ranked on such important criteria as the caliber of the guests, the exclusivity of the location, and whether Melanie would be fawned over.

She sashayed into the bathroom and turned on the tub's faucet, pouring a generous amount of jasmine-scented bubbles under the steaming blast. Drizzled rose oil over the water's undulating surface. The urgency of the chores floating away on a cloud of scented steam.

She doffed her robe and let it pool on the white tile floor, casting the appointed hook only a quick glance. *Someone else will pick that up,* she fantasized, settling into the warm water. *And they'll clean the tub too.* Warmth pooled in her nether regions.

Her fingers wandered down her bare breasts, lingering on the nipples. Dan hadn't touched them last night, but her imagination gave him a freer hand now. She stroked the dark pink circles until they hardened, poking out through the bubbly froth. With one hand still teasing a nipple, she let the other descend slowly down her body. *His* fingertips, awakening her skin and her desire inch by inch.

"Dan." Breathing his name across the iridescent clouds. "Oh, Dan." Reality didn't dare broach the walls of this magical bubble. No one could see; no one would know. Anything could happen.

Gently massaging her skin, traveling down and down at a measured pace, fighting the urgency. When her fingers at last dipped inside, feeling the slippery smoothness, her body floated with the bubbles, her head growing as fuzzy as the white mohair throw rug awaiting her dripping feet. Thoughts of him mingled with thoughts of the household help attending to her every need and whim: "Shall I tell the Dinkelmaers yes for the 12th, Mrs. Hightower?" "Would you like the crème brûlée for dessert or the tiramisu, Mrs. Hightower?" "The carpenter you hired for your custom shoe closet is here, Mrs. Hightower." Homemaker Barbie morphed into Royal Barbie with the solicitous attention of the help, and Royal Barbie reveled in Dan's driving touch.

You're so beautiful. Putting the words in his mouth. *You make me so hard. Only you, Melanie.* Her hand moving rhythmically in and out, faster and faster. She couldn't fight the urgency any more. *I want you, only you.* Images of his yearning eyes and the staff awaiting her orders and the custom shoe closet filled with Manolos and Jimmy Choos all merged in one deliriously rich moment, sending her over the top in an orgasm so powerful, water sloshed over the tub's sides. *Someone else will clean that up,* she reminded herself dreamily, closing her eyes and sinking back into the water's warm embrace.

ANOTHER HOUR of procrastinating put Melanie no closer to finishing any chores. But how was she supposed to focus? Her head was swimming in day-after bliss; she drifted along, noticing but not fully grasping all the real-world items drifting by: a bowl of low-fat yogurt, a cup of tea, email messages that suddenly all lacked urgency. Netflix lured her in with the promise of an award-winning French film, but the subtitles flashed faster than her languorous brain could process. Last night's footage ran on an endless loop in her head, the real blockbuster.

Dan's fingers entwined with hers in the restaurant. His voice, so deep and self-assured: "There's just something about you." His hands running up and down her body against the car, pinning her wrists. As if trying out a new purchase. She shivered with pleasure at the thought.

OK, Melanie, enough's enough. You can't waste your whole Saturday mooning around like a love-struck teen. Besides, you're going to jinx it if you keep this up. The line between visualizing intentions and jinxing everything was thinner than the film of soap still clinging to the bathtub's sides.

Trying not to think about Dan any more than necessary, she dreamily got dressed and wafted out the front door. Delightfully buoyant, such an unnatural feeling. An almost unbearable *rightness* of being. Is this what normal people felt like? People unplagued by anxieties and inadequacies? She wanted to skip down the street, to sing her joy to anyone and everyone. Anyone except her mother and sister, that is. Talk about a jinx, not to mention instant bubble-bursting. Either of them would skewer her joy like a shish kabob.

The radiant sun in a cloudless sky shone its approval. How considerate that it mirrored her mood. Didn't she deserve a little bliss after all the constant toiling, all the waiting and hoping and preparing for the right man? And now, maybe, just maybe....*Stop! Don't even think it.*

The café teemed with hordes of regular people, unaware of the divinely blessed girl treading a higher plane in their midst. The poor unenlightened masses with their trite existences, mainlining caffeine to jolt themselves into a semblance of life. Melanie didn't need caffeine; she could have subsisted on air and Dan's touch.

She ordered a rose-petal herbal infusion, a perfect princess drink. Alit on a black ironwork chair at a table for one as if it were a throne, facing the park across the street—the scene of last night's wonderment. Her indignation rose as a dog sniffed around the very spot where Dan had pushed her against the car—how dare the dirty creature defile such hallowed ground?—but magnanimity won out. Petty resentment didn't suit a princess.

All around her, people acted out stories for her entertainment without realizing it.

A young couple drinking matching iced coffees. Hm, were they even a couple? Hard to tell; they seemed more enamored of their cell phones than each other, texting and checking email. Not even the excuse of too many years together leaving them with nothing left to say. The girl stroked the guy's leg absentmindedly with a foot under the table; the typing paused as they shared a smile. Then the devices reeled them back in.

A slightly older couple at another table, complete with baby and dog but surreally still. Nestled into the woman's chest in a Baby Björn, the wee one snoozed; the dog followed suit at the husband's feet. No words passed between the husband and wife as they stared blankly past each other, slumped into their chairs. Distracted? Bored? Just plain exhausted?

The wife's hair needed a wash; stubble dirtied the husband's face. A doughiness around both their middles. *Letting themselves go already,* Melanie judged. *Not gonna happen to me. No wonder people have midlife crises. They wake up one day and realize they're bored and, even worse, fat and ugly.*

No, that would not happen to her. Good time management would help her rise above letting herself go to pot. And yoga—for the fitness as much as the flexibility for bedroom maneuvers. And a team of professionals dedicated to keeping up her appearances, courtesy of Dan's—er, her future husband's, whoever that may be—well-padded paycheck. Her mother had taught her at least one useful thing: Looking naturally young and fresh took a lot of work.

Homemaker Melanie of the future not only stayed gorgeously slender and wrinkle-free, but always proffered stimulating conversational tidbits. Her Ken, now sporting Dan's face instead of a vague blob, would eagerly engage. After all, he had been away from her so much of the week, working hard to give her everything she deserved. Weekends were for gazing at each other and their little cherubs adoringly, not staring off into space dreaming of lives not lived.

The thought of Dan staring at her adoringly made her girl parts throb again. Already? Hadn't they had their fill in the bath that morning? Her girl parts had a mind of their own. *Well, no harm in daydreaming,* Melanie thought, keeping her hands on the table but letting her mind wander to all the dirty places it loved rolling around in.

"Penny for your thoughts." The interruption shocked her out of the reverie like a bucket of ice water. Melanie frowned at the intruder, annoyed and displaced. His expression flickered sheepishly. "Yikes, that wasn't very original, was it?"

Melanie blinked several times, struggling to remember the name of this handsome waiter gazing at her. Freshly shaven and without his dog, he looked even more gorgeous than Melanie remembered from their meeting last Saturday in the park—if you overlooked the telltale barista's apron, broadcasting his lowly life status. "Scott," she came up with finally. Mental high-five. "How are you?"

"I'm good, just working. It's been a busy morning here. How are you?"

I'm fantastic! Melanie wanted to shout. *I went out with the man of my dreams last night.* But of course she didn't. No one could burst your bubble if you didn't blow it their way.

"Very well, thank you." Trying to swallow the smugness.

"Good, good. Um"—he cast a glance at an empty chair near-by—"I'm on break for 15 minutes…"

Princess Melanie of the generous spirit nodded, approving the unspoken request. Scott the lowly coffee slinger pulled a seat up to her table. "But I thought you worked only on weekdays?"

"I needed the extra hours." His soft, apologetic look seemed at odds with his ruggedly masculine face and crisp white button-down. "San Francisco is more expensive than I figured."

"Mm-hm, it certainly is expensive." *Especially if your job is doling out coffee for minimum wage and tips.*

But who was she to judge? After rent and health insurance and IRA contributions, Melanie barely had enough to spend at the designer outlets way out in rural nowhereseville. Without regular parental handouts, she'd be buying lingerie at Sears.

"The economies of scale are stacked against single people," he commented wryly. "Don't you think?"

Economics crossed Melanie's mind even less than Third World politics or where homeless people went when it rained. *Lucky for him he's so good-looking. With lips like those, he can spout off on almost any boring topic he wants,* she thought, before reminding herself that a) he was poor, and b) she was taken.

"Oh, yes, don't even get me started on that." *Don't* you *get started on that.* "How's the book coming?" The logical next question, although she wasn't particularly interested in that either. All she really wanted to talk about, to think about, to fantasize about, was Dan.

"Good." He leaned across the small table, so close she could see a bit of fluff on his eyelash. Such intense, penetrating blue eyes. Ocean-deep eyes. How big would they get if they saw her naked? *Quit it, Melanie. Can't you stop for two minutes?* "The writing is all going right on schedule. And the plot is really cool. It's about…"

"Wait, don't tell me." Melanie held up a hand. "I'd rather just read it when it's published." She smiled, smoothing the edge off the words. Who cared about the plot? Probably some formulaic thriller or batty sci-fi novel about aliens that would never get published. "I'll even come to your book signing." *The one that will never happen.*

"OK, gotcha." No offense taken; still leaning in. "How's the tea?"

"Delicious." She meant it. Euphoria sweetened everything even better than Splenda.

If only she could be honest about her bliss. Have a real moment instead of dancing around the truth, afraid of missteps and jinxes and hurting people's feelings. But no. Doormats don't take those kinds of risks. Doormats don't take any risks at all.

No use blaming anyone else for her wretched timidity and self-loathing, either. True, her childhood teachers had always been harder on the girls—"Boys will be boys" excusing every behavior the girls were lambasted for. The boys earned a mere sigh for an infraction that sent the girls to stand in the corner.

True, her own parents had cut Alex so much slack, he could have hung the whole family with it, while Melanie lost TV privileges for sloppy handwriting on her homework.

True, Harper had been an enemy instead of a kindly older sister from day one, waging a personal war designed to conquer with contempt—a self-preservation instinct Melanie actually had to admire. Parental-affection rations were scant among the Merriweather troops.

Melanie had swallowed it all as unquestioningly as she had swallowed the canned baby formula served up by the nanny while her mother served up aces on the tennis court.

But blaming everyone else? Pointless. You can't change the past. You can't change people. You can only play the cards you're dealt and maybe try to hook up with someone with a better hand. All the self-help books said so.

So she sat there and looked at Scott, and he looked back at her, and Melanie racked her brain for a topic to talk about that didn't involve economics, boring book plots, or Dan.

"I hope you don't think I'm stalking you or anything, by the way," he said after a while. "I do work here."

Melanie mentally shivered, not entirely unpleasantly, at the mention of stalking. But out loud, she just laughed. "No, of course not." *Too bad. Being a stalker might have made you more interesting.* Stalkers desired things; stalkers went after what they wanted. "Anyway, I'm the one who came here."

"But it is nice seeing you again. I"—he swallowed hard—"I still don't know too many people here in San Francisco." Melanie glimpsed something—wistfulness? Sadness? A door in her heart swung ajar. She had a soft spot for people who let cracks in the armor show through.

Not to mention the sunshiny hair and sea-dreamy eyes. *Maybe I could go for him,* she considered. *Just for fun, not for husband material. Everyone deserves some fun, right?*

"Well, you're very friendly." She leaned toward him encouragingly, close enough to inhale the clean scent of his pressed shirt. Rested her cheek in her hand. "And handsome too. I'm sure you'll have a harem soon enough."

"Ha, sure!" He snorted, amused, but his suddenly searching look betrayed his true feelings. *Go ahead,* Melanie urged silently. *Ask me out. You can do it. You know you want to. Be brave.* She couldn't do the asking, of course. Asking was even harder than not feeling inadequate.

"Hey, maybe sometime when I'm not working all day and writing all night, um…" he began, eyes sliding off her to a vague point beyond. *Would I let you wine me and dine me and throw me down on the bed? Yes, Scott. Yes, I would. Just tell me you want to take me out. Tell me you won't take no for an answer.*

But Scott just sat there ironing his apron with sweaty hands, every second of hesitation deflating her bubble of interest. And when he finally puttered around to, "Maybe we could have a coffee somewhere else, sometime, if you're not too busy," Melanie could only toss out a mere nod and an "Mm-hm," knowing that she had a better chance of being named Businesswoman of the Year than of their ever sparking it up in the sack together. A low-paying job made a poor catalyst, but wishy-washiness was an invincible spark-snuffer.

As she watched him sidle back to the counter, collecting dirty coffee mugs and crumb-strewn plates along the way, Melanie sighed. *What did you expect? He's not working here to pass the time. No confidence, no ambition, no passion.*

Not like Dan. Not at all like Dan.

Ohhhhhh, Dan. The thought of him lifted her heart instantly above the Scott disappointment. Why fret about boys when she had a real man, a man who knew how to take charge? And speaking of charging, time to go put a wedding gift for her cousin on her already overburdened credit card. The junk drawer could wait. Cleaning the fridge could wait. Someone else would be tackling all her unpleasant chores soon enough.

SURE, MELANIE could have ordered Grace's wedding gift online at work, between bouts of porn-surfing and client-brownnosing. But so much better to fondle the high-end merchandise in person—the creamy coolness of Lenox bone china, the iciness of Waterford cut crystal. You can't touch on the Internet, as dissatisfying a truth for housewares as for man meat.

Besides, Tiffany & Co., where Grace had registered, lay not too far from Kate Spade and Prada and all of downtown San Francisco's other sanctuaries of sumptuousness. Melanie was only too happy to worship at them even if the tithing put the goods out of reach.

Were the high-end stores designed to make you feel like perfection was only a handbag or wineglass purchase away? Everything so beautifully displayed, so seamlessly arranged. Their siren song humming in every perfect stitch and luxurious material, never a speck of dust on the shelves or a hair out of place on the salesgirls. *Isn't our world wonderful?* everything whispered. *You can't live here, but you can take us home.*

Her mother's and sister's endless critiques echoed in Melanie's ears:

"You can't make a silk purse out of a sow's ear, but I'll do my best"—Harper's offer to do her hair for the prom.

"Do you really need that dessert, Melanie? Nothing tastes as good as being thin feels"—her mother after countless dinners.

"You'd be so much [better off, happier, more popular] if only you'd [lose weight, stop slouching, get better grades, listen to me]"—either one of them on any given day.

Now, eyeing the rows of domestic bliss incarnate in the Tiffany china section, she couldn't help but picture the jaws of every single family member dropping as she introduced her future husband, a wildly successful *and* gorgeous financier. Who'd dare slap a put-down on her then? Presiding over the mansion staff and hosting Silicon Valley's movers and shakers at dinner parties, she'd make her lawyer sister look like a McDonald's manager.

No more criticisms. No more being second-rate meat in the bargain bin. No more penny-pinching on eBay and BlueFly and those God-forsaken Vacaville shopping outlets. She'd sail through the Kate Spade and Prada stores on Dan's plastic instead of giving in to the familiar tides of envy and longing.

Sure, she wished it could be her own plastic, backed by her own paycheck. But the high-powered career gene had skipped her. It had passed from her HR vice president dad first to her brother, Alex, probably celebrating some multimillion-dollar financial deal with a stripper on his lap right this minute, then to Harper, scratching her way up the law-partner post while other people raised her kids.

Harper toiled at the office like a madwoman. Their dad had put in reasonable hours and retired early just last year; he was only 58. Alex, though obsessed with money, hardly seemed to work at all, unless you could call tossing back beers with the Japanese while fake boobs jiggled in your face "working."

And then of course there were people like Melanie's boss, Violet, living off inheritances and never having to lift a finger for anything. Totally unfair! Melanie hadn't been gifted with Harper's ambition or Alex's money-making magic or her dad's luck, and certainly not Violet's inheritance. All she had was the hope of marrying a man who had one of those things.

And it's not like she wouldn't contribute to the marriage. She'd make their home comfortable and gracious enough for a king. She'd ensure her husband's immortality by bearing his children. She'd be his virtual sex slave. Wasn't that a fair trade for a big house and a platinum Amex card?

She ran her fingers admiringly over a Lenox china platter on the Tiffany display shelf. Eyed the cut-crystal glasses, lit to twinkle. Peered at the prohibitively expensive silverware, imagining her cousin unwrapping one fork—all Melanie could afford on her own salary. The longing for everything was so strong, it made her bones ache. For the love missing in her life. For the nice house filled with children and the help and expensive furniture. For all the things that would announce to the world that she was accomplished. That she was someone who mattered.

She bought a white stoneware gravy boat off Grace's registry. One of the least expensive pieces but still $65. Ouch. She'd have to bring lunch from home to work for two weeks instead of ordering out.

Someday she'd be able to afford full place settings for 12.

Someday maybe very soon.

VIOLET BREEZED back into the gallery from Fiji on Monday, ready to resume ordering Melanie around. Brimming with energy and stories of her yachting adventure. She had frolicked in the lagoon where they had filmed *Blue Lagoon*! She had gotten high in a kava kava ritual, and did Melanie know where one could procure kava kava stateside? She had skinny-dipped in the starlight with a shipping magnate, and if you've never swum naked under the Fijian stars, you truly have not lived! Never mind that the native Fijian yachting staff slept six to a bunkroom, saw their families only once a month, and had no health care—they had all those tranquilizing herbs and that energizing starlight.

The yacht had been chartered by one of Violet's many jet-setting friends for a vacation. But could you even call it a vacation if someone barely worked the rest of the year? Melanie gritted her teeth even as she ate up the tales of lobster served beachside and champagne flowing like waterfalls. Violet's circle turned a blind eye to the desperation of the poverty-stricken people serving them, the random-chance inequality doled out at birth. Melanie ached to have that blind eye instead of her desperate heart.

"Well, darling, we did boost the local economy—we spent lots of money there." Violet's rejoinder anytime someone remarked on the awful conditions of the locals in exotic locales. "World poverty is for the presidents to solve."

True, Violet spent money like it was going out of style—everywhere except on gallery staffing, as Melanie's paycheck could attest. She'd drop 10 grand at a charity fundraiser like it was spare change, hire a private jet on a whim, hop halfway across the world to escape the fog, but 3 percent annual raises atop an average salary were all she deemed fit for Melanie. Charity was for organizations that threw lavish galas, not servants at home or abroad.

Those charity fundraisers...what a farce, Melanie often thought. People can't open their wallets unless someone rolls out the red carpet? Just a bunch of social climbers and bored trophy wives with nothing better to do—and it killed Melanie not to be one of them. Violet always lamented the quality of the food at those events, but rubber chicken still tasted better than sour grapes.

"Maybe someone should have a fundraiser to help the Fijians," Melanie murmured, peering at Violet's photos of ramshackle island huts and toothless natives on her iPad.

"Oh!" Violet snapped her fingers and adjusted the new hand-painted shawl she had picked up from a toothless Fijian for $4. "That reminds me, I had to buy a table at the Children's Hospital gala—you know how I feel about children—and you would do me the loveliest favor by being one of my guests. Of course I hate asking a favor outside of working hours, but for some reason everyone is either out of town or otherwise occupied. I'm absolutely desperate. It's not this weekend but next."

Melanie did indeed know how Violet felt about children: She considered them adorable accessories as long as they were dressed nicely and didn't misbehave.

"On a weekend? Ummm..." Melanie had planned to leave the next two weekends open in case Dan asked her out again. For *when* Dan asked her out again.

"You can bring a date if you like," Violet urged.

"No, it's not that. I just..."

"*Please*, Melanie." The tone implied that this was not a request. "I wouldn't ask if the circumstances were not dire. You wouldn't resign me to the embarrassment of sitting at a half-empty table, would you?"

"Is it Friday night or Saturday night?"

"Saturday."

Melanie sighed. Prime date time. But how could she say no to her boss? Saying no was even harder than asking for things. "All right, Violet. I'll come. But without a date." No ordinary guy could fill Dan's Bruno Maglis; running into Scott at the café had made that clear.

Violet hopped up and down, clapping her hands like a 12-year-old, her raven-black bob swishing and settling perfectly. "Hooray! You've saved my life. And it'll be a fun night, you'll see." Conveniently forgetting her laments after the last one: dreadfully dull speeches, stultifying conversation, barely passable food. Violet, like Melanie's sister and mother, had a selective memory.

Melanie knew there was little "fun" in "fundraiser," but what choice did she have?

In any case, hooray for Violet's being back! Sure, it meant a dry spell of no porn-surfing at work, and no sucking down the self-help hope in any of her books either, but Violet's presence meant a busier gallery: clients who'd deal only with the boss, friends stopping by to chat, social climbers looking to claw up to another rung. Real-life liveliness was certainly better than the virtual kind.

Fascinating, these people who popped in to sip champagne and exotic teas on the pristine white sofa of the gallery's lounge where Violet held court. You couldn't make them up if you tried. Simon Hooverton III, the handlebar-mustachioed event designer whose ever-present poodle, Voltaire, was always sniffing around for treats. Sophie Wannamaker, a young bottle blonde with perfectly lasered skin, always sniffing around for chances to boost her social status. Edward Elkthorn, the plaid-clad octogenarian who doled out gossip like candy, sniffing for more juicy tidbits to add to the stockpile...

Yes, more humdrum folk dropped in too, VPs and marketing execs and PR flacks, and even people off the street just actually looking to acquire some art. But the colorful characters fascinated Melanie the most. So bravely bucking convention, so fearlessly thumbing their nose at expectations. Where did they get the audacity? Only a few had enough wealth to guarantee admiration. Were they born with it? Or just following in the footsteps of the great rebels before them?

Melanie tried to glean insight as she fetched everyone their champagne and iced coffees and sparkling water, proffering them on a silver tray like a well-trained servant in a high-class whorehouse. Contributing to the conversation would have been inappropriate, but she felt included even in her subservience; stars needed a rapt audience to shine brightly.

The drinks sometimes went untouched. Who needed beverages with such savory gossip to feast on? These gatherings were like a catty dinner party: a fork in the back, a knife in the eye, and dish, dish, dish.

As the week of Violet's return sashayed on, however, with no call, email, or text from Dan, Melanie's anxiety grew, dampening the merry bustle like a sweat stain. On Friday, a full week after their date, a full-blown funk set in. Melanie's movements slowed; her smiles grew forced. The once delicious gossip suddenly seemed stale.

Did he misplace my number? she wondered. *But he knows where I work!*

Could he be out of town? she considered. *As if everywhere doesn't have email.*

Is he too busy at work? she pondered. *Too busy for a 10-second text?*

Nothing made sense except the unthinkable: disinterest. Melanie had failed to intrigue him. Thoughts of Dan consumed her, but clearly she had been a morsel he didn't care to taste again.

She dragged herself home after work on Friday night and crawled into bed. Set the cell phone on the nightstand with the ringer on high, just in case. Lugged her TV into the bedroom and settled in for some quality veg time. Some Ben & Jerry's Chunky Monkey ice cream too—just add porking out to the list of her failures.

"Now this five-bedroom Beverly Hills mansion just sold for $12.5 million," trilled the perky blonde in the red power suit on the random home show Melanie clicked on. "Today we'll take an in-depth tour through its 5,500 square feet of pure luxury, including the Carrara marble pet bath, the all-white lacquer-walled gift-wrapping room, and the organic citrus garden. Only the best went into this stunner."

Sure, rub it in my face, Melanie lamented. *How am I ever going to live in a place like that now?* She clicked the remote dejectedly to change the channel.

"On this episode of *Travel Envy,* we'll be visiting the 10 most expensive resorts around the world." A brunette with gleaming teeth and model legs this time. "From Abu Dhabi to Patagonia, these getaways get away with charging up to $10,000 a night during peak season, making them exclusive playgrounds for the rich and famous."

"In other words, not us poor schlumps," Melanie snapped back at the TV announcer futilely, slumping farther under the covers. Maybe TV wasn't such a good idea. But she clicked again, one last chance.

"Nooooo, you cain't take mah baby from me! I'll go to rehab. I'll do whatevah it takes!" A greasy-haired young woman with rotting teeth screaming at a sheriff while the trailer park residents gaped. Reality TV, bingo! Nothing like the lowest common denominator to lift a person's self-esteem.

"My orders are to take the baby, ma'am. We can do this the easy way or the hard way." The sheriff looked barely old enough to drink legally.

The easy way. Such a joke. Nothing came easy unless you were born into riches or gifted with some special talent. What special talent did Melanie have? Nothing! Her only hope had been latching on to someone who did, and now it was dashed. She may as well just give up, buy 12 cats and take up knitting. Just accept that she'd be poor and alone forever. She gulped down another bite of Chunky Monkey. Easing a broken heart beat out dreaming of thin thighs.

The tears began gushing before she knew it, plopping into the ice cream. And it was only 7:30 p.m.! How would she get through the night—get through the rest of her life, for that matter—without Dan? Without any man to love and to cherish, to give her mind-blowing orgasms and set her up in a big house with a walk-in closet?

She had to call someone; the misery was too awful to bear alone. But who? Deena, her best friend, wouldn't be able to talk in her noisy bar. Ginger, her club-hopping *compadre*, would be out... well, club-hopping. Her brother, Alex, would be hopping into bed with the exotic dancer of the week. It was Friday night, after all. Everyone she knew had a life. Everyone except...

Don't do it, her inner protector warned. *Don't put yourself on the chopping block. It's not worth it.* But there was no one else. Only one person aside from Melanie's parents would be reliably sitting next to the phone on a Friday night, grinding away amidst paperwork and takeout cartons. Who might actually be pleased to hear from Melanie, if only to revel in her misery.

Melanie *had* to talk to someone. Reluctantly, she tapped out the numbers on her iPhone.

"Harper Landon." Her sister's voice sounded brusque and professional. As if Melanie's name and number hadn't flashed on the caller ID. Did Harper really need to one-up her right from the get-go by boasting her married name to someone so obviously and painfully single? Weren't the successful career and the Audi and the two kids enough?

"Hi, Harper, it's me."

"Melanie! What a…pleasant surprise. What's up?" Papers rustled in the background.

"Nothing much. I was just having a rough night and wanted to talk. How are you?" Melanie muted the TV, still half following the trailer-trash drama.

"How am *I*? I'm working, that's how I am. Some of us don't have the luxury of Friday nights off." Ice cubes wouldn't have melted on her voice. "But surely you didn't call to talk about *me*. So why don't you cut to the chase and tell me what you want? I have a lot to do tonight before I can go home and see my family."

What a dumb idea this call was. Sympathy from her sister? Like blood from a stone. But Melanie pushed on. Harper was familiar. Being talked down to was familiar. There was a certain comfort to it, being treated badly.

"Harper, how did you know your husband was The One? Your soul mate?"

A pause. "Soul mates are only in romance novels, Mel." Dismissive. "Good relationships are based on similar goals and interests. We wanted the same things out of life. That's really all that matters."

Melanie swallowed another bite of ice cream, considering.

"But also," her sister continued, jumping at the soapbox opportunity, "I wasn't waiting around for someone to complete me or take care of me. I was already in law school. I was a complete person."

"And you think…"

Harper quickly cut her off. "You're 26, and you still act like a baby, always looking to other people for answers. When are you going to grow up? When are you going to start living your own life?"

I'm trying! Melanie wanted to argue. *But I don't know how! I don't have your career ambition. I'm not as smart as you or Alex. I'm not anything.* Tears rolled down her cheeks, spoiling the creamy comforter's pristine expanse. On the TV, the young mother was sobbing too. Two losers who would never amount to anything.

"You never took my advice before, so I'm not sure why I'm even bothering now." Harper's softened tone almost masked the bitterness. "But I highly suggest you work on yourself instead of looking for a man to fix all your problems. Develop your talents. Advance your career. Success is attractive, but even if it doesn't land you a man, no one can ever take it away from you."

Melanie gulped back the tears. Sniffing loudly. "And what do you think my talents are, exactly?"

Harper snorted. "Well, you certainly have a talent for getting people to do what you want without even asking, don't you? Look at how you have Dad wrapped around your little finger, even though I work harder and gave him grandchildren. And those clients you get to shell out ungodly sums for overpriced art they probably don't even like. That's a real talent, wouldn't you say?"

"Right, so I'll just put that on my résumé and watch the offers roll in." Melanie felt justified being bitter now herself. "'Job skill: excel at getting people to do what I want.' Even if it were true, which I highly doubt, how am I supposed to do anything concrete with it?"

"That, you'll have to figure out for yourself. Just like I had to figure out how to stand out as the middle child between a brother who could do no wrong and a sister who was the pampered baby. Now I really do have to get back to work."

The phone line went dead before Melanie could barely get in, "OK, bye."

She unmuted the TV, now playing a reality show about female prisoners. Tried to digest what Harper had said, but the ice cream and inmate drama went down easier.

A talent for getting people to do what I want? What kind of job is based on that? The question still swirled through her thoughts as she finally shut off the TV and closed her eyes. Maybe one day she'd figure it out, but not tonight.

THE BED and TV sucked Melanie in all weekend. She could have gone to yoga. Could have updated her online dating profile. Could have eradicated the unidentifiable reek in the fridge. But no. The siren song of junk food and reality TV overrode all motivation to do anything healthy. Healthy or unhealthy, she'd still be a loser singleton.

"Do you need anything?" Her mom clicked into pretend care-taker mode on their weekly phone call. Even though Victoria needed to be needed, actually caring wasn't her strong suit. "Are you taking your vitamins? Eating healthy? You always did have a sweet tooth..." Melanie realized too late that she should have let it go to voicemail. During childhood bouts with colds, her mother had always made her feel like it was her fault. Victoria, of course, never got sick. What cold would dare lay siege on such a strictly regimented body?

"I'm fine, Mom." *No, I'm not! I'm going to die alone and unhappy, a haggard spinster. A horrible failure at everything.* "Really, there's no need to worry." *Why start now?*

"Well, try to get some exercise. It'll boost your spirits. I'm going to send you something from Dr. Phil's website about weight loss too. It doesn't take much to make you feel worlds better!"

Melanie wished she could tell her mother the truth, but you don't give the enemy extra ammunition.

She wished she could snap back into action instead of acting like a broken-hearted sad sack, but she didn't have the strength.

And most of all, she wished she could dial Dan's number and tell him how she felt. But if he had wanted to contact her, he would have. Silence wasn't golden in this case; it was crystal clear.

She would just have to get through it until time healed the wound. On Sunday night, as she laid out her work clothes for the morning, she resolved to forget Dan and move on. Disappointment tasted as familiar as ice cream anyway. All she could do was keep hoping, keep trying, and maybe if she were lucky enough, life would toss her a bone someday.

THANK GOODNESS at least for the Children's Hospital gala coming up on Saturday, a welcome distraction. Never mind that single men at fundraisers were as rare as white tigers. Only one problem.

"Violet, what's the dress code for the gala?" Melanie asked her boss as soon as Violet waltzed in late Monday morning. Just in time for lunch, except she barely ever ate.

"Whatever you like, darling." Violet waved a hand breezily. The other held a steaming china cup of Moroccan mint-lavender tea—the only stress reliever one really needed, she claimed. The $500 spa days were apparently just to support the economy.

"No, really," Melanie persisted. Violet could get away with flannel pajamas—writing huge checks had its privileges—but the common folk had dress rules. "What will everyone else be wearing?"

"Why do you want to be like everyone else, lovey?" Violet flipping through a copy of *Interview* magazine, her gel-perfect magenta nails flashing. "Why not celebrate the extraordinary uniqueness that is you?"

Easy for you to say, Melanie bristled. *If I were an heiress, I'd lord my uniqueness over everyone too. But since I'm just an heiress's lowly assistant, let's cut the crap.*

"Violet, please," she begged out loud. Trying to hide the desperation. But it was suddenly very important—even more important than usual—to get this right. If she couldn't even get clothes right, what hope did she have for getting her life right?

Violet sighed and closed the magazine. "All right, Miss Crowd Pleaser. Black tie. That means an evening-length dress, but a smashing cocktail dress wouldn't raise eyebrows. Go for Ralph Lauren or Oscar de la Renta if you want to blend in, Versace if you want to stand out."

Melanie's jaw dropped. Like she had a couple spare grand to drop on a gown for one night? She grasped for ideas as she paid invoices, responded to emails, and checked on orders while Violet lounged around with a stack of new art books, waiting for the glitterati to descend. Could she borrow a dress from Violet? Violet was four inches taller and 20 pounds lighter. Borrow from Ginger? Hookers 'R' Us didn't do evening gowns. And even second-hand duds from the consignment store would consume too big a paycheck chunk. Melanie's salary barely covered essentials like rent and mani-pedis.

Tears gathered slowly, steadily, as every idea quickly sputtered and died. Oh, for a fairy godmother! Or even just a credit card not maxed out.

She unwrapped her chicken salad sandwich brought from home, now soggy, nibbling discreetly at the desk while Violet fluttered between her cell phone and the art books. Oh, *why* had she agreed to go? Why had she let Violet *bully* her into going?

"Violet." A sob threatening to choke Melanie's speech, or maybe it was just the gloppy chicken lumps. "I'm sorry, but I can't go after all. Hopefully you can find someone else to fill my seat."

Violet looked up, surprised. Oblivious to Melanie's hand-wringing dress tragedy. "Why, darling? What's happened? Just an hour ago you were asking what to wear..." Realization dawning. "Ahhh. Why didn't you just *say something?*"

Because I hate asking for things. Because you'll look down on me even more. Because suffering silently is easier.

"I didn't want to bother you," Melanie said.

"My goodness, it's no bother. The least I can do since you're doing me the favor of attending is help you find something decent to wear!" Violet scrolled through her cell phone contacts. "I'm going to text you the number for Yvette at Calvin Klein. She's an old friend and a dear. Just tell her I sent you to borrow something."

Melanie swallowed her pride with the last bit of sandwich. "Thank you so much, Violet. You're a lifesaver." Better to be a groveling slave in borrowed finery at the ball than sitting home alone, wallowing in misery and Chunky Monkey.

"Nonsense. You're the one doing me a favor, lovey. Now I just need to fill two more seats, and we'll be all set." An enigmatic smile. "By the way, I think you'll especially like a certain other guest."

"Oh, really? Who?" Melanie felt obligated to ask. Although unless it was Dan, who cared?

"Now don't get too excited. You know I would never set you up on a date officially. I'm merely sitting the only two single people at my table next to each other, as any good hostess would do."

"But who is it?" Melanie repeated. *Cut to the chase already!*

"His name is…" Violet's eyes held a delicious secret, her voice breathy. "Very Well Known. And that's all you get for now."

Fine, whatever. Not Dan. Pain stabbed Melanie's heart. The memory of their date came barreling back: him pressing her into the car door, running his hands over her. The insistent, penetrating kisses. Melanie forced the images and the tears back. No use crying over spilled passion.

"All right, have it your way." *As if there were any other way.* Melanie forced a smile. "And thank you again for the dress help. I really do appreciate it."

"It's nothing, darling. Really. You don't have to keep thanking me." Subject dismissed, Violet went back to flipping through magazines to learn the latest artists she should like. A kindergartener had a longer attention span than Violet.

But it *was* something to Melanie. After all the years of being fed insults and criticisms, she lapped up tidbits of kindness like a homeless person at an all-you-can-eat buffet. She wished she could repay Violet, but what do you get a woman who has everything? Flowers from the corner deli wouldn't cut it.

The week staggered on, taking any remaining hope of Dan's calling with it. Tuesday's and Wednesday's *Maybe he was in a car accident and half his face is disfigured* turned into Thursday's and Friday's *Time to move on, sister.* Two weeks went beyond playing it cool into the icy reaches of Clearly Not Interested.

Saturday afternoon Melanie went all-out getting ready for the Children's Hospital gala; looking good is the best revenge. Hair and nails, check. Tastefully sexy makeup, check. Borrowed finery, check—God bless Yvette at Calvin Klein, who had come up with a shimmering silk honey-colored number that complemented her brown-sugar hair and flowed to her ankles like water. Every part of Melanie was buffed and polished and glowing—good enough to eat. Would her date step up to the taste challenge?

And who could the mystery man be? A baron with a manor on the moors? A hotshot CEO of a dot-com start-up flush with VC funding? The potential to be on the arm of so much money—er, such a fascinating man—made her girl parts shiver with anticipation.

Eat your heart out, Dan, she thought, eyeing the results of her primping efforts in the mirror. Appropriately elegant and yet smoking hot. The right makeup and a good pair of Spanx could make anyone look naturally beautiful.

Royalty Towncar Service arrived promptly at 6:45 p.m., compliments of Violet. ("Trust me, darling, waiting behind hordes in the valet line in four-inch Louboutins is a *nightmare*.") Melanie carefully picked her way down the stairs in the exquisitely high heels, her legs looking a mile long. Taking her time also gave the neighbors and any passers-by a chance to goggle enviously. Unfortunately, only old Mr. Stalerman was puttering around, sweeping the steps of his gingerbread Victorian; the neighborhood's yuppie parents were settling down to family dinners, and the yuppie singletons were hitting the restaurants and bars a few blocks away, escaping the strollers and chalk-drawn sidewalks.

Violet actually whistled when the uniformed driver opened the door. "You look gorgeous," she proclaimed, nodding her approval. Having gorgeous guests reflected well on her.

"And you look..." Melanie began. *Like a loon.* "Gorgeous too." Some kind of bizarre kimono dress, awash in Day-Glo graffiti, shrink-wrapped Violet so tightly, how could she breathe? Her boss was perched on the edge of the towncar's seat at an angle, unable to sit straight. But no one would utter a peep against it. Buying a

10-person gala table at $1,000 a head gave Violet the right to wear a trash bag if she wanted.

"Darling." Violet tossed her freshly salon-blown hair. "A girl would much rather be expressive than merely gorgeous."

"Violet, you look enormously expressive." Melanie grinned and leaned over for an air kiss. The lighter-than-air silk swished with her. She felt so lighthearted and happy for the first time in…she couldn't remember when. *Yes, you can—admit it. Since two weeks ago. Since Dan.* Amazing what looking smoking hot and having a posh party to go to—not to mention potentially meeting rich suitors— could do for one's mood. Had Cinderella dreamt only of the prince on her pumpkin ride to the ball, or had she strategized for sidling up to any available duke and baron too?

Their chariot pulled slowly away from the curb, leaving the prettily painted homes with their tidy flower baskets and side-walk-strewn toys behind. Leaving Mr. Stalerman to sweep his immaculate steps.

"Now will you tell me about my mystery table companion?" Melanie tried to maintain contact with Violet's eyes—difficult given the blaring green and orange dress.

"Surely you can wait 20 minutes more?" Violet's eyes glittered mischievously. "Good things come to those who wait."

Ha, I've been waiting my whole life and nothing good has come yet.

"As you wish," Melanie said.

A red carpet led from the street to the San Francisco Design Center's entrance. Two beefy security guys in dark suits flanked the doors. Quite a few guests hung around outside, some dressed quite down from Violet's description. *Maybe she doesn't even notice the "others,"* Melanie mused. *Or maybe she just didn't want me to embarrass her.*

Beefy security guy No. 1 checked their names on a clipboard. Opened the door with a curt nod.

"Why the Secret Service treatment?" Melanie asked as they sailed through. "It's not like there's any threat of danger." San Francisco's wealthy social butterflies might hiss about strangling someone for wearing the same dress, but none would risk breaking a nail in an altercation. "And no celebrities are going to be here either, right? The invitation didn't list any."

"Mmm-hmmm…oh, look. How beautiful!"

Scarlet-cloaked tables and chairs filled the main level of the four-story atrium, save a dance floor and the stage; lush crimson bouquets spilled over, petals scattered across the tablecloths. Rosy light cast an alluring glow on even the wrinkliest crones and withered widowers. The gala's chairwomen knew their stuff—flattered faces meant opened checkbooks.

"You'd think the Children's Hospital would have gone with something more demure." Melanie had been expecting something like a white wedding. What else did she have to compare it to? Galas aren't on the everyday agendas of underpaid assistants.

"The official theme is 'Follow Your Heart,' Violet said. "And hearts are red. But who doesn't love a sexy party?"

Especially the bored-housewife chairwomen, Melanie suspected. *Desperate to spice things up with their Viagra-popping husbands.* But charity parties, even sexy ones, were such an indirect route to spiciness. She would keep the flame alive in her man the reliable, old-fashioned way: playing sex slave.

"Let's get a drink." Violet nodded toward a group gathered near the front bar; only a few elderlies had parked themselves at tables already, their canes hanging off the chair backs. "Then we can mingle until dinner is served." She glanced around the expansive room, which could easily seat 300. "No sign of our special guest yet."

"You searched the entire room in two seconds?" Melanie followed her lead.

"Oh, we'd know if he were here. He tends to cause a stir." Violet winked. Geez, who was this guy? Simon Cowell?

Whatever. Melanie knew where getting her hopes up would lead—right back to vibratorville. No one in eyesight seemed worth getting excited about either, at least physically; paunches and receding hairlines ruled the roost.

But even so, several of the male guests cast appreciative glances her way, paying nonverbal tribute to the curve-hugging dress.

And being desired was the next best thing to actually getting laid. Melanie sent out a silent gratitude to Yvette at Calvin Klein for the shimmering floor-length frock; for once she didn't feel second-rate in some last-season designer outlet castoff. Tonight she was a thoroughbred, not a stuck-in-the-gate cow.

A DJ—no wedding-style string quartet, another surprise—spun '80s and '90s dance hits: The Spice Girls, Britney, Christina Aguilera. Not cutting-edge, but not falling terribly short either.

"Do you think anyone will be dancing later?" Melanie longed to shake it up. After two weeks of moping around, letting loose might lift her spirits.

She eyed the wine and champagne selections at the bar, draped in black satin and sprinkled with ruby rose petals. All pricier than her normal choices, but the $1,000 tickets thankfully entitled them to sucking it down for free. Violet ordered a pinot noir, while Melanie chose champagne. No red-wine stains on the Cinderella gown on her watch.

"Sure, there'll be dancing after everyone has tossed back a few." Violet took a sip and made a face. "I should bring my own bottle to these things." She accepted a mini dumpling proffered on a silver tray, never mind the barely breathable shrink-wrap dress. "Mmm, not bad. Try one."

Melanie cringed in horror at the bowl of brown sipping sauce, a disaster in the making. Shook her head and stepped back. Eating was the privilege of those who owned their clothes.

Violet worked the room as much as walked it, stopping frequently to chat. Mentioning upcoming exhibitions at the gallery, inviting people to drop by. Flirting even with the old codgers, who ate it up. Teasing too, both gentle and ballsy. Her heiress's fortune bought her the right to say what she pleased.

I could be fearless too if I were filthy rich. I could tease and joke and order people around. Until then it's "Yes, of course" and "As you wish." Melanie felt that old twinge of inferiority.

"Melanie, would you be a dear and bring me a sparkling water?" Violet deposited her empty wineglass into Melanie's hand.

"Yes, of course." Melanie hurried to the bar. *A borrowed dress doesn't make you one of them,* she reminded herself.

"I see retirement has been treating you well, Henry," Violet was trilling at an old coot as Melanie returned. Possibly a genuine compliment, possibly a taunt about his sizable girth. But suddenly a stir of excitement came in a wave from the front doors, which she and Violet had their backs to.

"Oh...my...God." Henry's petite wife, Tiffany—substantially younger and better-looking than her husband—widened her eyes. "Don't look now, but unless it's his double, Jaden June just walked in."

"From Double Sided Coin?" Melanie swiveled excitedly to look, her heart skipping. One of her favorite bands! And Jaden was the delectable lead singer, endless material for Melanie's dirty fantasies. She had borrowed his face so many times for her wet dreams, she felt like she owed him royalties.

Violet grinned, a cat with a fresh bowl of cream. "Those rock stars have no sense of time." Theatrically nonchalant. "He was supposed to be here 30 minutes ago."

It took Melanie a second to register Violet's comment. When it did, she simply gaped. Not Simon Cowell. Not Steven Tyler. Better than either. Better than both put together. Jaden June. *Jaden June!*

Melanie couldn't form a coherent sentence. She focused on removing her jaw from her cleavage.

Violet turned only when Jaden reached them. "Naughty boy." They air-kissed affectionately. "You're quite late." Melanie blushed furiously at the chiding. *Jaden June can show up whenever he wants!*

"I needed my beauty sleep to keep up with the likes of you, now didn't I?" Jaden parried good-naturedly. Millions of screaming fans must make for an unshakable ego.

Jaden gazed down at Melanie with greenish-blue catlike eyes, ringed in a hint of black eyeliner. And that British accent—*swoon.*

"Jaden, may I introduce you to my associate, the lovely Melanie Merriweather? Melanie, this is Jaden June."

"Of course." *As if I didn't know!* Melanie bravely stuck out her hand for a shake. Her panties dampened.

"Charmed." Jaden raised Melanie's hand to his lips. His eyes danced over her, taking in everything at once. Looking pleased, thank heavens.

"And this is my very dear old friend Henry." Violet lightly touched the large man's tuxedoed shoulder, "and his wife, Tiffany. We have the pleasure of their dining at our table tonight."

"Ah, splendid." Jaden shook both their hands. He and Henry were a study in contrasts: Henry a short fat cat in a well-cut designer tuxedo and dress shoes, cropped hair shot through with gray; Jaden a panther all in black, a slim-fitting jacket over a black button-down and leather pants, onyx hair curling rebelliously toward his shoulders. Black leather boots adding two inches to his six-foot frame. No tie at all at this black-tie event.

As the servers ushered everyone to the tables, Melanie felt everyone's eyes on them, watching in that deliberate not-watching way. This crowd was too sophisticated to brown-nose a rock star—at least until dessert.

"Well, you made it in time to eat." Violet continued her ballsy patter. "Probably not as good as your usual fare, though."

"What, Chinese takeaway on a bus?" The George Clooney way of setting the commoners at ease. Everyone laughed gratefully—well, Tiffany tittered too loudly, and Melanie put a hand to her mouth like a Japanese schoolgirl, remembering one of her favorite dirty fantasies: Jaden screwing her in the back of the tour bus. Thank goodness he was only a heartbreaker and not a mind reader.

Salads appeared all around. Melanie eyed the raspberry vinaigrette with dismay. This could be a new diet: Eat only what won't stain honey-colored silk. She'd be skinny in a week! She reached for the champagne and racked her brain for interesting things to say, but her brain was still partying like a groupie on the tour bus.

Just act normal. He's just a guy under it all. Picture him in his underwear. No! Don't do that. Picture him brushing his teeth, not in underwear. In pajama bottoms. His naked torso all lean and muscled…ack, help!

Thankfully, Violet began introducing the tablemates. Ten altogether. Violet's companion, a middle-aged male friend known for adoring younger men, sat to her left. An elderly couple unruffled by the fuss over Jaden (did they even know who he was?) and a younger dot-com-rich pair rounded out the group. Melanie guessed she was the only one with a net worth lower than the GDP of a small country.

Jaden thoughtfully acted self-deprecating, likely to appear human. He told Melanie about being homesick and missing his mum's kidney pie. About the challenge of having to be "on" even when you were bone tired. About waking up in a different city every night or two on tour being more disorienting than glamorous. Even the fanciest tour bus couldn't compete with the comforts of home.

"But the perks must be great." Melanie craved the fantasy. "The groupies and so on."

"Ah, yes, the girls." Jaden actually grimaced. "Let's just say they don't care who I *really* am."

Melanie didn't believe it. How could anyone not care about getting to know what lay beneath the godlike aura? She wanted to know everything about him—starting with what he looked like under those leather pants.

She listened raptly to his tales of life on tour. One time those leather pants had actually split during a stage-antic move; he just pulled them off and kept going in his Calvins. Another time he'd tripped over a cord and fallen flat on his face; he smeared the blood gushing from his lip on the guitarist's face in a pretend frenzy, and the crowd ate it up.

By the time the beef Wellington and rosemary potatoes arrived, Melanie was enraptured. Jaden led such an exciting life, despite his protests to the contrary. And homesickness would never hit her, since on her home turf she was considered a worm. On the arm of Jaden, she'd be a glamorous goddess in every Podunk city with a concert venue.

She prickled with jealousy now as other women dared to approach here and there, simpering and fawning and giggling like

12-year-olds. Had they no self-respect? *He's not interested in you, you conniving slut,* she seethed at each one silently. *He's my date, not yours.* She wanted to tell them to take a hike but stewed quietly instead, numbing the anger with yet more champagne. So what if all those free drinks would cost her in the morning?

Jaden ate heartily, drank little and treated the brazen hussies graciously. He didn't hog the conversation either, pressing Melanie for details about her own life. *Ha, maybe at bedtime. My life story is so boring, it would put you to sleep.* Then she remembered the night with Ginger at Warehouse, the human menagerie and the pole dancer and the half-naked partygoers in fetish wear. *Now there's a story worthy of telling a rock star.*

"Of course, that's probably a walk in the park for someone like you," she said, after regaling him with the juicy tale. Maybe even embellishing a wee bit—how would he ever know she didn't actually dance topless on a table?

"Mistress Gardienne and human dogs, eh? You don't say." A gleam in his eye. "Is that something you're into, then?" Leaning a smidge closer.

Melanie caught the gleam. Counted to three silently. "Only on weekends," she said slyly.

Jaden looked at her keenly. "What a rare bird you are." His breath tickled her ear, his lips grazing her cheek.

Could there *be* a worse moment to have to pee? Damn all that champagne! Jaden surprisingly stood up as she excused herself—a superstar *and* a gentleman. Double swoon. She hoped he wouldn't be as gallant in bed later on; manners had no place in her version of bedroom etiquette.

Melanie tried to gather her wits in the ladies' room stall, but her mind raced. Would hopping into bed with Jaden on the first date make her wild and uninhibited or a common slut? It was imperative not to come off as a groupie, but she couldn't let this magic evening slip away without snagging him, either. The situation called for a delicate balance, but guzzling all that champagne on an almost empty stomach didn't bode well for walking such a fine line.

She leaned her dizzy head on the cool stall wall just as two young women entered the restroom. Through the door crack she saw them: a leggy bottle blonde with a fake tan and collagen lips, and a plain-Jane brunette in last season's Burberry. Whispering, but loud enough for Melanie to hear.

"Oh, my God, did you see him?" gushed Blondie. "He is to die for. I could eat him up with a spoon."

"Who needs a spoon?" Burberry Brunette twittered. "He's even hotter in person than in his videos."

Obvious who they meant. Melanie's ears pricked up.

"I hear he has the security guards search the crowd for hot girls to invite backstage at his concerts." The blonde bimbo greased her hot dog lips with pink lip gloss.

"I hear he's seeing what's-her-name, that supermodel. Natalya." The brunette patted powder on her nose from a Cover Girl compact.

"We've *got* to figure out a way to meet him. Something not too obvious."

"Sure, like he doesn't have girls 'accidentally' bumping into him all the time." Brunette Bimbo made a rueful face. "Let's face it, we're probably going to have to settle for him just being eye candy."

"Well, maybe *you* can settle. But I like to actually lick my candy." They both tittered as they tottered out in their high heels, leaving a trail of drugstore perfume.

Melanie fumed. How dare they talk about Jaden that way? *Her* date. If anyone was going to be doing any licking, it should be her. But how to separate herself from the masses of fawning groupies like those two? She had to convince him she liked him for who he really was, to ignore the fame and the riches and the glamour—at least until he made her breakfast.

She washed her hands and reapplied lipstick, strategizing. Pushed the bathroom door open more forcefully than intended, a woman on a mission. And ran smack into...

Dan.

Impossible. And yet there he stood, the man she had been agonizing about every day for two weeks since their date, immaculate in a Ralph Lauren tuxedo. Clean-shaven and not a hair out of place. Staring down at her. No, not staring. Glaring. *Dan.* Dan? Dan.

Melanie straightened up and took a step back. His eyes bored into her as confusion and tipsiness washed over. What on earth was he doing here? And why the glaring?

She was too stupefied to speak.

"You work fast." Dan crossed his arms, frowning.

"What do you mean?" Too many thoughts were tumbling around in Melanie's buzzing head. Suddenly she wished she were home, tucked in bed in pink flannel PJs with a teddy bear. "What are you talking about?"

He grabbed her elbow and pulled her in, squeezing hard enough to hurt. Melanie didn't pull away. He nodded in the direction of the dinner tables. "A rock star? Seriously? Such a cliché." Shaking his head. His hand like a vise. Close up, Melanie could feel the anger radiating off him like heat from a furnace.

"Wait, why are you so mad at me?" Melanie couldn't believe her ears. She had been waiting for two weeks for him to call, text, anything, and he was mad at her? What the hell?

"You really don't know?"

"No, I really don't know." Tears welled up. Her arm throbbed under his digging fingers. From thrills with Jaden to chills with Dan—too much of a roller coaster for one night.

"You could have at least messaged to say, 'Thank you, not interested.'" Dan scowled but loosened his grip by a fraction.

"Wait...what? Me not interested?" Understanding slowly penetrated the champagne fog. "You were waiting for me to call you."

"Most girls would communicate interest afterward. Or at least call to say thank you." His eyes still pinned down her face; she felt trapped under his ruthless gaze.

Melanie didn't know whether to jump for joy or cry. Such rage meant he really cared—*he liked her!* Such anger meant she had done the wrong thing—*she had really fucked up!* And had no idea how to

fix it. She wished she could stop time, go home, and analyze everything from the comfort of her bed, then come back and turn time
back on again. All of that self-help training and she still felt helpless.

"Dan, I...I'm so sorry," she came up with at last. *Lame.* She
made her eyes big, arranged her facial features to look as repen-
tant as possible through the champagne haze. "There's been a big
miscommunication here. I had a wonderful time with you and had
really been hoping we could get together again. I'm sorry I didn't
call to say thank you. I should have."

"Is that so?" The ice melted slightly from Dan's eyes. He loosened his grip a fraction.

"Is everything all right here, Melanie?" Jaden suddenly appeared
next to Melanie, eyeing Dan warily. "Thought maybe you'd
drowned in the loo." He held a hand out to Dan. "Jaden June." As
if anyone could possibly not know.

"Dan Hightower." The two shook hands like businessmen but
looked more like boxers squaring off. A thrill pulsed through Melanie's veins.

"Everything's fine, Jaden. Thank you for checking." Melanie
smiled, but her emotions were tumbling around like bits of colored
glass in a kaleidoscope. "Dan and I were just catching up." The
biggest kaleidoscope shard: guilt. Over how much she was enjoying
being a prize worth fighting over. Anger meant affection, but
bloodshed meant passion.

"Glad to hear." Jaden gave Dan a curt, dismissive nod and
wrapped an arm around Melanie's waist possessively. "Shall we
return? They're about to announce the silent auction winners, and
I bid on something for you."

"You did? Oh, my...yes. Yes, of course we should get back."
Melanie cast an apologetic glance at Dan, begging his forgiveness
yet again with her eyes. Torn between the two, not wanting to lose
either. "I'll call you tomorrow. OK, Dan?"

"Of course," he said smoothly, all the rage simmered away. So
handsome and polished in his expertly tailored tuxedo. Melanie wished
she could make everything else disappear and make him kiss her again

right there. Lie down on the carpet and hike her dress up around her waist like a $25 hooker and take all of him inside her. Prove her interest the best way a woman could—by spreading her legs.

"Right, then." Jaden angled her back toward the tables, his arm tight around her waist. The two men did not say goodbye.

Back at the table, the conversation was restricted by protocol: Only quiet murmuring was allowed during the announcing of the silent auction winners. Thank goodness. Melanie was relieved to be able to process everything in silence: the confusion, the elation...the longing for Dan that had come rushing back, knocking her over like a wave. He could have had her flat on her back in no time if not for Jaden.

Then again, she'd spread her legs for Jaden in a heartbeat too! His hand rested on her upper thigh now, under the table. Not claiming ownership the way Dan's tight hand on her elbow had. Lightly, more a question than a declaration. And with Dan back in the picture, she wasn't sure how to answer. Dan didn't seem like the sharing type—more the conquering, take-no-prisoners type. *Mmmmmm, conquering...*

Melanie hadn't bid on anything in the auction—Tahoe trips and baubles and fine wines on her salary? Ha, not a chance. Jealousy pricked her again. She might be at the ball now, but on Monday the gown would disappear, and she'd be scarfing down homemade chicken salad at her desk again instead of beef Wellington and champagne at a linen-draped table.

The fat cats could lap up whatever treats they wanted and not think twice. And they did. Violet "won" (read: paid a ton for) a private dinner for 10 by a local renowned chef. Henry snagged some blingy earrings for Tiffany and golf lessons for himself. The elderly couple, holding hands now, got a romantic weekend trip to Napa Valley. Rich *and* in love. Melanie burned with jealousy, until she spied the walker parked next to them. At least she wasn't at death's door.

Jaden landed...a day at Elizabeth Arden's Red Door Spa?

"For you, of course." All the force of his star power lit up his features as applause rang all around them. Louder than for anyone else. "Violet said you'd like it."

The scale tipped immediately in his favor. Dan might have set her girl parts atingle, but such a generous present on the first date made Melanie's whole body tremble with lust. Impulsively, she kissed his cheek, her lips drunkenly lingering. A flashbulb went off. Jaden wrapped an arm around her shoulders, pulling her in. Desire tugged at her insides.

Maybe she wouldn't have to choose between Dan and Jaden, at least not until she'd had her fill of one. Or maybe they would be OK with sharing her. Sure. And maybe the wrinkly old couple with the walker would hop on the table and do a striptease.

But for now, for this one perfect night, the rules of reality were suspended. After tonight, the dress would disappear, the towncar would return to ferrying the rich, the beef Wellington would be a mere juicy memory. But right now, she could snuggle into Jaden's sinewy arms and dream of Dan's seductive kisses. For just this one night, she could have her cake and eat it too.

The most delicious cake Melanie had ever tasted. If there were hell to pay tomorrow, she'd pay it still dreaming of tonight.

DRESS SAFELY stowed in its protective garment bag, face washed, teeth brushed and flossed, Melanie lay in bed. Short pink satin nightie caressing her thighs. Jaden had strongly hinted at hooking up in bed after the gala, but too-eager sluts clearly didn't capture his heart. No, Melanie had to smother her lustful impulses in service of the greater goal: an actual relationship. Either Jaden or Dan would put a ring on her finger, if it was the last thing they ever did. Not even four or five glasses of champagne could tip her strategizing off balance.

Tick tock, tick tock. Time was running out to make her Homemaker Barbie dream happen. At age 26, she couldn't afford to fool around anymore. She just wasn't sure yet which man would put an end to her girlish fooling around and start her on the right course of mind-blowing passion, a mansion with a pool, and platinum credit cards etched with her name.

Thank God for vibrators. All the pent-up energy came rushing out as she recklessly thrust the vibrator tip inside her, a heat-seeking missile. No flower-opening gentleness tonight. She shoved it in over and over, the growing wetness making each push a little easier. First it was Dan's manhood, then Jaden's. She switched them like that, back and forth, back and forth, until the waves of pleasure brought her over the top and she lay there shaking with the aftershocks.

Whose face did she see in those last precious seconds? Impossible to tell in the blinding white light of gratification. Maybe both, blurred together.

Chapter 7

"Like It's Your Favorite Lollipop"

MELANIE BROKE slowly through sleep as if she were swimming up through warm turquoise waters to a sun-dappled surface. Mmmmm, why such a lovely feeling? The sweet haze blurred her memory momentarily; she knew only that something wonderful had happened. Languorously stretching her arms and legs, then curling into the pile of pillows next to her, hugging one close. Hugging...a strong hand grasping her elbow...a sinewy arm draped across her shoulders...ohhhh, yes. Had it all been a dream? In such a paradise, the doormat didn't usually make it inside.

But yes, look: there on the closet door, the Calvin Klein garment bag. Real! She *had* to tell someone. But who, on a Sunday morning at 10 a.m.? Ginger, her club-hopping friend, would be sleeping off a club-hopping hangover. Her best friend, Deena, would be sleeping off serving the club hoppers at her bar until 2 a.m. No way was she letting her mother or sister in on this until either Jaden or Dan was a sure thing. They could burst her bubble in the blink of an eye.

There was really only one person she wanted to talk to anyway. But no, too early. Coming off as too eager was as bad as too aloof.

Instead she made some English breakfast tea and toast with gourmet raspberry jam. Two Tylenol to chase away the champagne headache. Not hell to pay after all, just a slight hangover.

How soft her silk nightie felt this morning. How delicious the jam. Buffing her face with an apricot scrub, it seemed prettier. Radiant.

I could get used to this.

Melanie lazed around as long as possible, killing time until she could call him. Ignoring all the mundane little tasks begging to be completed. Someone else would do all the chores soon enough. Soon enough she'd be trading this one-bedroom flat for a big home with housekeeping help. The only cleaning she'd have to do would be throwing a towel over the wet spots on the sheets.

At 12:10 p.m. she snuggled up back in bed, cradling the cell phone to her ear, and carefully dialed his number. Her stomach fluttering.

"Hello." So deep and self-assured, that voice. Melanie couldn't tell if he recognized her number, if he even knew it was her.

"Hi, Dan." Softly. A sudden attack of shyness. "It's Melanie." They hadn't actually spoken on the phone before, and she felt awkward. "Uh, is this a good time to talk?"

"Yes. I just got back from a run a little while ago."

"Oh, you run?" *Duuuurrrrrr.* Stupid thing to ask. Who cares about running anyway, unless it's into someone's arms?

"Yes, a few times a week." Again not helping the conversation. *Jeez, give me something to work with here!*

"I do yoga," she offered desperately. "Three times a week." *It's not lying. I did do it three times a week for a few months last year.* "Do you ever do yoga?"

"That's not my thing," he answered. "But it's good for you. You should keep it up."

What an odd thing to say. Why wouldn't she keep it up? (Assuming she had actually been doing it in the first place.) It sounded like a directive. She squirmed in the uncomfortable silence that followed.

"Dan..." she began, just as she heard, "Melanie."

"Sorry, go ahead," she said.

"What did you want to say?"

Melanie gulped. "Look, I apologize if I gave you the wrong impression by not calling. I just figured if you wanted to see me again, you'd let me know. I didn't want to be presumptuous."

Another pause. "Go on."

She breathed deeply. "I had a really good time with you. I'd really like to go out again. Would you?"

"Now was that so hard?" Dan's tone softened.

Yes, yes it was! You have no idea how hard it is for me to ask for things!

"I guess not," she said.

"Good girl. And yes, we can go out again. Tonight."

"Tonight?" Melanie's heart sped up.

"I'll pick you up at 5:00. We'll have dinner."

He really likes to dictate things, doesn't he? Her stomach flipped.

But zero notice *again* for a date! Did he think she should just drop everything when he wanted to do something? She had a life, you know—well, sort of, considering her *real* life, the one she was meant for, hadn't started yet.

It wouldn't be the first time Melanie had swallowed her pride. At least this time it would actually help her get what she wanted: more of Dan's delirium-inducing kisses.

"OK." She gave in. "I'll rearrange my plans." *Not a lie. I was planning to catch up on email.*

"'OK' doesn't sound very enthusiastic," he chided gently. "Is that your final answer?"

Geez Louise, couldn't he cut her the tiniest bit of slack? Was he really that sensitive? Fine, whatever. Everything would be right as rain once he pressed her up into the car again.

Melanie took a deep breath. Let it out slowly. "Dan, I really would like to see you tonight. I'm glad we're going out." The words sounded forced to her. They were. Dan had pulled them out of her.

"Good girl," he said again, as if she were a child. Sounding pleased. "Be ready at five sharp. Wear something casually dressy."

"Where are we going?"

"You'll see."

Napa Valley, about an hour north of San Francisco, boasted the vineyards of Robert Mondavi, Domaine Chandon, and many other world-famous winemakers. Dan ushered her gallantly into a silver Mercedes convertible this time, not the black Lexus. Just how many cars did his venture capitalist income provide for? Melanie slid in, smelling that refined air again, feeling the smooth leather on her bare legs. She arranged her flowy skirt demurely, imagining him hiking it up later.

They drove to a private tasting room at St. Adele, an exclusive winery. Dan knew one of the vintners. Two other couples already sat around a big wooden table, lit by candles and set with simple creamy plates and thick cloth napkins. Rustic and elegant all at once. Dan pulled her chair out and scooted her in, a gentlemanly gesture from a not-gentle man. His hands fleetingly traced the sides of her bare shoulders in the sleeveless, low-cut silk top, sending trails of electricity to her heart and between her thighs.

They had spoken little on the drive up, mostly small-talk attempts by Melanie that had led nowhere. Dan seemed to choose words carefully and ration them out, as if they were a commodity. Even now, the wine loosened everyone's tongues but his. Still, his eyes and gestures spoke volumes: his gaze dipping to her cleavage, his hand roaming possessively on her leg under the table. A touch equaled a thousand words.

Between the caressing and the wine and the meal—farm-fresh field greens drizzled in vinaigrette, rosemary rolls with olive oil, Cornish hens with crackling golden skin—Melanie sank into bliss. Oh yes, she could definitely get used to this. By the time dessert arrived—mini pastries, cookies, chocolates, each one a little jewel—she felt positively spoiled. And, if her instincts were right, the best was yet to come. Anticipation fluttered up and down her spine.

"Listen, Melanie," Dan began, the two of them back in the silver convertible. The sleek dashboard clock read 10 p.m.

Here it comes, Melanie thought delightedly. *It's "Your place or mine?" time. At last!*

"I think we should stay in a hotel here tonight." He turned to face her directly. Curled his arm around the back of her headrest.

"A hotel? Now? I have to work in the morning. I don't even have a toothbrush." A quickie in a hotel room? Not what Melanie had envisioned at all. But the excuses tumbling out rang hollow. She would call in sick to work; she would crawl naked to the drugstore for toiletries if he asked.

Dan took her face in his hands. "It's late," he said, slowly. "I am not expecting anything from you physically—we can get two separate beds or even two separate rooms if you prefer. But given the wine and the hour and the dark drive back, I think it's best that we stay here in town tonight. There's a very comfortable place right nearby."

Wait, no action at all? Even worse than a quickie! Melanie was baffled. Did he want her or not? Should she agree to the hotel or not? If only someone would tell her what to make of this, what to do.

Then she realized: Someone *was* telling her what to do. Someone she wanted to please very badly. Why waste time waffling?

"Alright," she said. "Yes, I mean. Yes, let's get a room."

"Good." He nodded, satisfied. Started the car. "Anything you need for tonight, they'll have at the hotel. We'll get a good night's sleep and get up early enough for you to be on time to work tomorrow."

Thirty minutes later, the plushest white bathrobe Melanie had ever felt enveloped her. Two queen-size beds laden with down pillows and thick comforters lay for the choosing. A gas fireplace flickered in the corner, its light playing on two damask-upholstered armchairs and a low mahogany table. Two cut-crystal glasses and a decanter of sherry stood on a demilune table in another corner. The rug felt lush and soft beneath her bare feet.

Dan moved toward her, intently watching her face. A fascinated lover or a predator in the wild—impossible to tell which. Dreaminess took over as he led Melanie silently to one of the beds, laying her down as gently as if she were a child.

"Dan," Melanie blurted in a whisper, suddenly panicking at the intimacy of it. At how she might blow it, like she always blew everything. "Wait..."

He immediately pulled back, searching her face. "What?"

"I...I haven't had much experience. In bed, I mean." Losing her virginity at 18 to the country club's pool lifeguard in 15 minutes didn't count. Fumbling sack time a few times in college and afterward with guys who had more eagerness than skill didn't really count. Solo time letting her fingers do the walking definitely didn't count.

He probed her eyes with his, gauging her sincerity. "Is that true?"

Melanie nodded mutely, ashamed. Wishing away the burden of her inexperience. Wishing she could just tear her robe off and gyrate like a lap dancer, like a normal 26-year-old girl. But she didn't know how. Watching porn and having the courage to act like a porn star were two entirely different things.

Dan smiled then, and everything righted itself. Melanie's anxiety melted away like shoulder tension on a sunny beach. His expression exuded kindness and warmth.

"Don't be afraid." He stroked her hair gently, soothingly. "I'm not going to fuck you tonight. But you're OK with...other things? Touching?"

She nodded silently again, eyes wide with desire.

"Is that a yes?"

"Yes," she managed to get out.

And with that he landed a kiss on her so hard and deep, it was a devouring. His tongue almost crushing her mouth. He circled his fingers around her wrist and pulled her arm up above her head, pinning it to the pillow. Turned her body ravenous in one swift move.

Melanie almost cried with relief. Finally! A man who set her soul on fire. How long had she waited for this moment? She gave herself to him eagerly. Tried to keep up with his tongue. Tried to reach for him with her hands, but he quickly joined her wrists together in his grasp.

Resistance is futile. The expression wafted across her mind. But why try to resist something so heavenly anyway? She sank into his kisses, her arching body telling him, *Yes, don't stop. Please don't stop.*

His free hand, the one not pinning her arms, moved under her robe now, finding her bare breasts, their nipples tightening quickly under his fingers as he played with them, taking his time. Melanie's breath came in low rasps. She struggled to free her hands—habit telling her she should give back, should caress him—but his grip held them firm. Nothing to do but lie back and take it.

His mouth found everything it needed. His free hand caressed the length of her body. Melanie moaned softly, urging him on without words. Suddenly everything else fell away; nothing mattered but his touch, right here and now. The exquisite sensations. Her body was an instrument, being played by a maestro.

His fingers finally dipped inside, her warm folds giving way so easily, so readily, slick with wetness. A gasp escaped her mouth. She would have come right then, but he moved quickly back to her inner thighs, massaging. *No! Go back! Please, please, go back inside.* She wanted him so desperately, she could barely contain herself.

He continued to alternate like that, inside, outside. Watching her face, assessing her breathing, her moans growing louder and lower. Her hips rising to meet his touch. Inside, outside. More devouring kisses. The nipple-tugging turned harder by barely noticeable degrees, such lovely torture.

Nearing the final precipice, everything slowed even as her heart raced. His hands and lips paused, the eye of the storm. "You wouldn't come without telling me first, would you?" So low, his voice, almost a growl. It sent shivers down her body like magic tendrils in an enchanted forest.

"No, of course not." A ragged whisper. She would have promised anything for the satisfaction of release. *Just please don't stop!*

"Good girl." And then his touch was everywhere at once, his hand and his tongue invading her. His fingers turned to steel around the wrists pinned above her head.

"Oh, God, I'm going to come." Her voice sounded so unfamiliar in its desperation, the wanton need.

"Come for me, Melanie. Come now." Commanding, insisting, although she needed no urging. The explosion racked her body so hard, consuming every inch, that she lost all sense of time and place. Bucking and shuddering in the waves of pleasure that broke over her and knocked her deep into the bed.

He released her arms slowly. Pulled her body into his, cradling her. Petting her hair.

"Your face while you were coming...priceless." Obviously pleased.

Melanie hid her face in his chest, suddenly embarrassed by the carnal beast he had released. Had she screamed in abandon? She couldn't even remember. And what about him? Didn't he want pleasure too? So selfish of her to just take it all for herself and not give back. Tentatively, she began stroking his leg, crossed over on top of her now, holding her tight.

"Not tonight." His voice kind but firm. "Maybe next time."

"But..." It made no sense. Why wouldn't he want her to return the favor? What guy didn't want sexual gratification?

"No 'buts.' Just seeing your face was enough for tonight. There will be plenty of other opportunities in the future."

Plenty of other opportunities. The phrase was almost as pleasing as the physical ecstasy. Melanie snuggled happily into Dan's arms, completely spent. His hand stroked her hair, his kisses now so soft on the top of her head, lulling her into the sweetest sleep she had ever known.

Only in the last second before she slipped into sleep did she remember another piece of the puzzle. That gorgeous face flashing behind her heavy eyelids.

Jaden.

INEXPLICABLY, INEVITABLY, Melanie felt like she belonged to Dan from that night on. Juggling both him and Jaden without dropping the ball sent daggers of fear into her heart; plus, she couldn't shake the weird feeling that Dan might still be playing spying games. She did go out with Jaden a few times—how could any girl resist a rock god? But the whole thing went just like you'd think:

Their first date, dinner at a hot new restaurant downtown, was riddled with interruptions by fawning autograph seekers and star fuckers. And phone calls. And texts. Everyone looking right through Melanie as if she didn't exist. Who cared about a mere mortal with a rock god around? Jaden's boots got more attention than she did.

Their second date was even worse. Why had Melanie thought being backstage at a concert would be glamorous? The thrill of entering the inner sanctum, elevated into a position of envy by the commoners stuck on the other side, couldn't make up for her being seen as the bimbette du jour. The other band members, the security team, even the skanky *real* groupies barely acknowledged her presence. A piece of furniture at best, invisible at worst.

"Jaden wants…"

"Can you tell Jaden…"

"Did Jaden get my…"

Every single sentence addressed to her was about him. She may have been in the inner sanctum, but she ranked as a second-class citizen. A glorified servant. And Jaden could do nothing from his place on the stage.

Not that he could even off it! Performing onstage powered him, made him a deity. Offstage he was a mere boy missing home, landing inexpert kisses on Melanie and letting his greasy weasel of a manager, Harvey Ratmueller, pull all of his strings. His eagerness to please his manager, his fans, and even Melanie herself left her unpleasantly unaroused.

In the end she just felt sorry for them all. Sorry for the desperate fans, so deluded about the magic of their golden idol. Sorry for Jaden, deflated and weak when not powered by the energy of a crowd. But most of all sorry for herself, because no one paid her any attention—and, in fact, Dan gave her the stone-silence treatment for a week when the paparazzi caught her and Jaden in a lip-lock. Melanie didn't want to be a napkin on anyone's table; she wanted to be the main course. Dan's main course.

Jaden didn't beg her to stay, of course, though he did seem shocked. Everyone seemed shocked. How could any girl, let alone a lowly gallery shop girl, let a gorgeous, rich, and powerful rock star go without a backward glance? Most girls would claw each other's eyes out just to get near him.

But while Jaden was gorgeous and rich, he *wasn't* powerful. He was a weak little boy who never ordered Melanie to get out of the limo so he could push her up against it. Never ordered food for her in a restaurant without asking what she wanted or tested her with last-minute invitations. In fact, he seemed to like it when she took control of everything. No, that would *not* do. Money and looks only went so far, and Melanie's sexual attraction to him wouldn't have gone the distance.

Dan, on the other hand…Dan commanded every situation. His power didn't depend on slavering fans or blinding stage lights. Everywhere he and Melanie went—from four-star restaurants and high-end boutiques to the produce aisle at Whole Foods—people responded to his quiet strength and raw magnetism. Even the otherwise aristocratically haughty Violet fell under his spell.

"Scurry along now, darling," her boss urged once, seeing Dan's Lexus idling in front of the gallery. Still 15 minutes until closing. "You don't want to keep that one waiting, hm?" Dan had come in the first time and introduced himself to Violet, then waited outside thereafter. "Maybe you can persuade him to buy one of the new Eindorfer prints, if you're not too gobsmacked," her boss added, conveying less an early dismissal and more a business deal.

Melanie ceased making advance plans with friends, to be available for Dan on a moment's notice. She'd drop in to visit Deena at her bar on nights he chose not to get together, or tag along with Ginger for club-hopping at the last minute, but the sense of killing time dampened those outings like fog at a picnic. Dan became the center of her world; without him she felt adrift. A fragmented person only partially there.

But with him...oh, with him! Being at his command made her feel useful, gave her a real purpose. And how lovely to have the burden of choice removed! You can't mess up if you do exactly what you're told.

She felt the force of his will and attention even when his gaze shone elsewhere. He told her exactly what to wear on their dates. He picked the restaurants—always French or Japanese, never Mexican or Indian. He picked their weekend outings—long walks through San Francisco, never mountain hikes. Maybe brunch on a yacht around the bay, never paddling around Stow Lake. And shopping, from Target to Emporio Armani to Victoria's Secret. His face would light up in delight at the aisles of things to choose from. The more, the better. Always soliciting her opinion as if it mattered.

Shopping, in fact, seemed to be the *only* thing he asked her opinion about, as if women were genetically predisposed to know more. Instinct. Shopping. Women. Some kind of law of nature in his mind...

"Soy or beeswax?" he asked once, proffering two candles for her inspection in Whole Foods. Their cart already brimmed with organic steaks and artisan olive oil and enough other gourmet goodies to last a whole family a week, even though it was just the two of them for the weekend. Half of it would rot in the fridge. Who cared about cooking when so many blowjobs and mind-blowing orgasms awaited on the table? Melanie's favorite mealtimes had quickly become Dan's noshing on her pussy.

"I think beeswax has some medicinal properties," Melanie answered, as serious as a scientist pondering the minor question. "And maybe its wax is hotter than soy? I could do some research."

"You do that." Dan looked thoughtful, piling five soy candles into the cart. "Beeswax hotter; good to know." Moving down the aisle, he left her to push the heavy, overflowing cart.

What gives? Melanie wondered again and again about moves like this. Men were supposed to handle the heavy stuff. So confusing, these random buckings of tradition. Lack of cart pushing was not the only odd thing, either.

Dan never offered to carry her suitcase on weekend stays at his place. He either ignored or savored her struggle up the front steps to his house.

"Please" and "thank you" never, ever crossed his lips. "Hand me the remote, baby," he would say. Or the water glass or his cell phone from the other room. "What's the magic word?" she had teased once, early on. His annoyance was so visible, his glare made her feel so petty and ungrateful, that she never brought it up again.

He refused to hold hands, ever. Deemed it silly and childish. Who didn't like to hold hands, except maybe lepers and priests? Befuddling.

But Melanie counted quirks like these as a small price to pay for Dan's generous attention. And his out-of-this world passion and sexual prowess. They still hadn't played the actual hide-the-salami game yet—another mind-boggling oddity; what the hell was he waiting for?—but what he did do…well, she'd crawl to the ends of the earth for it.

They would lie in his king-size bed for hours, kissing and touching, his fingers creating trails of lovely shivers down her spine and into that warm, wet, secret place. He was thorough beyond belief. Tickling her earlobes with his tongue, lapping at her neck, teasing her nipples, pinching with a range of firmness from sweetly tender to a roughness that made her gasp. Nibbling her thighs, once biting her so hard so that she actually yelped, his teeth leaving tiny red marks. She didn't like these painful jolts, not one bit, but afterward the caresses seemed even more pleasant. Made her sink into a dreamy, otherworldly place where nothing else existed but Dan and his touch.

He took her shopping for sex toys, scooping up vibrators and dildos, "ticklers" and Ben-Wa balls, like they were going out of style. Melanie had no idea what some of the things were even for (anal beads—why on earth?), but they seemed harmless enough at first.

At first.

And then came the DVDs.

"I want you to watch this with me." Dan popped a disc into the player, the title flashing across the 64-inch flat-screen: *Pandora's Punishment,* starring Lacey LaRue.

Dan kept switching his gaze between her face and the screen. Lacey thrown into a hogtie, a blindfold tied on quickly as she struggled helplessly in the tight red ropes. A bare-chested man in jeans and a crew cut slapped her face over and over while he shoved his manhood in her mouth. Another man pounded her from behind, Lacey's moans muffled by the flesh filling her mouth.

Melanie's own mouth dropped open too—in horror and fascination. Shocking. Outrageous. Really, really hot.

But no. No, no, *no.* She shook her head as if her life depended on it. For once Dan looked askance at her instead of demanding or instructing.

"This is what you like?" Melanie could barely get the words out. The video had subverted everything she had ever been taught was OK for a man to do with a woman. *To* a woman. No way could she ever do something like that.

"I like many things." Dan seemed not the tiniest bit ashamed or regretful. "I would never make you do anything you didn't want to do, Melanie."

But she *did* want…maybe someday…no, never. Maybe.

Besides, why mess with a good thing? No, not a good thing—a wondrous, astounding, divine thing. His tongue had superpowers. His fingers were magic. His cock was glorious, a thing of beauty. It hadn't actually entered her yet, unless you counted her mouth, but the rest of her exploded to shreds under his expert touch.

She would lie on the bed, or the couch, or the floor—once slumped in his arms against the kitchen counter—completely spent. Her body no longer felt like her own on these occasions, no longer even in the same galaxy. It floated away into the ether, dissolved into the air like evaporated dew.

"How do you do that?" she girlishly murmured into his ear once. Afterward. Curling a shaky, jellified leg over his.

"Do what?" His mouth showed a hint of a smile.

"That. You know. To me. Where did you learn all that stuff?"

"Boy Scouts." A barely straight face. "They offer a badge in it. Magic Mountain Exploration Skills."

No matter that his erotic talents outshone her own by a mile—you don't acquire top-notch blowjob skills in bed alone with a vibrator—because his instructions had the same precision in bed as out of it.

"Stick your tongue out. Relax your throat. Look at me while you're going down—I like you staring like it's the best thing you'll ever do. Good girl." Directing her in the same tone as he might say, "Wear the red skirt. You'll have the scallops. Let your hair grow longer." Melanie was amazed at his naturalness at instructing her in these unnatural (to her) acts even as she struggled to follow his wishes. She often gagged as his largeness hit the back of her throat, swallowing tears of frustration. But she willed the vomit down. And he never chided her, not once. Offered only positive encouragement and compliments, between issuing instructions.

"Spread your legs. Stick out your ass like the little whore you are. Suck harder, like it's your favorite lollipop. That's right—such a sweet, sweet girl. Such a good girl."

A little whore and a good girl. Oh yes, he had Melanie pegged. Dan knew her deepest shame and her highest aspiration.

And thank goodness he had "earned a badge" in how to please a woman. Because she could never, ever, not in a million years, instruct a man so specifically in how to make her come. "Oh, yes, that's nice" or "A little harder please" were all she could ever manage. There was a better chance of there being a black female lesbian president than of Melanie demanding, "Lick it like it's your favorite candy."

Dan picked up on all of her insecurities early on, sniffing them out with a preternatural instinct. Making it his personal mission to eradicate every last one—while somehow still using them to his advantage, to make sure Melanie did his bidding. Her face was "beyond beautiful, and don't ever let me hear you say otherwise again." Her body was "magnificent, a work of art, and you'll get no dessert if you say you're fat." Her hair was "silky smooth, a cascade of honey." He drank in her kisses as if they nourished him. He deemed her job perfectly appropriate, although insisting the artworks paled in her presence. For the first time in her life, Melanie felt like something exquisite, valuable. Something *worth* something.

Melanie could never repay Dan for that, for making her feel wanted. *Treasured*. She could only devote her life to pleasing him, and even that might still not be enough.

Chapter 8
"The Only Word I Want to Hear Is Yes"

MOST OF the time, Dan treated her like a princess. Besides the four-star restaurants and the door-holding and the compliments that flowed like wine at a wedding, he showered her with little presents. Not flowers or chocolates, the unimaginative standard of the commoners, but jeweled hairpins and exotic spices and silk scarves. One big, delightful gift came only a month into their dating.

"Are you seeing anyone else, Melanie? I assume Jaden June is out of the picture." Their thighs were touching in the upstairs corner booth during dinner at Jardinière, an alluring French restaurant near the opera house. The votive's candlelight dancing against the thick white tablecloth.

As if she could see anyone else! She already belonged to Dan, body and soul, in her mind. Not even rock god Jaden June. Not anyone. She could no more imagine wanting to be with anyone else than quitting her job to be a traveling pole dancer.

But she couldn't tell Dan that. Men didn't like it when you got serious too soon. He'd probably run so fast in the other direction, her head would spin. Why risk scaring him away? Melanie was hoping to make Dan fall in love with her before he discovered all of her faults.

"No, no one." She put her fork down gently next to the white china plate topped with perfectly golden scallops and braised greens. *I want you and only you,* she added silently. *Please, please don't break my heart.* "I'm not seeing anyone else. Um, are you? Seeing anyone else?" How intrusive and nosy it felt, asking him the very same question he had just posed to her.

"Would it matter if I was?" He cocked his head to one side.

Yes! I want to be the only one. Say I'm the only one, that you'll adore me and only me forever. I would give anything to hear it.

Melanie counted to three in her head. "N-no, not exactly." Clutching the napkin hard. "I just...I just want you to be happy." The simple truth. Her needs were secondary in the end, as always. She wanted to please him more than anything.

"Is that a fact," he declared. Leaning back into the booth and folding his hands on the table. A pose of deliberation. "Do you mean that?"

The blush traveled to the roots of Melanie's hair. She twisted the corner of the heavy cloth napkin, wringing it to relieve the tension. Looked everywhere except at his eyes, drilling into her. Could she lay her cards on the table so soon? How could she not? He would find out one way or the other anyway. That unnerving ability to draw out her darkest secrets, to get whatever information he wanted. If interrogation wouldn't work, then spying would.

"Yes. Yes, I do."

Oh, why did she choose "I do"? Melanie twisted the napkin harder in her damp hands. All of her hopes and dreams lay in those two small words, words that meant everything. How many times had she already pictured herself intoning them at the altar? Her snowy dress flowing like icing, a lush bouquet trailing ribbons, friends and family radiating their approval and joy from the pews? Only goodwill and compliments would peel off her mother's and sister's tongues for once, their venom stayed by the sweetness of the occasion.

And lately, of course, Dan's face filled in above the groom's sharp-cut tuxedo in her reveries. Promising to love, honor, and cherish her until death do they part. No, beyond death. Forever.

Please don't be scared away by my overeager devotion. Please forgive my faults. I can improve with your guidance. I can be a better person, she thought desperately. *Please, please, please don't leave me.*

"Well, well, well." Dan reached a hand out, tucking a few strands of Melanie's brown sugar hair behind her ear. Stroked her cheek so tenderly. "What a sweet, sweet girl you are." He landed a hard kiss on her right there in the corner booth at Jardinière in front of all the waiters and stylishly dressed restaurant patrons. Melanie melted into the kiss. God was in his heaven and all was right with the world.

How many times had women responded to that term, "girl," so derisively? Rolling their eyes, shooting daggers. ("Is this the 1950s? Wake up; we're women now, asshole!") Lecturing the poor guy until he wished he'd never even opened his mouth.

But when Dan called her a girl—*his sweet* girl—tingles danced over every inch of Melanie's body, the kisses of butterfly wings. Tickles of fairy dust. Only he saw her true self, and he accepted—celebrated, even—all of it. All of it he knew after a month, anyway. She sparkled from the showerings of those "sweet girl"s.

The day after that dinner, when Melanie had bravely bared the truth, an enormous box awaited her at the front door of her apartment after work. At first she thought it was for someone else. *Strange, I haven't ordered anything.* She read the address label twice, baffled. Then she realized it could only be from one person. One very generous person.

Melanie opened the big box slowly, savoring the moment. Cherishing the idea that he had thought of her while picking something out. It could be his Goodwill castoffs, and still she would cherish them.

But no, not castoffs, of course. Dan trafficked only in the best, the newest. The most luxurious. Melanie carefully removed the bubble wrap to see…Frette sheets and a down comforter nestled inside. The softest bedding ever, the color of cream churned by a dairy maid. Unbelievably extravagant. She shuddered to think of the cost. Delighted to think of the cost.

TO KEEP YOU SNUG IN YOUR SWEET LITTLE GIRL DREAMS. The message, in Dan's own handwriting, was penned on heavy card-stock. Melanie kissed it, pressed it to her heart.

She stripped her bed right away. Lovingly smoothed on the new bedding, making every corner perfect. Then, unable to resist, she stepped out of her clothes and climbed naked into the bed. Tucked the enormous fluffy comforter up under her chin and snow-angeled her arms and legs up and down, reveling in the decadent softness.

Impulsively she grabbed her cell phone. Curled up in a sex kitten pose on her knees, a pinup girl with arched back, the sheets caressing her thighs and wound around to cover just the salacious bits. Snapped a photo and messaged it to Dan.

ENJOYING YR GENEROUS GIFT, Melanie texted. SO BEAUTIFUL, THANK U.

NOT AS BEAUTIFUL AS YOU, came the immediate response. ENJOY.

She laid the phone on the nightstand, but then another message pinged through:

I'M GOING TO CALL YOU NOW, AND THE ONLY WORD I WANT TO HEAR IS YES.

Almost before Melanie finished reading, her cell phone rang, humming in her hand. She read the instruction again, took a deep breath, and counted to three.

"Yes?" She answered the call just as he had told her to. That familiar shiver. Her nether regions throbbed knowingly, anticipating.

"Are you naked for me, Melanie?"

"Yes." Her vocabulary had shrunk to one word at his command. She cradled the phone to her ear, trying to bring him closer.

"Put the phone on speaker, then set it down next to you and lie back." Melanie obeyed, then waited. The faint sound of his breath came through the speaker. "Are you lying down?"

"Yes."

"Good girl. Are you comfortable?"

Ohhhh, so comfortable...amazing sheets! I don't deserve them. No, I do deserve them. But I wish you were here with me. Someday we'll never have to be apart. Someday...

"Yes," she said.

"Good. Run your hands over your breasts for me. You're going to do exactly what I tell you. Nothing more, nothing less. Is that clear?"

"Yes." Her hand trembled. Strange how it, along with her words, no longer belonged to her.

"Pinch your nipples. Are they nice and hard?" His voice so low, a seductive growl.

"Yes."

"Play with them for me. Your hands aren't yours anymore; they're mine. Do you feel my hands all over your breasts?"

"Yes." Her breathing turned shallow, her heart beat so fast now. Wetness surged between her legs.

"Run one finger over your lips and lick it. Now spread your legs...keep your other hand on your tits. Is your finger nice and wet?"

"Yeth." Melanie's finger was still in her mouth, because he hadn't told her to remove it.

"Such a sweet girl. Such a good, obedient girl. Now take that finger and dip it into your pussy for me. It's not your finger anymore. It's mine." His own breath grew thicker, heavier. Melanie didn't need to guess what he was doing on the other end.

"You just keep doing that. Touch yourself for me." God, she could barely stand it! The sensation felt so keen, the pleasure so intense. Lying stark naked on his gift, obeying his instructions, the raciness of it all, and the sun hadn't even set. Her neighbors would just be sitting down to dinner, gulping down meatloaf and prattling on about their uneventful days. Melanie moaned.

"You're not to come without asking me. Is that clear?" No moaning on Dan's end, only his breath turning louder by degrees. "For that, you can use words besides 'yes.'"

"Yes."

"That's a good girl. Such a special girl. You're so precious, Melanie…such a beautiful, precious girl. You make me so happy." He repeated this over and over, varying it just enough for every phrase to sound new, until Melanie could no longer contain herself.

"Dan…" So hard to ask, but what choice did she have? "I'm going to come. I mean, can I come, please?"

"Beg for it."

Melanie groaned. *You've got to be kidding! Beg? No way am I begging—it was hard enough just to ask! Begging, absolutely ridiculous.* "Dan, really, please, I can't hold it…" Almost whimpering now.

"Beg me, Melanie. You can do it. I believe in you."

Goddamn it! I can't say no to him. Why even try? "Please, Dan, please may I come now?"

"Hm, not yet."

What? No. No!

"PleasepleasepleaseDanIreallyneedtocome, pleaseplease may I come right now, I'm begging you, please…let…me…come…"

"Come for me, Melanie. Come for me right now."

Her body jerked so violently then, exploding into stars, shooting into space. She heard him groan too, from somewhere so far away, back on earth. So far and yet so close. Melanie had never felt closer to anyone in her life.

Only much later did she realize that Dan had never answered her question in Jardinière, about whether he was seeing anyone else.

She wanted only him, but he could have a whole harem for all she knew.

THE NEXT year drifted by, a surreal dream. Melanie glowed in the spotlight of Dan's attentions, so gratifying in the bedroom and out that she started to forget they hadn't actually consummated their relationship, that he had never entered her properly. He would when he wanted to, and that was that.

Started to forget she was a doormat too. Other people even started treating her less like a doormat. Her mother's pointed comments softened to the stab of a butter knife. How could she skewer a daughter so near to closing on such a big score? Even Melanie's dad started asking her what she thought of the new British prime minister and which emerging markets looked promising. Dan fed her the answers, told her what to think, but still.

Her sister, Harper, stopped the endless haranguing. Single friends cheered Melanie's romantic success. Even people she didn't know, salesgirls and waiters and whatnot, treated Melanie with respect, as if she mattered. Maybe she mattered only by association, but she savored the taste of it, like she savored all the unknown, exotic delicacies Dan fed to her.

Melanie didn't quite understand this change in attitude toward her by her family and friends. She still wore the same clothes and had the same haircut and job, and treated them the same as always. She was still the same person. Or was she?

"Have you had work done? You look really good," Deena observed keenly one night at the bar, her bar. Backslash. Deena was Melanie's best friend still, if you didn't count Dan. The two of them sat in a booth, Melanie guzzling a Cosmo and Deena sipping water, just as in the old times, the pre-Dan era. The dark ages.

"My goodness, of course not! Do you think I need to get work done?" Melanie made a mock-horror face. A 27-year-old needing cosmetic intervention? This was San Francisco, not L.A.

"Not at all. You always look good." Deena rushed to reassure. "But there's something different. I can't put my finger on it." She squinted, scrutinizing Melanie's face, propping her own in her hands as her elbows rested on the worn wood table in the booth. Her long onyx hair waterfalling over the heavily inked shoulders and arms. Then Deena leaned back as the realization hit. "Ahhh, I get it. You're in love." Nodded knowingly. "Of course."

Melanie breathed deeply. She had not even said the "the L word" to Dan yet, not out loud anyway. She told him with every order she obeyed, every pinch and bite she endured. Every look up into his eyes as she serviced his hard-ons on her knees. *I love you, I love you, I love you,* her eyes and hands and screaming orgasms told him.

Melanie feared breaking the spell by giving her thoughts a voice. Feared shattering the dream by forcing it into human form.

"Ummm…" She averted her eyes. Took a sip of her Cosmo.

"I knew it!" Deena smacked the table with an open palm, grinning, making the drinking glasses jump. Then a shadow crossed her face. She looked away, the silence hanging like an ominous cloud. "Melanie, how long have we been friends?"

"Too many years to count." Melanie smiled affectionately at her best friend, part of her life since elementary school.

"So you know that I would never, ever stick my nose in your business unless I truly believed that it was for your own good, right?"

Uh-oh, here we go. How have I screwed up now? "Of course."

"Good." She nodded, as if the momentum of her head moving were propelling her. "Well I have to tell you, then. There's just something about Dan…" Deena's mouth tightened, steeling for unpleasantness. Her fingers drumming lightly on the worn wooden table. On the carvings of hearts and initials of couples long broken up.

Melanie's skin prickled defensively. She stared at the long latticework of vines and symbols tattooed on Deena's arm.

"Just try to keep an open mind," Deena hedged.

"What is it, already?" Melanie's eyes narrowed. She had already guessed what Deena wanted to say. She just wasn't prepared for her to actually say it.

"You know, when you're a bartender, you see all kinds of people. And you listen to their stories all the time, and you develop a kind of sixth sense for reading people."

"And…?" How could Melanie keep an open mind where Dan was concerned? He controlled it from every corner, his to shut or open at will. And she liked it that way. Where had free thinking gotten her? A lame job, a small apartment. A thousand lonely nights with only a vibrator for company.

"There is something"—Deena strove to choose her words carefully—"*off* about the way you are when you're with him. You're not really you." Her face looked pained.

"Actually, I think I'm *more* like myself when I'm with him," Melanie said, curtly. Straightening her spine, squaring her shoulders.

Deena shook her head. "I know you, Melanie," she pushed on. "You're fun and smart and witty; you've got a thought about everything under the sun even if you can never commit to any of them. But those times we've double-dated with him, you completely deferred to him on everything. Like you had forgotten how to think for yourself."

Free thinking is overrated, Melanie retorted silently. *If I never think for myself again, it'll be too soon.* "That's not true," she protested out loud. "I do defer to him on certain things, yes. Because I don't care about the little things, like where we eat or what we do on a date. I never cared about those things or about…"

"And the way he treats you." Deena rushed to talk over her, recognizing the quickly shutting window of opportunity. "Like he owns you. Like you're a thing rather than a person."

If only, thought Melanie. *Sign me up.*

How nice would that be? To be owned, to just do what you're told and be cherished, rewarded for obedience, instead of having to figure out the right way to behave all the time. To no longer be responsible for outcomes, good or bad.

Then something snapped inside. Finally Melanie's Homemaker Barbie dreams were crystallizing into reality, and her friend—her *best* friend, who should have been happier for her than anyone—disapproved? Outrageous!

"You don't know anything about our relationship," she said icily.

Deena's face registered surprise, then softened. "I'm scared for you, Melanie. I'm scared he's going to erase you and remake you into something else. Someone not Melanie. I'm scared I'm going to lose my best friend."

"Ohhh." Melanie saw a track to switch to and hopped on it instantly. "I get it. You think we won't be friends anymore if I get married."

"No, that's not what…"

"Well, that's absolutely not going to be the case." Melanie forged ahead, desperate to leave Deena's disapproval, her vision of a future sans Dan, behind. "We've been friends for ages, and we will be friends for ages more."

"Melanie." Deena reached across the table and grasped Melanie's arm. "You're a guy magnet. You attract guys left and right—in bars and restaurants and at work and even just on the street. You dated a rock star, for Chrissake! You can do better than this one, I'm telling you."

"A guy magnet?" Melanie stared at Deena in disbelief. "Are you kidding me?" Anger surged. She pulled her arm away roughly. "You and *your guy* have been magnetized at the hip for so long, you've forgotten what it's like not to have someone to hold at night. Someone who really cares about you. Even if I had dates every weekend, which I assure you was not the case before I met Dan, it's not the same as having one constant, wonderful man who really appreciates you."

"And you think Dan really appreciates you?" Deena's face was heavy with concern.

"Of course he does!" Melanie's eyes blazed. "No one has ever appreciated me the way he does. No one has ever *seen* me the way he does. Every date with him is like being Cinderella at the ball." She pushed back all the images of her lugging suitcases up Dan's steps without his help, of doing his laundry and cleaning his apartment with not even a "thank you." He thanked her enough with his tongue.

She would lug a thousand suitcases alone, would fold his socks and shirts every day of the year without being thanked, if it meant being Mrs. Dan Hightower. Deena didn't understand what he did for her in return, more even than the mind-blowing orgasms. He *saw* her. Without him, she'd still be a loser waiting for her life to start.

Deena searched the ceiling as if she'd find the right words written there. "If you say so," she said finally, dragging her eyes down sadly to meet Melanie's again. Not convinced, but recognizing the hopelessness of her cause. "In any case, I can see your mind is already made up." Deena sighed. "I really do hope he makes you happy."

"He does. He makes me happier than anyone else ever has," Melanie said miserably. Her best friend, her longtime protector and confidante, disapproved! She wished she could take Deena's implications and disapproval and stuff them right back where they came from. Wished the conversation had never even started. Wished she weren't so angry and hurt. Why all the anguish over one person's opinion? One person who had, let's not forget, been dating the same boyfriend for three years without snagging a wedding ring.

"If you say so," Deena repeated. Her mouth twisted as if to hold something in, then opened again. "But please know that I'm here for you if he ever doesn't. You can *always* come to me for help, OK?"

"It's not going to come to that." *Could it?*

They tried to shift to other topics after that, to lighthearted small talk, but the negative energy lingered like bad breath in an airless room. Why couldn't Deena, her *best friend since the third grade*, just be happy for her? Why did she have to rain on Melanie's parade? So many people had rained disapproval on Melanie her whole life, she was soaked in it.

Why, oh why, did her oldest and dearest friend have to water those damn seeds of doubt?

ON THE one-year anniversary of their first date, Melanie sat with Dan nibbling oysters in the exquisite French restaurant Fleur de Lys. Microwaved Lean Cuisine solo on Thursday nights, haute cuisine for two on Fridays. Her life had split into black and white and Technicolor over the past year. Two distinct worlds had developed: Without Dan and With Dan. Time in the former dragged at half speed and held a dim approximation of color; time in the latter, always in too short supply. Without Dan, Melanie merely killed time.

She reached for her champagne glass, noting as usual how gorgeous he was, all fierceness and unbridled passion simmering behind the carefully composed façade. She longed for dinner to be over so they could get to the *real* main course: "Oh, oh, oh" with a side of "Yes, yes, yes!"

Did Dan remember that this was their anniversary? Elegant restaurants with sky-high prices had become par for the course, so that indicated nothing. Would he get her something extra special? A shopping spree at Kate Spade or even just a Prada purse?

A year ago, Melanie had been a nobody. A year ago, people had ignored her, insulted her, walked all over her. She marveled at how Dan had changed all that. The spotlight he shone on her followed her everywhere now, for everyone to see.

Yes, it was enough. But a little anniversary gift—say, a spa day or a long weekend in the tropics—would be nice too. Maybe the gift box lay wrapped and waiting in the trunk of the Lexus. Maybe it could fit in an envelope and hid in the inside pocket of his perfectly tailored Armani suit jacket. Maybe…

And then Melanie saw it. Her breath caught in her throat.

A ring.

Nestled at the bottom of her champagne glass, bubbles dancing around it. A dazzler—three carats at least. Set simply, perfectly, on a silvery band. Platinum, she guessed.

"Melanie, will you marry me?" No bent knee, of course. Dan would no more get on his knees to her than wear plaid polyester or take the bus. Besides, theatrics weren't necessary when you already knew the answer.

Words failed her. All the waiting and hoping and dreaming of this moment, and still Melanie felt caught unprepared. All the rehearsing of her spontaneous reaction, and now she just froze. She waited for the wave of joy to lift her up and carry her to the appropriate natural expression of ecstasy, but felt only…

"I'm tired of being Mr. Hightower by myself." Dan reached for Melanie's hand across the table. "Be my Mrs. Hightower."

Flat. That's how she felt. Dan sat there so casually, as if he had just asked the server for the dessert menu. A mere formality, the asking. The biggest anticlimax ever.

Time slowed. Deena's warning flashed in her mind, how Dan might erase her. Memories too. Her sister, Harper, bringing the twins home for the first time as babies, her proud husband snapping photos. Melanie's mother practically planning the wedding since meeting Dan, dishing out generous helpings of advice about him like it was shrimp at an all-you-can-eat buffet: "Don't act *too* eager; mysteriousness is attractive." "Keep your nails and shoes immaculate; men like that notice the small details." "If you let this one get away, you'll regret it forever."

Remembering his bedroom skills, his bringing her to uncharted worlds of pleasure without ever even entering her with his manhood, always saying it would happen at the right time. Maybe he'd been waiting for this all along. She ached to know what his conquering the final frontier would feel like. How could such a dreamboat not send her out of this world when he took her in the most ancient expression of possession? Not to mention, the ring bathing in her champagne could easily have cost 20 grand. Hesitation had no place in the land of $20,000 diamond rings.

Every bride-to-be has doubts, she reminded herself. *But this is the right choice. I know it. Right?*

No going back now.

"Yes," she answered at last, feeling odd. More like a task had been accomplished than a cause for celebration. "Of course I'll be Mrs. Hightower." She summoned a radiant smile. "We're going to be so happy together."

Fishing the ring out of the bubbles, she slipped it on. It fit perfectly.

THE WEDDING was a dream come true, right down to the doves released upon their "I do"s. Her parents and Dan spared no expense. The dress: an ethereal Vera Wang silk sheath—Melanie had starved for weeks to look good in it. Bridesmaids Deena and Ginger looked so chic in their elegant champagne frocks that brushed the floor; their satin slingbacks just peeking out as they swished down the aisle. Beribboned peonies in every shade of pink tumbling over their hands. Pride and joy for their friend setting their faces aglow, aided by the $100-an-hour makeup artist.

Melanie has wrestled over choosing Harper as the matron of honor. Her sister, her nemesis. In the end, magnanimity won out. Landing a rich and handsome husband who adored her was the best revenge.

The sun shone brilliantly in the Magritte sky, generously bathing the Napa Valley in its light. St. Adele winery, the scene of that dinner date with Dan so long ago, now witnessed Melanie and Dan's vows. Guests wore their finest, the women in their pretty pastels like sugar sprinkles dotting the manicured lawn.

Dan's best man: an old college friend, backed by business-associate groomsmen and, a gesture of goodwill, Melanie's brother Alex. Melanie purposefully avoided learning any details about the bachelor party.

"Do you, Daniel Hightower, take this woman, Melanie Merriweather, to be your lawfully wedded wife, to love, honor, and cherish, in sickness and in health, for richer or for poorer, as long as you both shall live?" The Unitarian minister radiated kindly authority.

"I do." Dan's voice carried across the lawn, clear and firm. His eyes stayed locked on Melanie's face.

"And do you, Melanie Merriweather, take this man, Daniel Hightower, to be your lawfully wedded husband, to love, honor, and cherish, in sickness and in health, for richer or for poorer, as long as you both shall live?"

And to obey, she added silently. *Forever.* Her stomach clenched.

"I do." Her voice sounded unfamiliar, not heard beyond the wedding party. She willed her knees not to knock.

The rest went by in a blur. So many well-wishers (247, to be exact) to hug and thank—Melanie didn't even try to commit the names of Dan's myriad business associates to memory. She barely tasted the winery chef's artisanal offerings or the generously flowing champagne. The cake, five tiers of fairy-tale fondant and pink crystallized flowers nestled like gems on a princess's tiara, melted on her tongue with only a moment's savoring. So much to take in, so much to remember to tell her grandchildren!

Certain moments flashed like snapshots, burning instantly into her memory:

- Gliding down the aisle on the arm of her father, gently trodding on rose petals in her white satin heels; his eyes wet as he handed her over to Dan. Pride and satisfaction on her mother's face in the front row; Melanie felt almost unnerved being the cause.

- Dan gorgeous and unimpeachable in his expertly fitted Tom Ford tuxedo, waiting at the altar. His waiting for her seemed unnatural, backward. Melanie should have been running to him, to kneel at his feet.

- Gazing out at the crowd of family members and friends— but mostly strangers. Dan's business associates. And was it love and support everyone radiated, or merely relief, obligation, and envy?

- Meeting Dan's parents, Harold and Ethel Hightower, for the first time, elderly and sweet in their pastels and Tod's loafers. How normal they seemed! How middle class and middle-of-the-road. They'd keel over if they had even an inkling of Dan's sexual tastes.

- And, of course, Dan's sweeping her over the threshold of their hotel suite. The same hotel where he had first shown off his bedroom skills, staking a claim without words. His lips now touching every inch of her body. His mouth saying, "Give your hair to me, Mrs. Hightower; it's mine now. Give your mouth to me, Mrs. Hightower; it's mine now. Give your neck to me..."

And finally the moment she had been waiting for forever: giving herself heart and soul and body to someone who deserved it. Her husband. Her prince. No, her king. Melanie breathed deeply and tried to relax. Her hands fluttered nervously, unsure where to land.

She expected him to be gentle for their first time together, as he had been so gentle and patient over the past year and a half. But no. Once Dan had claimed every part of her with his lips, he shoved himself inside her with such swift force that Melanie let out a half scream. A hand shot out, clamping over her mouth.

"You want this." His voice guttural in her ear. "You've wanted this since the day we met." Every thrust like a knife stab. *Of course* she had wanted it, but not like this! Not this kind of pain. Tears poured from her eyes, but they only seemed to turn him on more.

"You're mine now," he reminded her. "Mine to do what I want with, mine to love and cherish and use, as long as we both shall live." Driving into her, faster now, his hand still pressed to her mouth, pushing her head into the pillow. She struggled to breathe through her nose, stuffy from crying. Tears ran down the sides of her face. Her body grew numb from the waist down.

"You're mine, Melanie Hightower." And with that repeated declaration, he let out a raw animal groan, a low roar, as he came inside her.

Thank God. Melanie wiped her waterlogged cheeks. She had never been so happy to see him finish.

Dan lay on his back, his head propped up on folded arms against the pillow. Melanie curled into a ball beside him, hands clenched into little fists. Shocked and confused. *What the fuck?*

Then, after a few minutes, Dan reached over and stroked her hair, as if calming a wounded puppy. Reached down and unpeeled her fingers from their fists gently, one by one. Kissing each tenderly.

His hands felt so light on her bare skin now, teasing out little shivers. Replacing the roughness with only the softest, sweetest caresses. Kissing her neck, breathing in the scent of her as if it were the world's most expensive perfume.

Ever so slowly, Melanie's body loosened. Relaxing into the familiar seduction. Dan knew her body better than she did. How to please her like no one else. And as he worked his fingers down into her warm, wet places, she opened up to him again. How could she not? She would forgive him almost anything for the deliciousness of this.

All the pain set adrift now from this island of pleasure. Melanie melted into his hands and tender kisses, thinking only, *Yes, yes, yes.* Yes, she belonged to him—she *wanted* to belong to him. Yes, she had married the man of her dreams—finally, she *mattered.* She was a wife.

The blinding force of the climax that shot her body into the heavens paled in comparison to the joy of her exalted new status, enhanced identity. After so many years of waiting and hoping and dreaming, of feeling like an utter failure, she had finally succeeded.

Melanie had found the man who gave her life meaning. Who made her whole.

She was his now. To use as he pleased.

Part 2

MISS M

Chapter 9

Any Port in a Storm

"Mommy, why Daddy not back?"

Sammy's eyes were impossibly big, questioning. Filled with longing. Melanie had tucked his brightly colored Thomas the Train comforter up under his chin, snug as a bug in a rug. She had just finished reading his favorite bedtime story for the hundredth time. Trying not to notice how Sammy had gotten Dan's eyes from the gene pool.

She slipped the book back into the low bookcase by the bed. Tucked the blanket tighter around her son lovingly. As if busying her hands would stay the tears. She couldn't bear to tell Sammy yet. He was only three years old—it would break his heart. How do you tell your little boy, your angel, that his father isn't coming back? That his "business trip" had been extended permanently. That he did not want to be part of their family anymore. Such cruelty should be reserved for grown-ups.

"Daddy will be back soon, honey." The lie slipped out before Melanie could stop it. She smoothed Sammy's hair with the palm of her hand, bent over and kissed his soft cheek. "He's in another city for work." She turned to flick on the Thomas the Train nightlight on the wall, surreptitiously flicking away a tear too. Switched off the lamp, but the glow of the nightlight and moonbeams let her still see.

"Wub my back Mommy, OK?" Sammy yawned and rolled over onto his tummy.

"Of course, honey." Her favorite part of the day. All the stress and chaos of the waking hours melted away as Sammy slipped into dreamland. No one prepared you properly for motherhood, for all the times of raw terror and nail-biting tension, for the love that filled your heart to bursting. For the roller coaster of emotion. But here, rubbing Sammy's back as his eyelids grew heavy, everything seemed right with the world.

Everything except, of course, that Dan—the love of her life, her husband of five years, the father of her son—had abandoned them.

DAN HADN'T ever really wanted a child. Yes, of course they had talked about it. Yes, he had agreed to have children when the time was right. But the "right" time, Melanie quickly discovered after she signed the marriage certificate, existed somewhere between the far-off future and "forget about it." And how could she be Homemaker Barbie without children? Who else would fill the long hours when Dan toiled at the office, if not children? Shopping bags and gardening tools don't hug you back.

A year into the marriage, she decided to take matters into her own hands. It was the only way. And once Dan held his child, felt that magical little bundle so sweet and innocent in his arms, he would see the light. Would see the baby as the perfect piece to complete their family puzzle. And then would want more pieces to make the puzzle even bigger.

So Melanie began popping each birth control pill from its packet every night and flushing it down the toilet. Justification *almost* outweighed the guilt at the deception. What choice did she have? It was either flush the pills down the toilet or watch her dreams go down it instead.

"We didn't plan this, Melanie." Dan had glared at the positive pregnancy test stick as if it were toxic waste. He never, ever yelled at her, but the quiet anger seemed worse—nothing to defend against. "You can't keep it. We're not ready."

"*You're* not ready!" *Don't whine, don't whine. Talk like a grown-up.* Melanie choked back tears. "I'm almost 30 years old! I'm more than ready. And I'm beginning to think you will never be ready, that you knew all along you would never really want this." She placed a hand protectively over her tummy, shielding the embryo from feeling unwanted. The past, her own experience of feeling unwanted, would *not* repeat itself.

"Are you calling me a liar?" He towered over her menacingly. Would he actually hit her?

"Of course not." She rushed to placate, actually fearing him. *Liar, liar, liar. You knew all along.* Melanie had never seen him this angry. She glanced around and moved closer to her cell phone. "I just think it's possible…maybe…you aren't so in touch with your feelings on this. A little."

Dan didn't answer at first. Melanie felt the heat of his simmering rage. She placed both hands on her tummy now, buffering, as if she could cover the little seed's ears. When he spoke, Melanie almost didn't recognize his voice. So twisted and clipped.

"I. Am. Perfectly. In touch. With my *feelings*." The sneer contorted his usually handsome features, turning them sinister. "It's *you* who is disregarding *my feelings* on the subject. Luckily, this is fixable. I will give you one week to reconsider. Think carefully. Your decision will have ramifications."

"Alright." It came out a whisper. But she had no need to take a week. A lifetime of considering would not change her mind. *Besides,* she buoyed herself, *it will be different when the baby comes. He won't be able to help falling in love with it. This will all be a bad memory when he cradles his child.*

Rubbing Sammy's tiny back now as he drifted off to sleep, almost four years after that awful day—the first and only time she had ever defied Dan—Melanie knew she had made the right decision. Even if she never saw Dan again, never felt his passionate grinding inside her or his tender kisses, never felt the pride of being on his arm or the joy of his attentions, she had this incredible angel. So innocent, so precious. She and Sammy were connected in a deeper way than she could ever have imagined. He was a success no matter what else failed.

"I love you, Mommy," Sammy slurred sleepily. "To infinity and beyond," he added, echoing his hero, Buzz Lightyear. He shifted to his side, then sailed off instantly to dreamland.

"I love you too, Sammy," she said softly, even though he could no longer hear. "To infinity and beyond." She leaned over and kissed his sweet little-boy head.

And then the tears came pouring out, as Melanie watched her angel sleep. Her body shook with the force of her sadness, the betrayal and incomprehension. How could this child, so beautiful, so special, have cost her the only other love of her life?

Melanie stumbled down to the kitchen, her floor-length silk nightgown swishing against the polished hardwood floors. Made a beeline for the fridge with its promise of relief: an open bottle of chardonnay. Any port in a storm.

Dinner that night had been a handful of raw carrots. Lunch, a small bowl of miso soup. Her life was falling apart; food brought nauseating waves to her stomach. But at least she could still suck down wine for comfort.

The buzz set in quickly. Melanie savored it. The buzz numbed the nightmare feeling, let her examine it from arm's length instead of being consumed by it. How had her life taken such a wrong turn? She perched on a dark leather bar stool at the island and took in the spacious, modern kitchen. Top of the line, of course: Sub-Zero fridge, Aga stove, Carrara marble countertops. *Everything* was top of the line in their $2.3 million Palo Alto home, 10 minutes from Dan's venture capital office, but somehow Melanie's life was hitting bottom anyway. How had all of her patience, all of her careful efforts, led to such disaster?

She unfolded the note again, the one Dan had left on this same kitchen island three weeks ago. As if it might offer a new clue or a shred of hope.

```
Melanie,

We have not wanted the same things for a long
time now. Be free to explore what makes you happy,
as I will. Consider the house yours. I will be
taking an extended leave abroad and will contact
you when I return to discuss details regarding
closure.

      D.
```

Where had Dan disappeared to exactly? She didn't know. The date of his return? No clue. His office, if they knew, refused to spill the beans. *Of course, they know. Bastards. Protecting him. Obeying his commands like little puppets. Just like everyone else.*

Except me. And look where it got me.

With whom he had disappeared, however, she had little doubt. Melanie might still be a bit mousy, but she wasn't stupid. That waitress slut, barely even drinking age. Too many credit card charges to a diner well below Dan's standard had led Melanie there, a bloodhound tracing the scent of sex and betrayal. Must be that bottle blonde with the too-big tits. Proof? Who needed more proof than those porn-star looks? JASMINE, the slut's name tag read. Should be Jezebel. Melanie had sipped a coffee demurely, fantasizing about hurling the mug at the husband stealer's head.

When Melanie had discovered the note that fateful morning three weeks ago, she had run back upstairs flinging open closets.

Stared with disbelief at the emptiness where his clothes had been only the night before. Impossible! *Wake up, wake up, wake up. This isn't happening. This isn't real.* She had left bruises on her own arm from trying to pinch herself awake.

Every day since then, her heart sank a little more. Why had she ignored their problems for so long? Why hadn't she confronted him about that home-wrecking cunt? Why had she let it come to this? All her fault, as usual. Now no one would be able to hack through the thorny mess that had grown between them.

Melanie refilled her wineglass and stared dully at the kitchen mess. Dirty dishes towered in the sink. The detritus of frozen and prepared food cluttered the counters. Gnats buzzed around the compost. Maybe tomorrow she would clean up. Maybe tomorrow she would take a shower. Maybe tomorrow her strength and motivation would return.

Tonight, though…Melanie knocked back half the glass in two sips.

"Just let me make it through the night." A prayer to no one. The whispered words fell through the empty air, settling on the now grimy floor.

…Midnight already? The last dregs, where did they go? Melanie wove an unsteady path up to the master bedroom. How lovingly she had decorated this bedroom! Over there, the custom silk drapes the shade of Dan's eyes. Here the footstool upholstered in leather where she'd rubbed his feet with Italian cream. Suddenly she had the urge to slash through the drapes with a kitchen knife. Stab the twin overstuffed armchairs mocking her—*you'll need only one of us now, eh?* Tear up the $2,000 bedding on the king-size bed— all dressed up in Egyptian linen and no one to sleep in it with her.

But destruction…no. Not even in anger and despair. Instead, Melanie knelt down at the foot of the bed. For almost five years she had shared this bed with Dan. She clasped her hands on the thick down duvet, the prayer position unfamiliar but soothing. God had been a mere bit player in Melanie's childhood; her mother didn't welcome the competition.

"Please, God." Her voice barely audible. "Please make every- thing all right." She cleared her throat, feeling silly. Talking to someone who may or may not even exist. "Please help me. Help Sammy. Don't let him be scarred for the rest of his life." Her voice grew urgent, picking up the pace. Thick and guttural through the onslaught of tears. "God, please help us come out of this OK. I don't care what I have to do to make a good life for Sammy. Just show me what to do. Please. I'll do anything to make this right. Just tell me how. I'm begging you." Her head fell to the bed, damp cheek imprinting the duvet. One more stain to worry about tomorrow.

Lightning didn't crash. No doors slammed. No sign at all that God had heard or cared, just a car humming by on the street below. A minute more Melanie knelt, waiting, then got up, feeling foolish. What a gyp. God was a fairy-tale character, just like Prince Charming and godmothers who made wishes come true.

Melanie climbed into bed without brushing her teeth, the dry fuzz from too much wine creeping over her tongue. Sleep, when it finally dragged her down, offered little relief. Anxious dreams tossed her like a tiny boat on a roiling sea. She woke up in a cold sweat at 4 a.m., reaching automatically for Dan. Oh, right. That buoy had floated off.

Melanie felt utterly adrift. For the first time in her life, she had no plan. No idea what to do next. She would drown without Dan.

Wouldn't she?

Please, God. I'll do anything.

Help me.

Anything…for Sammy…

The thought loop ran in her head until exhaustion finally won out and her open eyes gave up the fight.

A BLEARY-EYED Melanie dropped Sammy off at preschool the next morning, her puffy red eyelids hiding behind oversize black sunglasses. She managed a wave to the teacher and a hug for her son, but relief chimed with the sound of the car door closing. Four precious hours of not having to smile and pretend her life hadn't fallen apart.

Nowhere to be, nothing to do. No job since Sammy's birth—per Dan's decree. No nanny could replace a mother, he'd declared. Fine by her. Who needed a job as an art gallery assistant when you ruled a house and a child? But she had no housecleaning help, either—another decree. Since Melanie would be "hanging around the house all day" with "nothing to do but watch the baby sleep," Dan had insisted she take over all the cleaning duties, replacing the service he had always used. A not-so-thinly veiled punishment. Punishments had replaced sex since her decision to keep the baby.

Melanie wandered around the house now, willfully ignoring the mess. The dirty clothes strewn everywhere. The papers and almost-empty teacups, rancid cream coagulating. She picked things up and put them down again. Just the thought of cleaning made her tired.

She caught sight of herself in the hallway mirror, shocked by the pale and sunken ghost who stared back. Ugly roots fouled her golden hair highlights. Puffy bluish half moons sat under her eyes. And were those crow's feet and mouth wrinkles getting deeper? She sighed and quickly moved on. First she lost her husband; now she was losing her looks. Once a loser, always a loser.

As she moved through the rooms, so stale and lifeless now with no one in them, Melanie thought of all her effort to make their place a real home. Here on the polished wood mantel, all the lovingly placed wedding and family photographs. Their first-anniversary trip to London. Sammy a newborn, eyes already full of life below the pink and blue hospital cap. That picnic at the beach, when the seagulls had snatched their sandwiches.

There on the coffee table, the hand-carved abstract sculpture bought on their Paris honeymoon for almost as much as the trip itself. Against the wall, the plush sectional picked for family snuggling. The kitchen open to the living room so she and Dan could keep watch over their brood while whipping up coq au vin together. Her heart was entwined in every part of the house, everything in it. Every corner now felt like an open wound.

But be honest, her inner self urged. *You were never really happy together since the wedding. Sure, the sex was amazing. But amazing sex does not a soulmate make.*

Why hadn't they broken through the initial physical passion to the realm of deep intimacy? *Dan's fault. Clearly incapable of emotional intimacy.*

But her fault too, certainly. She could never bring herself to try the shocking maneuvers in his violent porn videos—the rope bondage and the crops and whips. No matter how gently or persistently he urged. Normal people don't *do* that! *But you could have tried. For him.*

The way to a man's heart was supposed to be through his stomach— or even through his manhood. Not through S&M tricks.

Anyway, it didn't matter now, did it? Dan had fled to Europe with his floozy, who probably let him hogtie her from here to next Tuesday.

Five years of marriage, and all Melanie had to show for it now was a house filled with painful reminders of failure...and Sammy. Oh, God—a three-year-old to raise all on her own! How could Dan abandon his own child? Not one mention of Sammy in the note. Not "Tell Sammy I love him," not "Take good care of Sammy," not "Don't let Sammy forget about me." Who could be so heartless?

And did she even have the house at all? What did the note mean, "Consider the house yours"? The title held Dan's name only. *Everything* they shared was in Dan's name—the cars and credit cards and artwork. Melanie didn't even have her own bank account! Just as Dan, the control freak, wanted it. Impossible to refuse. Independence seemed like a fair trade for a husband, a four-bedroom house, exotic vacations...everything she'd ever dreamed of. Now she had nothing but her pre-marriage pittances and a child barely out of diapers to raise—alone.

Oh, yes, she intuited immediately that she'd be raising Sammy alone. Mr. "Your Decision Will Have Ramifications" apparently didn't give two shits about the child carrying on his genetic legacy. Selfish bastard. He cared more about sticking it to that big-breasted waitress slut, probably in some five-star hotel room. On a four-poster bed with iron rails for the rope bondage.

Stop, stop, stop. No more. I can't take it! Tears spilled again. Blurry-eyed, she stumbled down the stairs to their state-of-the-art temperature-controlled wine cellar. Grabbed a chenin blanc. Only 11 a.m., so what? Sorrow doesn't wear a watch.

Besides, who cared about propriety anymore? Look where trying to be proper had gotten her! She took the bottle out to the back patio, dragging a cushioned lounge chair to a secluded spot under the arbor. No need to give the neighbors gossip fodder.

The rosebushes she planted on their second anniversary. The barbecue that Dan had presided over like a commander in chief. The sandbox she had installed when Sammy turned two. Melanie took a big swig of the perfectly chilled white wine, barely tasting it. Citrusy notes, crisp finish, whatever. As long as it did its job.

Halfway through the second glass, the doorbell jolted her away from the memories. Pulling her away from the pity party. She guiltily stashed the bottle in the fridge on the way to the front door. Avon lady? No, upscale Palo Alto didn't go for lowbrow door-to-door sales.

Melanie peered through the sheer curtain of the front window. Holy shit, Deena? What the hell was her old best friend doing 45 minutes south of San Francisco at 11:30 a.m. on a Tuesday morning? So incongruous with her black jeans and tattoos in the Stepford Wives setting. And such a serious look. Oh God, did someone die?

Melanie unlocked the solid oak door apprehensively. Pasted on a smile.

"Melanie, thank God." Deena wrapped her arms around Melanie, hugging tight. "I've been leaving messages and sending you emails for at least two weeks! I know it sounds weird, but I thought something had happened to you. Why didn't you answer?"

Not weird. Exactly right. Deena knew her better than anyone, and she had the instincts of a tiger. Before Melanie could answer, Deena pulled back and sniffed.

"My goodness, is that wine I smell on you? Are you cooking with it?"

"No, I'm just marinating."

Silence. The lame joke to hide her embarrassment had fallen flat.

Deena opened her mouth, then shut it. Melanie's face crumpled. She could never hide anything from her best friend.

"Please, come inside." Melanie opened the door wider and waved an ushering hand. "There's something I need to tell you."

"WHAT A dick." Deena shook her head in disbelief, her long, obsidian hair lustrous in the bright daylight. "You should hire a private investigator to trace him."

"I can't. He emptied our bank accounts." Saying it out loud for the first time made it finally seem real. Melanie could barely admit it. "He left exactly $10,000. He's punishing me." She hugged one of the velvet toss pillows on the huge sectional as if it were a life raft.

"Of course he is, that fucking bastard." Deena would never say, "I told you so," but the unspoken thought hung in the air as clearly as the wine reek. "You can't let him get away with this, Mel. There must be something you can do."

"No, it's hopeless!" Melanie burst into tears. Reached for a dirty, crumpled tissue on the coffee table. A colony of them littered the glass surface already. "He's gone. I'm broke. I have no job and no income. Even if I could hire a PI, it would take ages to track him in Europe. If he doesn't want to be found, he won't be."

Deena considered this. "You'll have to get help from somewhere else, then, until either he's found or he comes back. Then the courts can deal with him. I know you're not going to like this idea, but..."

"No!" Not her parents. Oh, God, how could she even tell them, let alone go crawling back for help! *I would rather die,* Melanie thought. *The one thing I did right in their eyes, and now it's blown to pieces.* "I'm not asking my parents for help. In fact"—she took a deep breath— "I'm not even going to tell them. And you're not, either."

"Are you crazy? They could be your lifeline here. Why not?"

Melanie shook her head back and forth so hard, her neck tendons hurt. "You know better than anyone why not. Go back to being poor pitiable Melanie, taking handouts from Mommy and Daddy, useless without a man? Not a chance. They'd feast on my carcass."

Deena stood up, anger impelling her upright. She paced back and forth, her leather boot heels leaving little dents in the thick carpet pile.

"Then you're going to have to get a job. At least temporarily until the asshole is forced to pay support. It's your only option."

My thoughts exactly, Melanie agreed silently. *But then full-time childcare for Sammy. A stranger raising my baby! And who would even hire me?* A fresh wave of sobs racked her body.

"Look, there's no magic solution here. You got dealt a bad hand, and you have to make the best of it. But you're not alone. You know that, right?" Deena sat back down, enveloping Melanie in a tight hug.

But that's exactly how Melanie did feel. Alone. She had made this bed—or *not* made it—and now she would have to lie in it.

As she and Deena kept talking, though, a strange new feeling began to grow. She wasn't the pitiful third grader Deena had rushed to protect anymore. She was a *mother*. She had someone of her own to protect now. Someone whose life depended on her.

The urge to fight, to stand up instead of lying down and taking whatever abuse Dan chose to heap on her, took root. For the first time in her life, she felt an inkling of power. Melanie had a sense of purpose beyond other people's expectations now, beyond being the perfect little girl to Mommy and Daddy and the perfect Barbie doll wife to Dan.

Her beautiful boy, the boy *she* had brought into this world—he didn't deserve a doormat for a mother. *She* would be the provider. The nurturer. The one who took care of things.

Melanie would not let her son down.

Chapter 10

"A Ginormous Smorgasbord of Men, and You Can Stuff Yourself Silly"

MELANIE'S DREAMS took a violent, wanton turn.

On Monday, when the credit card bill came, she dreamed she walked the streets as a common harlot, pocketing fistfuls of bills. When a john tried to stiff her, she stabbed him with a switchblade. Cackling crazily as his blood ran into the gutter.

On Wednesday, when Sammy's preschool insisted she pick him up early because her son had bit another child, she dreamed she wrestled a half-naked woman to a mat. Oil everywhere, their bodies sliding off each other. Men leering, cheering on all sides of the ring. When the ponytailed enemy spat in her face, Melanie chewed off a piece of her ear.

On Friday, when the $4,000 property tax bill came, she sucked down an entire bottle of wine and dreamed she wandered through dark tunnels, a homeless beggar. Getting beaten and gang-raped by teenagers who left her for dead. Crawling through the mud, shreds of clothes clinging to her breasts.

Preschool tuition, food, car and homeowner's insurance, utilities, healthcare, gas, household supplies...holy shit, the $10,000 pittance Dan had left would be gone in no time! Property taxes alone would eat up almost half that; the goddamn government thought fit to punish her too. Everyone wanted their pound of flesh.

On Saturday morning Melanie marched through every room. Clutching a mimosa in one hand and closing heating vents with the other, to save on energy costs. Making piles of things to sell on eBay, from the Tiffany silver to Sammy's old T-shirts. Sammy himself trailed behind her, her perpetual shadow. Tossing random things on top, thinking it a game.

"I gived eBay my ABC blocks." He dropped them onto one of the mounds with his little hands. "Dey for babies."

Melanie had to stop and laugh. Her three-year-old, still and always her baby. He had heard her say "eBay" but didn't know the company from the president of Zimbabwe.

She scooped him up in her arms impulsively. "What a good helper you are, honey! Such a good boy. You remember that, OK? Always and forever. You are a good boy no matter what happens." Argh, those damn tears again—blame it on the booze, turning the tap on the tear ducts. Crying into his sweet, soft hair and hugging him as if her life depended on it. But he couldn't save her. *She* needed to save *him*.

"Why you crying, Mommy?" Sammy's little fingers wiped the hair and tears from her eyes. His own eyes wide with concern. Her sweet angel, so thoughtful and caring and barely potty trained. Clearly he didn't get this goodness from his dad.

Time to tell him about that dad, the man who had abandoned them both. A month already. *C'mon, Melanie, grow a pair! You've got to do it sometime. The longer you wait, the harder it will be.*

But no. Not yet. She couldn't shatter Sammy's world, his innocence, just yet.

"It's nothing, honey. I'm just a little tired." *Tired and hungover and a failure. Selling my toddler's T-shirts on eBay.* She kissed his cheek and set him down.

"I miss Daaaaaddy." Sammy clung to her leg, not ready to let go.

Melanie was about to second that, then stopped. No, she *didn't* miss Dan! She missed the *idea* of a husband and the financial security, not to mention the mind-blowing sex (at least before the pregnancy), but she *didn't miss* Dan! How bored she had been these past three years, without a job to go to, without nightclubs and bars, without all her old friends. Dan had only ever wanted to work or be at home with her alone. Never wanting to share her, never interested in hanging out with her friends. How lonely—how utterly bored and lonely—she had been since marrying him.

The realization knocked her to her knees.

Sometimes life knows better than we do. Where had she heard that? She would never in a million years have chosen this fate, but maybe, just maybe, life had something better in store for her than being a lonely accessory stowed safely on a shelf with the Wedgwood and the Waterford crystal.

Now if only she had an inkling of what that something better looked like.

SAMMY HAD a sleepover that night, his first. How bad Melanie needed a break, some downtime so she could think. Or at least sleep off the hangover on Sunday morning.

Benjamin, a friend from preschool—thankfully not the child her son had bit earlier that week—lived in a smaller house a five-minute drive away. His mother, Piper Lovejoy, was a gym-toned personal organizer with bouncy platinum hair and an impressive array of Juicy Couture track outfits in every color of the rainbow. Piper worked hard to look effortlessly put together.

Melanie swiped cover-up over the dark circles and dabbed some Benefit High Beam "luminescent complexion enhancer" on her cheekbones. Nothing like a pound of makeup to give a girl a natural glow.

The two boys ran off shouting the minute the front door opened, forgetting Melanie and Piper instantly. *So much for the clinging and anxiety the books warned about,* thought Melanie. Sammy's first sleepover, and he was acting like an old pro. Or did he just want to get away from his depressed, weepy, boozy mother?

"C'mon in, Melanie. Can you stay for a minute to chat?" Piper was perfectly composed as usual, looking at 6 p.m. like she had just stepped out of the shower. Hot-pink velour track suit and radiant milky skin setting off her sky-blue eyes. But something in her expression…

Uh-oh. She knows. Melanie felt the urge to demur, to beg off coming in on account of plans. But boozing it up alone in front of the TV hardly counted as plans.

"Sorry about the mess." Piper led the way through the immaculate living room to an aqua sofa under the big front picture window. "Our housekeeper called in sick this week." Now *this* was the real Barbie, in the flesh. Piper's impossibly flat tummy belied the girl and boy she'd popped out. Her home a candy-colored dollhouse with everything in its place. Purple and fuchsia and lime-colored canvas bins hiding toys on gridded shelving units painted sunshine yellow; walls swathed in colors so delicious, you wanted to lick them. Melanie felt her spirits lift even as she dreaded the coming conversation.

Piper patted the sofa, like calling over a puppy. Melanie perched on the edge of it reluctantly.

"So." Piper tilted her head to one side fetchingly. "Normally I would not butt in…"

But… thought Melanie.

"But I know what a difficult time you're having, and I thought maybe I could help. Can I get you anything, by the way? Oatmeal-raisin cookies fresh from the oven? And Howard and I just opened a nice bottle of rosé at dinner."

"No, thank you," Melanie demurred. No way she'd get sloshed and even sloppier. In her pound of makeup and unwashed hair next to Piper, Melanie already felt like an ink blot on an angora sweater.

"The thing is, Howard works with someone who invests with Dan, and he says Dan has been out of the country for a month. Which you haven't told anyone, which seems kind of odd." Piper raised a perfectly arched eyebrow. "So I'm putting two and two together here—and please stop me if I'm wrong and forgive the assumption—but I thought maybe you and Dan might be having some...issues." She gracefully swung her legs up and sat in the lotus yoga pose, facing Melanie with a sympathetic expression. "Am I right?"

"Ummmm..." So much for keeping it a secret.

"Well listen, I don't need the exact details, unless you want to share..." Piper paused and looked at Melanie expectantly. "No? OK, well then I'd like to share something with *you*, but you have to promise to keep it a secret."

Someone else with a secret, such a nice change. Melanie scooted her rear end further onto the aqua velvet couch, finally relaxing against the back cushion.

"I'm only telling you this because I know you won't judge. Some of those other moms at the school"—Piper made a face— "it's like they have sticks up their rear ends." She tittered. "And it might help your...situation."

You don't know the half of my situation, Melanie bristled silently. *But who am I to stop you from spilling a juicy secret?*

"You may not believe this"—Piper leaned toward Melanie conspiratorially— "but Howard and I once had major marital issues."

Impossible. The prom queen and king? Holding hands in public, sneaking kisses when they thought no one could see? Staring at each other like no one else existed. The dream marriage team.

Piper nodded at Melanie's shocked face. "Oh, yes. Right after Ben's birth. Postpartum depression, ugh, so horrible. Our sex life went into the crapper." Another giggle but this time a little snort escaped too, which made her laugh harder. Melanie stared in disbelief. The neighborhood's head cheerleader, snorting and saying "crapper"! This sure beat swilling sauvignon blanc in front of *Real Housewives*.

"Anyway, Howard and I went to counseling, which led us to actually start *communicating*, which led us to"—Piper made a show of craning her neck in every direction, confirming no one in earshot, and lowered her voice to a whisper—"swinging." She covered her mouth and stared at Melanie with wide eyes, nodding as if she herself couldn't believe it.

"Swinging," Melanie repeated. *In the playground? At the circus arts center? From the ceil...? Ohhhhhhh.* Understanding dawned. Super Couple were super sluts! Like a 1970s porn flick come to life.

"We were shy at first, of course, but it turned us both on so much, the idea. And we figured since the alternative was divorce, what did we have to lose? So we joined a swingers group. And it's totally amazing! Like there's a ginormous smorgasbord of men, and you can stuff yourself silly, guilt-free."

Piper's eyes darted around again, but they both heard the boys thumping around upstairs. "The funny thing is, everyone is totally normal, just like you and me. Looking to keep their sex lives spicy and whatnot. It's all very respectful—not creepy at all despite, you know, the, um, group setting."

At the mention of "group," Melanie pictured Piper on a round bed with red satin sheets and leopard-skin pillows, naked, sandwiched between two guys pumping into her holes. Melanie's own inner tramp had gotten almost zero action since the day she announced her decision to go through with the pregnancy. She was completely sex-starved, while the neighborhood prom queen was getting stuffed in sex sandwiches at a buffet of strangers!

"So, like, you just go to sex parties at random people's houses and say, 'I'll have you, you, and you?' And Howard doesn't care that you're...*fucking* other guys right in front of him?" If the prom queen could say "crapper," Melanie could say "fucking."

"Not exactly. I mean, everybody negotiates; it's not a total free-for-all. Although..." Piper grinned mischievously. "It sometimes ends up looking that way. And then when I'm in some boring neighborhood homeowners' meeting about how everyone can use only white Christmas lights in their front yards or whatever bullshit, I think to myself, 'I had an orgy last week!' It keeps me going. Not to mention, sex with Howard has never been hotter."

Melanie felt that old familiar tug in her nether regions, the warm pool stirred by a titillating breeze. Her pool hadn't been stirred in far too long. She shifted and recrossed her legs.

"Anyway..." Piper looked almost superior now. "I'm not saying it's for everyone, of course. Just that it made all the difference for Howard and me. It takes a certain mental shift."

Sounds like it takes a whole new mental gear set. "Yes, of course. It certainly does sound..." *Crazy. Bizarre. Normal people don't have orgies with strangers!* "...intriguing."

Piper put a hand over Melanie's, oozing sympathy and friendship. "Maybe it could be just the thing to help you and Dan too. You never know until you try, right? In fact there's a party next week over at..."

Melanie hopped up, letting Piper's hand unceremoniously drop. The room's candy colors suddenly seemed too sweet, too saturated. A carnival fun house with unsettling surprises lurking behind friendly façades.

"Thank you so much, but I've gotta run." Sammy's gleeful shouts wafted down from upstairs. "I didn't realize how late it was and I...I have plans tonight. Will you tell Sammy I'll pick him up at 10 a.m. tomorrow?"

"Of course." Piper rose from the couch smoothly, the composed mask lowering instantly over her face. That wave of icy-blonde hair settling perfectly back to frame it. "And I know you'll keep this conversation between us."

"Yes, absolutely. And I'll...uh, consider your idea." *I'll consider never thinking about it again.* Melanie made a beeline for the front door.

But before it shut behind her, Melanie caught the last look on Piper's angelic face.

It was pity.

SAFELY BACK at home, Melanie rushed to the fridge like a parched nomad to an oasis. She guzzled right from the open bottle of white wine, the fridge door still ajar. God, the smell! Moldy cheese, meat gone rancid, an unidentifiable pink liquid pooling around the milk carton. Melanie slammed the door shut with her heel. Out of sight, out of mind.

Someone else will deal with that. How many times had she dreamed of that? Someone else to clean the fridge and the toilets while she handled the important things: looking good and keeping her husband satisfied. Now the housekeeper had been booted, her looks were shot, and her husband had taken off with a low-class floozy. So much for good intentions.

The wine caressed her from the inside, loosening her tense muscles. Melanie's shoulders dropped from where they had been hovering up by her ears. She breathed deeply and pulled a wineglass from the cabinet, one of the last few clean ones out of dozens.

*The funny thing is, everyone is totally normal...*Piper's words swirled around her head. *Not creepy at all.*

Suddenly Melanie's body flooded with desire. The house felt like a lonely prison, too empty without even Sammy for company. Fuck *Real Housewives*; she needed to get *out* before the memories and regrets sucked her back into hell. Tearing through closets, searching for something sexy. Something that said "hot singleton" instead of "suburban soccer mom." Not easy after years off the market and more baby bibs than hot-babe minidresses.

A black leather miniskirt and clingy top, perfect. Perfume to cover the lack of a shower. In 20 minutes Melanie hurtled along the highway toward San Francisco in her Mercedes—make that *Dan's* Mercedes, per the title—heading for Deena's bar, Backslash. Deena wouldn't judge or even raise an eyebrow if Melanie slutted out; maybe she'd even facilitate. What were friends for?

"Hey, stranger!" Melanie grabbed a serendipitous seat at the bar just as someone vacated it. Addressing Deena too brightly in the bar's murky light. She felt reckless, unlike herself—a speeding car with no brakes.

"Melanie, hey! What are you doing here? Where's Sammy?" Deena lifted the bar top and scooted over to the customer side, the gathered throng parting for her like the Red Sea for Moses. She towered over the seated Melanie, the heels of her motorcycle boots adding inches. Had even more of her skin disappeared under tattoo ink since the visit last week?

"Sleepover. I'm a free woman until morning!" Melanie shouted louder than necessary over the low din. She didn't want to talk about Sammy. She wanted to forget, just for a night, motherhood and being abandoned and the bills piling up on the custom-made console in the foyer.

Deena squinted, taking in the slutty outfit, the troweled-on makeup, the cloud of perfume. "And you're taking a walk on the wild side, I see."

"Just having a little fun, like old times! Buy a girl a drink?" Melanie's face was unnaturally flushed, her eyes glinting in the low-wattage glow of the battery-operated candles lining the bar.

"Allow me." The offer came from Melanie's other side, a nice-looking man in…a brown tweed sports coat? Who wore rumpled tweed to a dive bar in the hipster Mission? He stuck out conspicuously amid all the jeans and knit skull caps but seemed oblivious to it. Or unconcerned.

"Clay, how sweet—and totally unnecessary." Deena smiled at him. "Melanie, meet my good friend Clayton Chumbley. He did some marketing for the bar a while back and refused to let me pay him. By my calculation, I owe him drinks for life."

"Nice to meet you." Melanie stuck out her hand, sizing him up. Entirely untidy outfit—wrinkled khakis and white button-down, scratched leather elbow patches on the rumpled tweed. *The poetry reading is down the hall,* she sniped silently. Receding hairline. But kind blue eyes and a handsome face. Not bad-looking at all for someone in his…early 40s? And certainly closer to her type than the skinny, pockmarked boys in torn black Ts lording over the pool table.

"So drinks are on me," Deena insisted. "Clay, another Scotch?

And Melanie, let me guess: Cosmo." She dove back under the bar without waiting for an answer.

Melanie angled her body toward Clay. "Soooo…" Polite small talk…no, not tonight. Save politeness for the gardening committee; tonight she was a woman on a mission, on the prowl. Besides, politeness seemed like a lie while trying to picture someone naked. *Not a bad bod. Maybe a little paunchy.*

"So." Clay slowly sipped the last of his old Scotch, savoring it. Another oddity in the room full of beer bottles. Looked at her, waiting. Waiting for what?

Neither of them said anything for a minute. Dan would have taken control of the conversation by now. Dan would have told her what to talk about, what to do. Then again, Dan was probably off fucking that graduate from Hooters University at the Paris Ritz.

"Look, I'm going through a rough time." Melanie nodded acknowledgment as another bartender slipped their drinks over, pointing at Deena dealing with a pool-table dispute. "My husband just"—she took a deep breath—"my husband just left me, and this is a rare night out." No sense beating around the bush. Her bush didn't have the luxury of patience tonight.

"Ah, I see."

Do you? Do you see how desperate I am? Practically off my rocker. Do you see how bad I need to get laid, to feel like something other than an open walking wound?

"I'm divorced myself." His face showed sympathy. "It'll be a year next week." His hands rested in his lap like a schoolboy's.

"Oh, I'm so sorry, Clayton." The autopilot response and a lie. Melanie's didn't care about his status—married, divorced, multiple Mormon wives—as long as he called out her name in the sack.

He waved away her apology. "Don't be. It's the best thing that ever happened to me. And please, call me Clay." Such a casual vibe he had, throwing Melanie's desperate heat into high relief. "Now I get to"—he eyed her meaningfully—"taste any forbidden fruit I like."

Melanie took an emboldening gulp. A lot of alcohol packed into that pretty pink drink.

"You're probably pretty angry, eh? I know I was." Clay leaned closer. "Lonely too. Those first few months, you think you'll never hook up with anyone again. You will, though. A beautiful woman like you."

Could it really be this easy? He may as well be turning down the bedsheets. But…a one-night stand with a stranger? *Why not? It's exactly what you want! Seize the day. He's not even a stranger; Deena knows him. He did free marketing for the bar.*

"Clay, you don't by any chance live near here, do you? It's kinda hot and crowded."

He gave her a long look. "As a matter of fact, I do." He stood up, laying some bills on the bar. Sweeping his arm, an ushering gesture. "After you."

THE DOOR opened on an apartment as disheveled as Clay's outfit. Empty glasses and water rings marred the coffee table; crumbs littered the carpet by the baggy couch. Books and magazines strewn everywhere. Dan would have never let Melanie get away with such a mess.

Dan is fucking that big-titted slut at the Paris Ritz, Melanie reminded herself. Forget actual proof of this. Who needed proof? It got more real every time she repeated it.

"Sorry about the mess." Clay hurried around with a brown paper grocery bag, sweeping in napkins and takeout containers. "Not expecting company tonight and all."

His embarrassed bustling oddly calmed Melanie. *Someone* had to be the cool and collected one here. She gathered a pile of magazines off the couch, set them neatly on the table, sat down. Patiently watched him rush around, a hawk sizing up its next meal.

"It's not usually like this. Been working too much lately, and I don't have a cleaning woman, uhh obviously….But oh, where are my manners? Can I get you anything to drink? Or a snack perhaps?"

"Clay. Sit down." Melanie pointed to the space next to her on the couch. She didn't want to watch him clean or make small talk or waste time having another drink. Only one thought consumed her. Desperate times call for desperate measures.

Clay sat promptly, looking relieved. His relief emboldened Melanie even further. The orders had been hers to take for so long, never to give; the never-ending need for other people's approval such a burden. And look where it had all gotten her: abandoned and impoverished. Tonight she would hold the reins, and if Clay didn't like it, then he could jerk off alone into one of the half-empty chow mein containers when she left.

"Why don't you start by taking off your jacket?" More an instruction than a question. He complied.

"Now the shirt."

"Well, I don't get to the gym much these days what with work and…"

"Clay. I said take off your shirt. Your body is fine."

"You don't waste any time, eh? Let me just lower the lights and, hmm, turn the heat up a touch."

That's my job, Melanie thought. *Gonna be blazing hot in here in a minute.*

"There, that's better." Clay relaxed in the darker light. Unbuttoned his shirt but left it on.

Between the alcohol and the unfamiliar setting, and her sexy outfit accessorized with desperation, Melanie felt quite unlike herself. Here, with this bumbling, sympathetic man who understood and didn't judge—oh, what a change not to be judged!—she could take charge. She could get from Clay exactly what she wanted as easily as ordering sushi à la carte: *Let's start with some eating out, followed by fingering and your cock thrusting inside me. Please.*

Then she spied it. Its thick spine jutting out from the bottom of a book pile. *SM101: A Realistic Introduction.* S&M. Sadomasochism. Melanie cringed, remembering Dan's hard-core porn bondage. His urging her to re-create it with him. Her every demurral widening the distance between them. Dammit, had she walked right into another trap?

But wait…Clay and Dan…as different as The Odd Couple. The only thing she could picture this kind, sympathetic, apologetic man tying up would be a pink box filled with croissants. Which meant…

"Clay." Melanie stood up and plucked the book from its half-hidden spot. "Tell me about this."

Clay turned 50 shades of red. "Oh, that's not…I mean it's just…the thing is, since my divorce…" Melanie flipped through the pages, absorbing random words: "erotic pain," "fantasy," "consent."

"It's OK, Clay. I get it. My husb—my *ex-husband* was into this stuff, not that we got very far with it." *And it drove us apart. I didn't want him to truss me up like a cow, and he found someone else to pork.* "What do you like about it?" Her curiosity overtook her horniness.

Clay was clearly torn about answering. Maybe a little pitiable too, with that untoned fish-white belly flopping over his waistband. Suddenly Melanie felt a wave of… motherliness? Commiseration? She wanted to reassure him. Punish his waffling. Protect him. And use him like a sex toy. Holy conflicting emotions, Batman!

It occurred to her that Dan probably had felt this exact confusing combo. And never let on. Always appearing decisive, always in charge. What would Dan do here?

"Never mind answering that for now, Clay. Come here." Melanie inched back on the couch, spreading her knees wide apart. Feet flat on the floor. Pointing to the space between her legs. "I'd like you to kneel facing me. Please." Halfway between an order and a request. Plenty of leeway for him to refuse.

Clay gazed at her thoughtfully, head cocked. Melanie could see the wheels turning. His eyes glazing over—the universal expression of male desire.

Melanie reached under her skirt and slowly slid off her black lace panties. Let them hover by her knees, then her ankles. Used a toe to scoot the bunched-up lace off entirely.

Clay's eyes slid down, attached to the panties by an invisible string. Oh, yes, Melanie had him eating out of the palm of her hand. But it wasn't her palm that needed eating.

"Do I need to ask you again to come here, Clay?" Opening her legs an inch wider on the couch.

He stared for a second longer, then shook his head. Awkwardly got down on his knees and waddled over on them. His face exactly level with her now-soaking mound.

Melanie wriggled her skirt up around her hips. What now—ask him to have at it? Order him? What would Dan do?

"Stick out your tongue, Clay. Close your eyes." He did.

I could get used to this, Melanie reflected, placing a firm head on the back of his head and guiding his tongue to lap up the wetness.

MELANIE BOLTED upright as the 9 a.m. alarm yanked her from sleep. Disoriented. Sammy usually snuggled her awake at 7 on Sunday mornings. *Sammy! Where's Sammy?* A stab of panic. *Oh, right, the sleepover.* She hit the snooze button, sank back into the king-size pillows. Too tired to be grateful for the extra sleep.

Pieces of the previous night snuck back. Piper's lascivious secret life. Guzzling wine right from the bottle in her kitchen. And Clay… oh, God. She had indeed used him like a sex toy, availed herself of every part of his body through three screaming orgasms. And they hadn't even had "the talk" about STDs, not that she had any. But maybe *he* did…maybe he got cold sores on his mouth and a little herpes army had marched right into her through the wide-open door. At least they'd used a condom. Melanie pulled the covers up over her head and tried not to think about what she'd done. Guilt and shame were hard habits to kick.

Her head throbbed. The soft morning light hurt her eyes. The alarm shrieked again, and she whacked it into submission. Wrenched the power cord from the outlet and knocked the clock to the floor. Didn't she deserve one goddamn morning to sleep in?

But Sammy would be waiting. She'd said 10 a.m. Can't have your kid thinking he's unwanted. *Unless you're Dan,* Melanie scoffed. *He doesn't give a shit how he makes anyone feel, including his own wife and child.*

You also don't want to piss off the only woman who can grant you those sleep-in mornings. *Note to self: Find more Sammy sleepover possibilities pronto.* With Dan gone, they'd be the only sleep-ins Melanie would get. She could barely pay for groceries thanks to the emptied bank account, let alone babysitting. How do poor people with kids not go insane?

Melanie got up and dragged herself to Piper's door right on time, smiling and thanking and offering to return the sleepover favor. Trying not to imagine the doll-perfect Piper, in sky blue velour hoodie and pants this morning to match her eyes, being tossed around in an orgy like a beach ball at a rock concert.

"Melanie, come in! Would you like a cappuccino? A homemade blueberry muffin, perhaps? The blueberries are organic."

No, Melanie didn't want coffee or muffins; who could eat baked goods with so much S&M research online to devour? For the first time, her mind blazed with the possibilities of it rather than shrinking away in revulsion. She burned with desire to know more, ignited by a one-night stand where she called the shots.

Maybe, the voice in her head observed, *just maybe, you've been coming at this whole S&M thing from the wrong side. Maybe you never let Dan do those things to you because you want to make people do things.* The thought terrified Melanie. Excited her. The world suddenly brimmed with new prospects.

"No, thank you. We've got such a busy day; we should really be going." *Busy researching perversions.* Hopefully Piper couldn't read minds in addition to her otherworldly housekeeping and man-pleasing skills. "Did everything go OK with the boys?"

"Oh, yes, Sammy's such a sweet boy! No trouble at all. He's welcome anytime." Piper looked as serene as if she'd just stepped out of a spa. Whew. Blow the first sleepover and you don't get asked back.

Sammy and Benjamin barreled down the hallway. "Mommy! No go, no go. I staying with Ben." He and Benjamin sported matching purple towel capes fastened with safety pins.

Melanie knelt down and wrapped her arms around her son. Kissed the top of his head—a whiff of bacon and maple syrup. "Sorry, little man. I'm glad you had fun, but it's time to go. You can come back another time."

"But who gonna fights the bad guys?" Sammy frowned as anxiously as if his adventures were real.

Melanie unfastened the towel and handed it to Piper. "Trust me, honey. There will always be more bad guys. A hero's work is never done." *And the biggest villain is your own dad. How's that for reality?*

"Thank you again. So much." She hugged Piper warmly. "Having a free night made all the difference."

What an understatement.

MELANIE'S MIND raced on the drive home. The sex-swinging Piper Lovejoy. The eager-to-oblige Clay Chumbley. So normal-looking on the outside, both of them, yet brimming with deviant secrets. Maybe perverted was the new normal. Maybe normal never existed. Melanie felt like Alice in Wonderland, except the real world lay on the wrong end of the rabbit hole.

She couldn't shake the financial distress, either. The $10,000 pittance was slipping away faster than G-strings at a strip club. She had to do something, and fast. If Dan didn't want to be found, she wouldn't find him without an expensive PI. She couldn't, *wouldn't*, borrow from her parents. Borrow from the bank? With what collateral? Nothing was in her name. Her mind kept circling around the same futile possibilities in an endless loop, finding no solution to land on.

Too much to think about. When she and Sammy walked through the front door, Melanie headed right to the kitchen. Who would begrudge a mimosa on a Sunday morning?

"Mommy, play wit me." Sammy tugged at her pants with his little fingers as she rummaged through the stinky fridge for OJ and champagne. The pinkish bacteria-ridden pool on the bottom shelf taunted her.

"Not now, honey. Mommy's busy." She threw paper towels over the meat-juice swamp and reached over a carton of expired milk to grab a champagne bottle. Not one single goddamn clean champagne glass in the whole cabinet? Fine, a water goblet then. Waterford crystal. How much could she get for it on eBay?

"Pleeease, Mommy?" Sammy trailed her from fridge to cabinet to counter. His face so eager, so needy.

"In a little while, honey." The champagne foamed over the top of the glass, puddling on the counter. Dammit! Another mess for her to clean up. Could she sue Dan for housekeeping support along with alimony and child support?

"Pleeeease play wit me, Mommy? Pleeeeeeeeeeease?" Sammy poked at her leg now. Poke, poke, poke. Yanked on her shirt.

"Sammy! I said *not now!*" Melanie snatched her shirt away from his tiny hand. Roughly. Watched him fall backward, plopping down on his rear end on the hard kitchen floor. Staring at her with sad, uncomprehending eyes. Then came the tears, pouring instantly from his eyes like they had waiting in the wings for weeks. Maybe they had.

And in that moment, the vision of who Melanie was turning into struck her harder than the floor on Sammy's rear. Horror and regret filled her to the core. She knelt down and pulled Sammy onto her lap, rocking him like a baby. Apologizing and hugging and rocking him until he stopped crying. Her tears mingling with his as he hugged her hard and patted her face. Her thoughtful little angel trying to make her feel better even though *she* had wronged *him*.

Melanie kissed his face and his head then, apologizing over and over. "I'm sorry; I'm so sorry, sweetheart. I didn't mean it." Apologizing not just for this incident out loud but in her head for his father's leaving for good, even if Sammy didn't know it yet. Apologizing for making the wrong choice in a life partner. For his having to live with her mistake the rest of his life.

But no, not a mistake. Nothing that had given her this amazing miracle, this gift of a son, could have been a mistake. She would thank God every day that she had Sammy, husband or no husband. Her new life purpose would be to take care of him. Nurture him, protect him, provide for him. Make sure he grew up healthy and happy, not bitter and deprived. He would not feel like the product of a broken home. Not on her watch.

When they had both dried their tears, she firmly placed the orange juice back in the fridge and dumped the champagne down the sink. She would not be that kind of mother, the kind who bought her kid cheap shoes and generic cereal to have more booze money. The kind who snapped at her kid in the morning because she was hungover. The kind who stuck her head in the sand instead of facing facts and fixing problems. For Sammy's sake, for her sake, Melanie would fix everything.

Failure was no longer an option.

"Let's play now, Sammy." Melanie's summoned a bright smile. "How about trains? You can be Thomas and I'll be…" She struggled to remember the other characters. "Emily. OK?"

Sammy grinned happily and took her hand, leading her into the playroom. Melanie squeezed his hand tight, feeling a surge of love so powerful that she wished she could stop time and bottle this moment. Keep it forever as a precious memory to take out again when grown-up Sammy had no use for her.

She would do right by him, no matter what. She would make it work.

And she would clean that goddamn refrigerator.

MONDAY MORNING, with Sammy safely tucked away at preschool, Melanie finally could plunk down with the computer for some serious Internet research.

> BDSM is a variety of erotic practices
> involving dominance and submission, role-
> playing, restraint, and other interpersonal
> dynamics....The term BDSM is unclear, and is
> believed to have been formed either from joining
> the term B&D (bondage and discipline) with S&M
> (sadomasochism or sadism and masochism), or as
> a compound initialism from B&D, D&S (dominance
> and submission), and S&M.

Gotta love Wikipedia. Why hadn't she looked this up before, when Dan had urged her to explore the fine art of being hogtied? Because being trussed up like a pig had as much appeal as cleaning refrigerators, that's why.

But having someone at your beck and call, to order around as a sex toy? Now you're talking.

> Regardless of its origin, BDSM is used as
> a catch-all phrase to include a wide range
> of activities, forms of interpersonal rela-
> tionships, and distinct subcultures. BDSM
> communities generally welcome anyone with a
> non-normative streak who identifies with the
> community; this may include cross dressers,
> extreme body mod enthusiasts, animal players,
> latex or rubber aficionados and others.

Blah, blah, blah. Cross-dressing? No way. Body mod and animal players? Ew and ew. Where's the good stuff, about how to get men to eat you out on command? Three minutes of Internet searching and the answer popped up: Kink.com. Hardcore S&M porn. Right below "Bound Gang Bangs" and "Device Bondage," she saw the "Divine Bitches" section. Here we go.

All the curtains in the den shut tight? Check. Door closed? Check. Sound on low? Check. Melanie took a deep breath. Pressed

Play on a Divine Bitches free video trailer. Title: "Slaveboy Games: Are You Worthy?" A pretty platinum blonde woman in a black micromini and stilettos informed an admirably hung young stud: "You don't use your dick. *I* use your dick." And use it she did, along with slapping him around, making him lick her stockinged feet, and fucking him with a strap-on dildo.

Another blonde, poured into fuchsia fabric, rode the stud's face while Dick User gave him a handjob, cackling. Melanie could hardly believe her eyes. Two minutes total and the trailer ended. The camera flashed on the blonde and the stud post-shoot, smiling, thumbs up. Enthusing, "Awesome!"

All this smut was available free to anyone with an Internet connection? Melanie made a mental note to figure out the web browser's parental control settings. And look at all those other deviant sections on the Kink.com website: "Electro Sluts," "Fucking Machines," "TS Pussy Hunters"...the list went on. Repulsive. Reprehensible. And yet...

Melanie's undies were soaking wet.

What the hell? So different from watching violent porn with Dan. So different from anything she'd ever imagined as a turn-on. And yet, the proof was in the panties.

Such power and attitude Dick User had! Following rules? Ha! She *made* the rules. If the guy didn't like it, fuck him. Literally.

Melanie put a hand on her hip and addressed Dan's favorite armchair: "You don't own your dick. *I* own your dick." The words sounded unnatural, forced. Her doormat mouth found the power position unfamiliar. She tried again.

"Did I say you could sit?" The empty chair gave no response. "You'll sit when I allow it." Better. But still something was missing. Dick User had wielded a crop.

Melanie snatched a ruler from the desk drawer. Brandished it at Dan's armchair. One of those old-fashioned chairs: thick, rolled arms and nailheads dotting the edges of the brown leather. A gentleman's club chair for an ungentlemanly bastard. How many times had Dan sat there with his iPad after dinner, lord of the manor, scanning news sites and stock prices, while she, the lowly servant, had cleared the dishes and given Sammy a bath? Too many times, that's how many.

"You're a lowlife." She whacked the seat with the ruler. "You don't deserve me." Another whack. "You're a selfish, evil, manipulative bastard." She hit the seat's back and arms now, the ruler making satisfying thunks. How good it felt! How freeing. Such a release—all of the frustration and confusion and anger, all of the unbearable pain, shooting out the ruler in one fell swoop. And again. And again.

Her hitting developed a rhythm of its own; Melanie felt the beat of it in her bones, almost as if it were moving her rather than the reverse. Losing herself in the yelling. The invectives flowed easily now, as if her mouth had been born to spew them.

"Arrogant prick! Try to cut me out now. Just try."

"Does that husband-stealing waitress cunt do your laundry or does she just do *you* on command?"

"Six years of my life you stole. Six years! I'm going to take them all back with interest, you thieving...conniving...manipulative...*asshole*..."

Small scratches popped up on the brown leather, snapping Melanie back to reality. She suddenly felt slightly foolish, like someone waking up from a drunken blackout, unsure of what had happened the night before. What had come over her? She soberly placed the ruler back in the drawer. Found some leather conditioner and set to work gently, almost lovingly, buffing out the scratches with the softest cloth she could find.

Poor armchair, she comforted it silently. *It's not your fault I've gone off my rocker.* Giggling then, feeling oddly lighthearted. Talking to furniture! So absurd, this entire scenario. Yet so completely right.

At least being absurd is better than being an alcoholic. As long as nobody gets hurt.

Nobody who doesn't enjoy it, anyway, she clarified. Giggling again in the strangely still air. The crushing weight had disappeared from her chest, dissolved into thin air by a hundred blows. Who knew violence could be so healthy?

Maybe Dan did. Not like they'd ever discuss it over tea and crumpets someday, though. Five weeks and not even a single text or email from him. Surely whatever five-star European hotel Dan was shacked up in had Internet. Probably too busy making money and sticking it to that gold digger. Money and sex, Dan's top two talents.

Kind of like my brother, Melanie thought for the first time. Oh, God, how could she ever tell Alex—and her sister and parents—about Dan's leaving, about being instantly impoverished and alone? Be the brunt of their pity and disdain again? No, no, no. Not until the world lay at her feet again. Not until she could rest her sugar-scrubbed toes on Dan's back and her family members' backs and her old boss Violet's back. On the backs of everyone who'd ever treated her like a second-class citizen.

The realization rose in Melanie so hard and fast, it almost knocked her over. *She didn't need Dan to be a success!* Not Dan, not Violet, not her family. She would give Sammy everything he deserved and more—give *herself* everything she deserved. She would build her own business and be even richer than Dan. *How about that, you selfish, controlling bastard? I'm never taking a back seat to you or anyone else ever again. You'll beg me on your knees someday, and I'll drink your tears for breakfast.*

The only question now: how? Building a megasuccessful business took more than Sammy's Legos and construction paper. Only one place Melanie could think of had all the answers, all the wisdom of generations of tycoons in every industry on earth.

The bookstore. She grabbed her coat and purse.

AN ECLECTIC throwback, the local bookstore, a stubborn holdout against Amazon and Half.com. Every wooden shelf and case crammed to sagging with books new and used, all thrown in together. The owner and sole worker was a quiet, elderly man who ran things exactly how he pleased. He kept unpredictable hours that depended on circadian rhythms, moon cycles, and whether Mercury was in retrograde. That's California for you.

Melanie kept her fingers crossed for an open door on this Monday morning at 10:30 a.m. Only a couple of precious hours with Sammy in preschool to start figuring out her multimillion-dollar business—or at least how to keep his tuition checks from bouncing.

The Open sign hung askew against the mottled glass. Whew, must be a good phase in the moon's cycle. The old man glanced up as Melanie entered, nodding curtly. Then promptly went back to doing his crossword puzzle. No other customers to punctuate the tomb-like silence. Just as well; the grapevine rivaled high-speed Internet in Palo Alto. Better to keep her plan a secret than risk failing in front of every dot-com millionaire's wife in town.

Now to find the business section, filled with the insight of gurus and titans and anyone who'd made it big. They would tell her what to do…no, wait. Melanie would never let anyone tell her what to do again. Guide her. That's it, guide. Offer insight.

But something drew Melanie to the "New and Noteworthy" table. Staring out from the back cover of a book was a face that seemed familiar, but she couldn't place it. A handsome guy with friendly eyes. A college classmate? An old art gallery client? Wait a minute…that barista from the café near her old apartment! The one she had met in the park. The one who had tried to ask her out eons ago, before Sammy, before Dan, but she had blown him off as a loser. Scott Forsythe, the cover shouted in huge type. Right next to the eye-grabbing gold sticker: "1 million copies sold!" *Nice going, Melanie. How off can your judgment be? You let Mr. Right get away for Mr. Right Now. Way to go.*

The President's Secret Spy was emblazoned in metallic letters on the cover. She'd refused to even hear Scott's description of his book that day in the park, trying to avoid a snoozefest. "Bestselling author Scott Forsythe lives in San Francisco with his wife and twin baby girls. This is his first novel," announced the bio blurb. From bussing coffee mugs solo to bestselling author and family man in, what, six or so years now? Melanie had clearly bet on the wrong horse.

Her shoulders tightened. Her eyes narrowed. Steely resolution slowly flooded her body. Yes, maybe she'd made a wrong turn. Maybe if Melanie had been less judgmental about Scott's barista status back then, *she* would now be Mrs. Bestselling Author, instead of an abandoned single mother with barely a pittance to her name. And yet…

And yet if Scott Forsythe—apron-wearing, dregs-clearing, working-for-tips Scott Forsythe—could turn successful in one fell swoop, so could Melanie. What did he have that she didn't have? An idea, that's all.

She just had to find the right idea.

Melanie put the book back and craned her neck around, looking for the owner. Gone—probably napping in the back. Fine, who needed him anyway? She'd find the business section on her own. She'd figure out everything on her own. No more waiting for salvation.

Cookbooks, nope. Self-help? Melanie snorted, remembering the countless hours studying them, trying to improve, to be someone worth loving. Had they ever helped do anything but pad the pockets of the authors? No matter now. Self-help books were for doormats, not rising business stars.

But hello, what's this? "Alternate sexual practices" read the shelf label. Melanie halted in her tracks. Peered around covertly. No witnesses, good—her deviant exploration would have made for meaty gossip at the coffee bars.

The titles on the five shelves read like a pervert's dream library: *Wild Side Sex: The Book of Kink*—the cover sporting a naked woman with legs curled around a typewriter. *Kajira of Gor*, a sci-fi fantasy starring a female sex slave on another planet. Books about boot fetishes and latex fetishes and foot fetishes, about how to be a proper dominant and how to tie someone up: sensually, roughly, Japanese-style, suspended in the air. Melanie laughed at one title: *31 Flavors of Kink*; 1,031 seemed more like it.

The Ethical Slut, now you're talking. Melanie's libidinous tigress, hibernating since Sammy's birth and Dan's gradual withdrawal, opened an eye. No husband and no more Miss Nice Girl meant no reason not to slut out. And *ethically,* no less. She chuckled, envisioning gifting a copy to Piper. Tucking it under the family's Christmas tree with the photo mugs and pasta necklaces and family board games. Then again, sex-swinging Piper and her husband had probably already read it.

Melanie squatted down to check out the lower shelves. *SM101,* the book Clay owned—yes, absolutely. *The Control Book*—maybe. *Sacred Submission*—not in this lifetime. Well, maybe on the receiving end.

"Can I help you find something?" Melanie almost fell backward from her squat at the lower shelves, startled to see the old owner looming above her. She flushed beet red.

"N-no," she stammered. "No, thank you. I was just looking for, uh…" He waited patiently, scratching his short white beard. "I was just…" *Just waiting for the ground to open up and swallow me whole.* "I don't need any help." He squinted thoughtfully, nodded. Turned to go.

But then again, he *owned* this bookstore. *He* had put those books there. Why should Melanie be embarrassed? People were meant to read these books; she wasn't doing anything wrong. She stood up to her full height. Cleared her throat, making way for the emerging confidence.

"Actually, I *am* looking for something in particular." Her voice firm and clear.

"Yes?" Amusement glimmered in the elderly owner's rheumy blue eyes. "What is it?"

"I'm looking for a book on female dominance and also the history of BDSM." There. She said it. Lightning didn't strike her down.

"Well now." A wry smile as he bent down toward the shelves. "You can't go wrong with Midori; she teaches a lot of classes right here in the Bay Area, and she's been around awhile. We don't have anything on female dominance in particular right now. But really"—he plucked a book out called *The Loving Dominant* and placed it in Melanie's hand—"I s'pose you could got a lot from the ones written from a male perspective too. I found this one particularly helpful myself."

"Hm." Melanie flipped through it, random obscene phrases jumping out:

```
"A spreader bar can be attached between the
ankles..."
```

```
"...shiny steel sliding over her breast and
caressing her nipple..."
```

```
"...the intense, localized stimulation of the
vibrating crop so arousing..."
```

But hang on a sec, did the old man just say *he* had found this book helpful? Melanie's eyebrows lifted as she looked him over, a skinny Santa Claus with cataracts. A walker seemed a more likely accessory than a spreader bar.

"As for history," the lovingly dominant bookstore owner continued, "to be honest, most folks aren't interested so much in that as the...practice. This one"—he lugged out the weighty *SM101*—is worth its weight. Lot of valuable stuff there for a newbie. Jay Wiseman knows his stuff."

Hey, she hadn't said anything about being a newbie! Did the lack of calluses on her riding-crop hand give her away? Or just her unfamiliarity with this section of the store? Melanie suddenly flashed on her last trip here; she and Sammy had chosen *The Runaway Bunny* from the children's section. Hopefully a bad memory accompanied the owner's cataracts; kink and motherhood seemed a more unsavory combination than hot sauce and oatmeal cookies.

"And the fiction is popular too." He tapped on the *Kajira* book Melanie had already spotted. "Far-out stuff and never gonna win a Pulitzer, but people do like their slave stories."

"No, that one's not for me." She shuddered. Hadn't she just

escaped a kind of slavery? *Never again,* she vowed. *I will never be beholden to anyone again.*

"Well, feel free to browse as long as you like. Sorry there isn't more, but it *is* a specialty area. Harry Potter, I got a lot of." The elderly owner hiked up his pants and strolled back to the front of the store, rearranging books along the way.

Melanie noticed that he had a limp. How many times had she been in here and never seen it? It occurred to her how many other things she'd never seen or even considered before—people like Piper orgying it up in secret; the potential of a mere barista for celebrity status. Melanie had been so focused on attaining the superficial—the big house, the rich hubby—that she'd been blind to the deeper, complex reality just below the surface.

What a hoax. I've been fed lies since the day I opened my mouth.

A sad thought. But freeing too. Now that she saw how bogus her life had been, she could change it. Be in charge of her own destiny. She took *The Loving Dominant, SM101,* and *Wild Side Sex,* plus a book on rope bondage called *Shibari You Can Use* by Lee Harrington, up to the counter.

"What happened to your leg, if you don't mind my asking?" she asked, forking over precious cash. Dan had cut off the credit cards, of course.

"Oh, just an old war injury. Vietnam. I can't complain—at least I'm still here." He slipped the books into a brown paper bag. "I'm Stanley, by the way."

"Melanie." She stuck her hand out. "So, er, Stanley, do you get a lot of buyers for books like these in person? Or do most people just order online—you know, from the privacy of their own home?"

He gazed at her keenly. "Your secret is safe with me. First rule of BDSM is not outing people." Handed her the bag. "Oh, and Melanie?"

"Yes, Stanley?"

"You might want to keep these out of reach of your little one. Pretty soon he'll be able to read *The Runaway Bunny* by himself, I'm guessing." And winked.

Melanie couldn't help but laugh as she sailed out the door, its metal bells tinkling. Feeling more buoyant than she had in a long time. *Every time a bell rings, an angel gets its wings.* Well, maybe life would turn out to be wonderful after all.

Only this time the angel might get a whip.

Only in the car did Melanie realize she'd never even made it to the business section.

Chapter 11
Hello, Goddess

MELANIE EASED the silver Mercedes SL into a spot a block away from the address Deena's friend Clay Chumbley had given her. Clay had already proved his S&M submissive cred the other night as she rode his face, so presumably he would know the credible kinky hot spots. The car stuck out amid the beat-up Toyotas and steely motor-cycles; filth clung to the man gazing at her disinterestedly from the floor of the doorway opposite. Of course San Francisco's one and only kinky café would reside in a seedier part of town. Perverts don't hang out at Neiman Marcus.

Oh yes, they do! Melanie corrected herself, thinking of her friend Piper getting it on gangbang-style in a stranger's rec room. *And they make awesome oatmeal cookies for the gardening club.*

She pinned up her hair and settled the black bob wig in place, adjusting it carefully in the rearview mirror. The exact opposite of her natural look, precisely the point. Disguise is crucial in finding your true self when your true self is a pervert.

The café's name danced proudly above the doorway: Grounds for Punishment. Two flags flanked the door: the rainbow pride flag and the other…Melanie had no clue. Black and blue and white stripes with a red heart. *I heart getting black and blue?* She giggled nervously at her own joke.

She worked up her courage as she neared the front door, the heels of her chic leather boots clicking on the dirty pavement. Maybe too chic, especially paired with the black Gucci leather jacket—the scraggly smokers out front sported torn black jeans, faded blue jeans, piercings. But no, she would do this *her* way. And her way did not include looking like a refugee from a homeless shelter.

"Mommy, why you painted your eyes?" Sammy had asked that morning, as they exited the car in the preschool parking lot.

"Can't a mommy look extra pretty sometimes?" Buying time to think of a good answer—the deviant truth was no business of a child's. She glanced in the driver's-side mirror. The black eyeliner crawling across her lower lashes. Maybe she *had* laid it on a little thick.

Sammy hugged her legs tight, burying his face in her crisp black Calvin Klein pants. "You aw-ways bootiful, Mommy."

"Oh, honey." Melanie's eyes welled up. *Don't cry; you'll smear your eye makeup.* "What a sweet thing to say!" Five days without any wine to dull the ever-present torrent of emotions. She felt like a walking open wound without alcohol's salve. But calmer too. Funny how not boozing it up every night could clear your head.

Melanie squatted down and hugged Sammy tight. "You are the sweetest boy ever. I love you so, so much. Be a good boy at school, and I'll see you later." Then he spied a friend and took off running without a backward glance. Kids and their happy oblivion—he had no idea that the mommy who lovingly slathered together his PB&Js was about to slide down the rabbit hole of S&M.

Stepping through the Grounds for Punishment café doorway

now, Melanie consciously straightened her spine. *Fake it till you make it.* Maybe she did look a little slick for 11:30 a.m., but she could dress how she damn well pleased now. *No apologies, no regrets,* she reminded herself. *Let someone else be the doormat.* She eyed the two dog bowls just inside the door: one labeled "animal dogs"; the other, "human dogs." *Shouldn't be too hard to find one.*

Thoughts banged around her head randomly. *That cage looked bigger on the website. Thank goodness no one is naked—can you even be naked in a café? Where is Clay? Mmmmm, something smells really good— cookies? Please let there be an empty table. Wow, that guy in the corner is really cute. Goddammit, Clay, where the hell are you?*

Erotic photographs lined the walls, naked men and women sprawled and splayed and crouched, lines of light dancing around them. Some lines coiled like bondage. Café patrons were perched at tables under the photos, blasé about the deviant art. Sipping coffees and teas, noshing on quiches and croissants, tapping away at laptops. As if this were Starbucks and not perverts central.

"What can I get you?" The coquettish girl behind the register sported a black corset and red schoolgirl miniskirt. *Wait, not a girl. A boy. Maybe. Nice skirt,* Melanie thought. *What's underneath it?*

"Double latte, please, with whole milk. And are those muffins fresh?" To hell with worrying about fat, sugar, and refined carbs; Melanie could eat what she pleased without dictatorial Dan around.

"Not as fresh as me." The girl-boy smiled. A tilt of the head, a sassy jutting out of a hip. "But they're damn good. Especially the blueberry."

Melanie laughed, her shoulders relaxing. "Then I'll take one damn good blueberry one, please." She combed her brain for something witty. "And can you make it hot?"

"Oh, hon, you know I can!" A shake of the hips. "It'll be about three minutes."

"I really like your skirt, by the way," Melanie offered. Exciting opportunities for a whole new wardrobe promenaded before her eyes. Clothes you couldn't buy at Prada. Was there a Sluts 'R' Us?

Clay was 10 minutes late and counting now. *Grrrrrr.* How dare

Melanie's guide make her wait alone in a foreign land, even for a single second? He should have been there already, smoothing her way with the natives. Or at least saving them a table.

Luckily a table sat empty in the back. Melanie doffed her $1,200 Gucci leather jacket and hung it gingerly on its beat-up wooden chair. Wandered over to the "boutique," a tiny area near the human-size cage: shelves with books and cards; glass-encased displays protecting collars and cuffs; leather paddles and floggers hanging off hooks on a rotating stand—a corrupted tie rack. She'd have to get used to corruption now.

Not much merchandise, more like a teaser taste, but lots of glossy postcard-size ads for events and classes. Melanie spotted one with Midori's name: FORTE FEMME—SENSUAL DOMINANCE INTENSIVE. YOUR COACH: MIDORI. Yikes, $700 for the weekend class! With Dan's credit card in the old days, she'd drop that on a single pair of shoes. Now she felt like a beggar sidling up to a pricey buffet.

She slipped the card in her handbag anyway, along with ads for Bondage-a-Go-Go (a "fetish-themed dance party") and a products company called The Frugal Domme. *Is that what they call dominatrixes these days, dommes?* When her multimillion-dollar business—whatever *that* would be—got going, $700 classes would be a drop in the bucket.

"Double latte and blueberry muffin for gorgeous!" School-girl Skirt winked at Melanie as she turned, then sailed off into the kitchen. Melanie grinned and gathered the goodies. *Although you'd think they'd have a servant to bring the food. Maybe I'll bring my own someday,* she fantasized wickedly. *And make him drink from the dog bowl.*

Clay hurried in five minutes later, rumpled and stubbled. Apologies spilling out: a client had kept him, he couldn't find his keys, his car wouldn't start. Melanie sensed an opportunity. Held up a hand.

"Clay, stop. I'm not interested in excuses." She stretched up taller in her seat. "This is the first and last time you'll keep me waiting. And you'll have to make it up to me for being late today."

How delicious those words tasted, rolling so easily off her tongue—even the freshest blueberry muffin couldn't top that.

"Is that so?" Clay gauged her sincerity, then gave a little laugh. "Well, good for you...*as you wish*." Music to Melanie's ears. "And how shall I make it up to you? Nice disguise, by the way."

"I'll think of something. In the meantime, would you get me a glass of water?" Melanie didn't even want water; she just wanted to make a point.

Clay nodded amiably and sidled up to the counter. Melanie sipped her coffee, nibbled the muffin—both excellent. She had assumed from the seedy neighborhood that the offerings would be subpar. She really had to stop making assumptions.

"I'm so glad you called," Clay said, setting down the water glass, along with a croissant and tea for himself, in an elegant black iron pot. "I really enjoyed our...get-together the other night."

"Me too. I think I'm hooked."

"On one-night stands with friends of your friends?" A corner of his mouth went up. Melanie recalled how just a week ago, she had pushed that very mouth against her pink parts, gushing all over it.

"On BDSM."

Clay's eyes glimmered. "Welcome to my world." The other mouth corner shot up. "We're the sanest nuts you'll ever meet."

"It's just...I don't understand why I'm suddenly so attracted to it. Wouldn't you think if I were meant to be in this world, I would have figured it out sooner? I'm 32. How could I have gone so long in life without realizing it—especially here in the Bay Area, the freak-flag-flying capital of the world?"

Actually, Melanie already knew the answer. *Be a good girl.* Her parents had drummed it into her before she could even talk. The mantra of well-meaning teachers. The expectation of the world. Not being a good girl meant swimming upstream.

Clay shook his head. "You never know what's going to open your eyes. My divorce did the trick for me. And many people *never* figure it out; they just go on being miserable and unfulfilled. You know that Oscar Wilde quote about temptation? 'The only way to get rid of a temptation is to yield to it. Resist it, and your soul grows sick with longing for the things it has forbidden to itself.' A lot of people are walking around with sick souls."

Clay gazed at her longingly. "By the way, you look beautiful. A little Barbie Does the Dark Side, but beautiful. If you want to explore this lifestyle, you would have no trouble finding people to be at your beck and call."

Was that an invitation? Melanie's heart flipped, excited and pleased. How long had it been since Dan had gifted her with any compliments? Too long. How hungry she was to be adored. She *deserved* to be adored.

"A strong, dominant woman who's also beautiful is a rare and precious thing," Clay continued. "You'd have men—and women too, if you wanted—literally begging at your feet for the chance to be with you."

Would you beg to be with me, Clay? She might have to test that.

Melanie eyed the photo hanging next to them: a woman lying flat on her back, legs up. Holding her ankles by her ears. Lines of light shot up from her nether regions to her face.

"And what makes you think I'm dominant?" She cast a sly look at Clay. "How do you know I don't want to be hogtied and beaten to a bloody pulp with my ankles by my ears?"

"Call it a wild guess."

"And how do I find these people exactly? The Kinky White Pages?"

Clay laughed. "They'll be beating down your door soon enough once the word is out. News travels fast in this community. Start with FetLife—it's Facebook for kinky people. Go to events; show your face around here. Give people something to talk about. Hey," he called out to a scrappy redhead in a black T-shirt and faded jeans. "C'mere a sec."

The guy amiably ambled over in his high-tops. "Hey, man, what's up?" He had a baby face with a trusting expression. Here in San Francisco, he could be a fast-food worker or a billionaire CEO.

"This beautiful lady, who for the moment shall remain nameless, is my new friend." To Melanie: "Start thinking of a scene name. I suggest something elegant, just like you."

Babyface chuckled knowingly. "Welcome to the kinky community, nameless beautiful friend of Clay's."

Had Melanie suddenly joined "the community" just like that? The ground seemed to shift under her chair. And what's with all the welcoming? Like a preschool social, minus the watery coffee and Costco doughnuts.

"Thank you. You can call me Miss M."

"Very original," commented Clay drily. Melanie shrugged. What did he expect? Nobody had said anything about needing a scene name to have a cup of coffee. Great names don't pop up on command, like Clay did.

"So what kind of spanking are we talking about?" Babyface split his gaze evenly between them both. "Bare-handed? Bare ass? Marks or no marks?"

Wait, what? Who said anything about a spanking? Is this guy on drugs?

"Who doesn't love a good spanking from a gorgeous goddess?" Clay offered, noting Melanie's confusion. "He makes Grounds for Punishment a home office just to be available for random spankings. His FetLife name is actually RandomSpanks."

"Get a lot of work done?" Melanie murmured in Babyface RandomSpanks's direction. In this foreign land, her new persona spoke sarcasm fluently.

The guy blushed. "Maybe I should just get back to work."

"Aaagh!" A female voice screeched from the front, drawing glances away from laptops and coffee. On the purple velvet couch a portly man was pinning her down, arms behind her back. Slapping her face deliberately: one side, then the other. They kissed, and everyone else went back to their business.

Melanie scrutinized Babyface. That creamy skin and ginger hair, a scattering of reddish freckles across his nose. She wanted to hand him money for ice cream, not a beating.

"Perhaps we'll do a spanking another time." She noted with a certain satisfaction the look of disappointment, and softened the rejection. "If you get all your work done." Flirtatiously.

Truthfully, all of this unnerved her. "Let's meet for coffee," Melanie had requested of Clay. Not, "Let's meet for some impromptu ass abuse in broad daylight with a baby-faced stranger"! Smacking an armchair with a ruler was one thing; smacking a live body with her bare hand, another thing entirely.

"Oh, my God, Clay!" Melanie hissed through her teeth when the guy moved out of earshot. "You could have given me a little advance notice. No more surprises like that, *ever*. You put him on the spot too. Totally presumptuous."

"Whoa, whoa, *Miss M,* slow down." Clay held up a hand to stay her annoyance. "First, I've known him for years. Not only are you very much his type—you're going to inspire a lot of MILF fetishes, FYI—but he is a very experienced player and would never do anything he's not comfortable with. Taking a light spanking by a newbie is his way of giving back to the next generation."

He took a slow sip of coffee while she digested this information. The coffees were lukewarm now, while Melanie still steamed.

"Second," Clay continued, "I was trying to do you a favor."

Melanie considered this. Someone doing her a favor—there's a change for you. But there went her shoulders tensing up again. What the hell was she doing here? She didn't belong in a kinky café, wearing a black lace thong and pretending to be something she wasn't, surrounded by photos of naked people bound by light. She belonged in her cushy suburban living room wearing a butter-yellow twinset and a hairband. Or in her top-of-the-line kitchen, cutting Sammy's sandwich with a dinosaur-shaped cookie cutter. Or in the playground sipping tea out of a Thermos, recapping the latest episode of *Real Housewives* with the other mommies. Stupid, this entire idea.

She swiveled around in her chair, clutching for her jacket and purse.

"Melanie." Clay reached over, grabbing her hand. "Don't be so hard on yourself. You're just getting your feet wet."

"Don't you think I know that?" Melanie's eyes blazed. She yanked her hand from his grasp. "Apparently I know nothing about anything! That's what everyone thinks, anyway. Dan thought he knew best about everything. My parents? Same thing. But I *do* know lots of things, and I know that whatever I don't know right now, I will figure it out." Almost spitting the words out. She'd held them back too long.

"Of course I have a lot to learn," she continued, aiming for a more restrained tone. "But you know what? I've always wanted this; I just couldn't see it. Now I do. And nothing's going to stop me."

How tired she was of being treated like a child who couldn't take care of herself. She'd show them all. She'd take of herself *and* Sammy, with money and love to spare. Unlike Dan, who just took off when he didn't get his way. No loving dominant there, only a loving-himself dominant.

The *Loving Dominant* book, hidden in Melanie's locked night-stand, said that loving dominants tended to be centered on others, not self-centered—in other words, not Dan. Dan had always assumed that whatever pleased him pleased Melanie. As if.

Clay looked distraught. "I didn't mean to upset you. I'm sorry."

"Oh, Clay, it's not you." Melanie sighed. Patted his hand. "It's everything."

"I've been there." He looked sympathetically rueful. "Breakups are a bitch. My ex tried to use my—ahem, proclivities—against me in court to gain full custody of our child. Luckily, I hadn't done anything she could trace."

Hmmmm, what's this? Melanie hadn't even considered it. But no worries there. She'd be lucky to get Dan even partially involved in Sammy's life, let alone have to fight for custody. Still, might be a good idea to snap photos of his porn stash, duffel bag of rope, and drawers full of sex toys. Just in case.

"Miss M, how can I help you? Just tell me what you need." Sweet Clay, so eager. So obliging. She wanted to hug him. And so messy. Croissant crumbs littered his shirt; one pants leg was wrinkled. She wanted to smack him.

In fact, she wanted to do lots of things to him. Nasty, perverted, deviant things. And she would. And he would like it.

But now she had to get back to Palo Alto and pick Sammy up from preschool. Perverted pleasures would have to wait until she could find a cheap babysitter.

"Clay, clear the table please. I have to go." He hopped up instantly, she noted happily.

Getting into the car, Melanie realized she was not the same person who had left the house that morning. *Good riddance, deluded princess.* She imagined her sorry old self getting smaller and smaller along with the café in her rearview mirror. *Hello, Miss M.*

Hello, goddess.

The thought made her so hot and wet, it was all she could do to keep her hands on the steering wheel.

As MELANIE pulled into the preschool parking lot, her cell phone rang. An unfamiliar number flashed on the screen. A wrong number? No…a premonition clutched at her heart. Her stomach lurched. The world outside the car went strangely silent.

"Hello, Melanie." That steely voice, devoid of feeling. As if she had just seen him yesterday. As if he had not torn their family apart.

Where are you? Is that home-wrecking cunt with you? When are you coming back? Do you realize you left your wife and child broke, you selfish bastard? The unvoiced thoughts collided randomly behind the barrier of her silence. If she opened her mouth, they would all come spilling out and drown her.

The phone line hummed quietly. Finally Dan spoke again: "Not speaking to me? Very mature." Melanie could picture his sneer.

"Well, I called to tell you that I'm enjoying my time away so much that I won't be back for at least six more months."

Six months?! She and Sammy would be penniless long before then.

"You may continue to live in the house, in *my* house, during that time, but you will not see one cent from me for yourself, per our prenuptial agreement. When I return, my lawyer will handle the details regarding child support."

"Where. Are. You." Melanie could barely get the words out through her clenched jaw.

"That's my concern, not yours. And don't bother trying to trace this number; it's Google Voice."

Suddenly the dam broke.

"How could you do this, Dan? To us? To your own child? Do you realize you're going to break his heart? And forcing me to handle finances when I haven't worked in years? Are you trying to punish me, Dan? Is that it? You want me to suffer because I didn't bow and scrape and do your bidding every second?" The tears clogged her throat, spilled from her eyes. But she cleared them quickly. Dug sunglasses out of the glove compartment and waved to another mom from the front seat. Nothing to see here.

"How could *I* do this? Of course you would see it that way." Dan's tone dripped with condescension. "When you grow up, little girl, you'll see that the whole demise of our marriage is your doing. Now you'll just have to find some other sugar daddy to latch on to."

"You won't get away with this," Melanie seethed. "I'll sue you for alimony. Prenups are broken all the time." She wiped more hot tears away, her fingers black with mascara. She probably looked like a raccoon by now.

Dan's laugh crackled like icicles falling on concrete. "Good luck with that. The prenup is ironclad, and my lawyers are the best in the state. Poor girl, you'll just have to make your own way now. You know, I actually thought if you apologized and offered to change, we might have worked things out. Clearly that's not going to happen."

So that's it. He wants me to come crawling back. To beg forgiveness. For what, having her own wants and needs? For having *their baby*? His leaving, and leaving her with no money, was a ploy to scare her into submission. *To hell with him.* That girl who would have apologized for breathing too loudly was as dead as her love for this heartless monster.

203

"Go to hell," she said. And pressed End Call.

No more Little Miss Nice Girl.

No more Please Tread on Me.

No more needing anyone for anything. Tonight she would tell Sammy that his dad had taken off for good.

From now on, Melanie and Sammy were on their own. And she would trample the heart of anyone who tried to stand in their way.

Chapter 12

"Do Bears Crap in the Woods?"

PARENTS AND grandparents, aunts and uncles and friends, packed themselves into the all-purpose room like it was a presidential inauguration and not a preschool show. Some perched on the hard metal folding chairs, some chatted while standing, some actually were setting up tripods with video cameras. Melanie rolled her eyes. Surely the next Broadway star would not be discovered warbling "Polly Wolly Doodle" off-key at age three.

"Melanie, thank goodness!" Piper slipped into the adjacent seat, one of the last empty ones. "Howard was supposed to save us seats, but he couldn't get out of work. Oh, wait, were you saving this one?"

Melanie shook her head. Just her. Better get used to it.

"Whew." Piper shook out her long platinum hair, picking invisible lint off her mint-green velour track suit. She settled her fuchsia

Juicy Couture backpack under the seat. "It's going to be hard enough getting through two hours of this without having to stand." Her features contorted in mock horror.

Melanie smiled. "Oh, it can't be that bad! I saw them practicing, so cute." Sammy played a squirrel, begging the woodsman not to cut down his favorite tree. No chance of getting out of this dry-eyed.

"Spoken like a true first-timer." Piper patted Melanie's knee knowingly. "Benjamin and I sat through Lilac's show last year. The 10 minutes your kid is onstage, it's cute. The rest—torture." She whipped out a pocket mirror covered in pink crystals and swiped rosy lipstick over her already perfect lips. Turned in her seat to face Melanie full on, bathing Melanie in her angelic radiance.

"So how *are you?*" Piper lowered her voice and gave Melanie the sympathy face. "I can only imagine how hard it must be with Dan still away."

And never coming back, Melanie added mutely. She had broken the news to Sammy the night before. Made him his favorite dinner, set out an extra-big helping of ice cream, let him watch two SpongeBob SquarePants videos. Count on SpongeBob to turn any tragedy into farce.

"Honey, there's something I have to tell you." Melanie had pulled him onto her lap, a mama bear's instinct to protect her cub. "It's about Daddy."

"Daddy, Daddy! Coming home, yay!" Sammy wriggled excitedly in her arms.

Melanie breathed deeply. Shifted her eyes away, seeing the Christmas cards that would never be sent, the anniversaries that would never be celebrated. She gazed at the three of them together, a happy family in a frozen image, in a place that no longer existed. That maybe never did exist except in her dream life. Time for them all to wake up.

"No, honey. Daddy's not coming home. It's going to be just you and me for now. But he loves you very, very much. You know that, right?" What a whopper of a lie. An act of mercy. Melanie planted kisses on his head like a toy bobbing woodpecker. Her son would be the only one to ever receive her mercy from now on.

"But Daddy come back when?" Sammy didn't look at all like he understood. His little face scrunched up in confusion.

"I don't know exactly. A really long time. I'm sorry I don't have a better answer. Mommy will take care of everything; don't worry."

"What? No Daddy? I want Daddy!" Sammy's big hazel eyes pooled with tears. *Be strong; you can do this. Keep breathing,* Melanie told herself. *Don't let him see how real this nightmare is.*

"I do know that you and I are going to have the greatest, bestest adventures no matter what, and I know that you are a good, good boy, the best little boy..." Her eyes welled up. *Don't cry, don't cry, don't cry,* she chanted silently.

"I's a supuh-hewo," Sammy corrected, the tears running down in rivulets.

"I know that you are a good, good superhero, and together we are going to fight crime everywhere." *Even if the biggest criminal is your father. I will hunt him down and make him pay for what he's done to us. I will never forgive him. And I will never, ever let you down.*

"But I miss Daddy, Mommy!" Sammy's eyes shredded Melanie's heart with their simple and pure longing. His little hands desperately clutching chunks of her hair. "No fair!"

"Many things in life aren't fair, honey. But don't you worry about anything. Mommy's here, and we're going to be just fine. Better than fine." *You're going to have all the love and good things you deserve, whether or not we ever lay eyes on your sorry excuse for a father again. You're going to grow up happy if it kills me.*

"I'm fine," Melanie told Piper firmly now, back in the preschool show's audience. Maybe too loudly, even considering the din in the packed room. "But...I'm thinking of going back to work."

"Good for you!" Piper beamed her approval. "Personally, my work as a personal organizer has kept me sane this whole time. You've got to have a bigger sense of accomplishment than having a spotless toilet, you know?"

How about six orgasms in four hours on Clay Chumbley's mammoth manhood? Beat that accomplishment! Melanie had put Clay's café proclamations about her desirability to the test in a marathon fornication session two days ago, and she was still sore. Clay might be a softie in life, but he was all hardness in the sack.

"But I don't know what work to do. Going back into the art business…that seems so stale now." Melanie frowned. What kind of job, the million-dollar question. So much more pleasant to think about straddling Clay on top of his coffee table.

Piper pulled her legs up and sat easily in lotus pose, her legs folded so neatly, they barely touched Melanie's knee. "Don't worry, you can always be a high-class hooker." Then, registering Melanie's shock: "Kidding! We're both probably too old for that."

"Attention, parents and guests!" The preschool's director had strode to the center of the stage, her pink pantsuit somehow energizing and soothing simultaneously. She gripped the microphone like it was a trophy, waiting for the shuffling and coughing to subside. "Welcome, everyone, to our annual spring showcase. It's wonderful to see so many loving, supportive people here today! Please know that it means the world to your kids, and give yourself a big round of applause." Piper rolled her eyes amidst the clapping. Melanie, thinking of Dan thousands of miles away, put her hands together. If she didn't cheer for herself, who would?

"Maybe we'll get a treat at the end," Piper sniped. "If we sit crisscross applesauce and keep our listening caps on."

Melanie laughed. Who knew that behind Piper's pristine exterior lay a sewer-mouthed spitfire?

"A couple of announcements before we begin…" The director launched into thank-yous and pleases and don't forgets. Piper's eyes glazed over.

"What are you doing after this?" Piper's voice in her ear again. "Do you want to come to the park with us? The kids can burn off all that pent-up energy from waiting backstage, and we can talk Help Wanted."

The unsolicited offer of help surprised Melanie. Since when did anyone do anything good for mere goodness's sake? But then again, what did she have to lose? Except maybe more assumptions about her new friend's normalcy.

"Sure." Melanie nodded. "Although I might not survive this entire thing, if this speech is any indication." The director droned on, savoring her yearly moment in the spotlight.

"Someone should gag her." Piper scrunched up her face cutely. "This is torture."

Melanie tittered. What did Piper know about torture? Melanie knew torture. During the past couple of weeks since she had met up with Clay at the café, she had dived head first into the deep pool of kink. Awash in knowledge from books and websites and two classes at the Stronghold, one of San Francisco's dungeons. And using the eager Clay as a practice target. Thank goodness Piper and Benjamin loved having Sammy over.

Fetishes of all flavors called out from the kinky corners; Melanie felt like a kid in a candy store. Flogging? Sign her up. Whipping? Just wait until the catsuit arrives. Peeing or worse on someone's face? Not in a million years. ("But never say never," one book had urged. "Your tastes will likely change.") Melanie couldn't fathom that someday her tastes might run to having a human potty.

So delicious, having a secret deviant side. A double life. Who cared if the other moms had husbands and multimillion-dollar houses with their name on the title? Winners at a game for losers. Melanie had moved on to a game packed with excitement. Let everyone else sleepwalk through life, dreaming in black and white. Melanie was wide awake in a world painted with red lash marks and pink welts and purple bruises, sex and violence bursting through in Technicolor passion and multiple orgasms.

But oh, how careful she had to be not to slip up! Not one drop of the kinky ocean must spill out in public. Not one glimpse of the deviant hellcat emerging. Incognito or bust. She had even set up a PayPal account to pay for her kinky purchases—no trail for anyone to follow. On the way: a liquid-looking cutout black minidress, $16.99 from China. A dress for enslaving consenting men, made by Chinese factory slaves with no choice. Sure it bothered Melanie, but poverty was a bitch. She'd probably have to sell some Prada to pay for it.

"So, in conclusion"—the bubbly director finally began relinquishing the spotlight—"you should all be very proud of yourselves and your children. Let's give everyone a big hand again!" Sheesh. Things sure had changed since Melanie was a kid. Parents back then didn't applaud and shower their kids with positive reinforcement. Kids did what they were supposed to do, or they got punished. *There's a sown seed for you.*

Melanie clapped and settled in. Wrangled her attention from thoughts of shiny dresses and what kitchen implements she could use for no-cost impact toys. The youngest group toddled out, a dozen girls and boys done up as flowers and plants, all younger than three. Only one even attempted to do the actual performance; the others waved at their parents in the audience or boogied to their own beat. One little girl promptly plopped down at the front of the stage and burst into tears, holding her arms out until her father scooped her up. She clung to his neck and immediately stopped crying.

A painstakingly slow piano number. A tremulous vocal rendition of "Somewhere Over the Rainbow." Three or four more wobbly, meandering dance numbers. Finally Sammy's group came out, and Melanie's heart swelled. Her little boy waved to her with his furry squirrel paw, then focused so seriously on his role. How often she had heard him practicing his lines, getting dressed in the morning or murmuring on the car ride to school. Speaking them now so clearly, even if he did have trouble with r's: "Please, Mr. Woodsman, leave ow-uh tree alone. It's ow-uh home." Such sincerity! Such earnestness! Melanie's eyes welled up. What a precious gift her child was. Even with Dan at their happiest, she had never felt anything like this. The bonds of a mother's love are stronger than anything man could invent.

Impulsively, Melanie clutched Piper's arm. "Oh, my God. I don't think it gets any better than this."

Piper smiled indulgently, stroking Melanie's hand on her arm. "I've been saying that every year since Benjamin was born. And somehow, every year it does get even better."

How perfect if the show had ended right there. But next up: a violin solo, a tapping trio, a *Toddlers & Tiaras* wannabe. Melanie slipped out to "go to the ladies' room," as she whispered to Piper. Her rear end ached from the hard metal chair; her heart ached at seeing all the happy, complete families. She needed to be alone.

She wandered into the church next door, empty save a few elderly women clutching rosary beads like lifelines. Melanie had been to church a couple of times in her 20s, weddings and whatnot, but that's it. God had merely been used as muscle for her mother's orders growing up ("So help me God, if you don't clean your room right now..."). Melanie had to hand it to her mother, turning the Lord Almighty into her personal henchman.

She looked for God now in the stained glass windows, in the vaulted ceilings meant to diminish the faithful. If God was infinite, why did he need to make others feel small?

Dear God, she began silently, the padded leather cool against her knees. *Please tell me the next step, show me the way. What kind of work should I do? What will save Sammy and me?* A cough echoed through the cavernous silence. The statues with their frozen stares.

Ten minutes and still nothing. The candles flickered in their red glass holders. God didn't live here; maybe he just stopped in every week for Sunday mass. The priests trotting him out like the good china.

You're on your own now. Get used to it.

Melanie's shoulders relaxed at the thought. The pressure that had been clutching at her heart eased, like air streaming from an overfilled balloon. No one to answer to anymore; no one to judge. She could finally choose her own fate. What did she have to lose now? She had already lost almost everything trying to play by someone else's rules. Wasted 30 years of her life trying to win at a game she didn't invent.

Melanie took a last look around. The widows' lips moving in unheard prayer. The altar inviting worship of someone with better things to do than answer a desperate woman's prayers. The colored windows with their ancient stories meant to educate, to intimidate.

She got off her knees and exited the church without genuflecting. From now on, Melanie would play by her rules alone.

"SUCH A great idea!" Melanie enthused. She and Piper watched the kids tear around the playground as if demons nipped at their feet. "They'll get all their jumpies out, and we get some fresh air after being cooped up in there for two hours."

"A fresh vodka tonic would be better." Piper sighed. "But that'd be an hour on the treadmill."

"Ha, as if you have anything to worry about." Melanie cast her eyes on Piper's slim legs crossed prettily on the park bench.

"If you only knew." Piper leaned in conspiratorially. In a lowered voice: "I used to weigh 250 pounds."

Melanie's eyes bugged out. Living Barbie was once a porker! She liked Piper more every time they hung out. Like unwrapping an onion, in a good way—another revealing layer peeling off each time.

"Just goes to show you can do anything if you set your mind to it." Piper nodded in self-affirmation. "Speaking of which, what do you have in mind for a job?"

"Ugh, that's just it. No clue. Something major—like, multimillionaire major—but I'm not trained for anything except art gallery work." Melanie's brow furrowed.

"Training is so 1950s. Nowadays you just need a good idea and even better marketing." Piper snapped into organizational/inspirational wonder mode. "What are you good at? What do you like to do?"

Visions of pushing her gushing nether regions into Clay's face flashed in Melanie's mind. Oh, yeah, that's what she liked to do. The sex. And the pushing. Turn that into a career, Miss Motivator.

Then again…Melanie stared thoughtfully at Piper's eager face. Piper had dished out her own honest tidbit about porking out—not to mention getting porked by strangers at parties. Of all the people in the world, Piper wouldn't judge. But could she keep a secret?

Melanie watched the kids dipping in and out of their games. Sharing laughs and secrets. Everyone needed a friend to share secrets with. But could she trust her new friend?

"Piper, can you keep a secret?"

Piper's eyes glowed. "Do bears crap in the woods? The things I know and never tell, you would be amazed."

Melanie considered this. True, Piper had only ever dropped shockers about herself. And as a personal organizer, she knew where the bones were buried. What people stashed in closets and under mattresses. But never once had she let on anything she knew about anyone. A walking Fort Knox of juicy secrets.

"OK then." Melanie breathed deeply, letting the air out slowly. Time to share her own shocker. "I just discovered S&M. It's all I think about, making guys do my bidding and hurting them if they don't. That and sex. Oh, and...Dan and I are splitting up." *How's that stash of secrets for your Fort Knox?*

Piper swiveled toward Melanie, propping an arm on the bench back. Face as unreadable as a poker pro's.

Relief and trepidation joined hands in Melanie's heart. How good to finally let the secrets out! So tiring, keeping up the happy-vanilla-housewife front. Even Batman had Alfred. *But Piper isn't an elderly butler. She's a mom. Your kids play together. Who wants their kid around a sex-crazed kinkster?*

Piper pursed her lips. Turned her head slowly from side to side.

Even Piper's group sex is still just sex. S&M is different. Deviant, perverted. Who wants to be chummy with a degenerate?

Piper's eyes focused on something in the distance. Too embarrassed on Melanie's behalf to even look at her?

Another minute of silence. "Piper, please say something!" *Even if it's, "Adios, pervert. Have a nice life."*

"Melanie..." Piper dragged her eyes back from the horizon. "I'm really, really sorry you and Dan are splitting up. You have my total sympathy. But..."

But that's no excuse to descend into depravity? But you can't associate with such a horrible deviant?

Piper placed her hands on Melanie's shoulders. Their faces were mere inches apart. A whiff of mint and strawberry lip gloss.

"But this is the most exciting thing I've heard all year!" Piper broke into a grin. "A dominatrix in the neighborhood—it's too rich. And speaking of rich, do you have any idea how much money they make?"

Melanie shook her head, too stunned to answer. Thank goodness no one could hear Piper's enthusiasm over all the shrieking kids.

"Buttloads! You want a job? Helllllloooo, if it were a snake, it would've bit you." Piper pulled a notebook from her backpack, its little gold zipper charms jingling. "Now, let's talk details. Wardrobe, equipment, marketing…do you have any clients yet?"

Clay's mouth and colossal shaft smeared with her juices flashed before Melanie's eyes.

"Not officially. And only the most basic skills too."

"How much skill does it take to crush someone's balls under a heel? You'll figure it out. Attitude is the most important thing here, I think." Piper uncapped a tiny silver pen from Tiffany's. "Have you got the attitude?"

Melanie recalled beating up Dan's armchair with the ruler, how happy—and wet—it had made her. How adeptly she had made Clay do her bidding. Attitude did trump training, apparently. Commands now flowed from her mouth as easily as apologies once had.

She smiled—a satisfied, excited, evil grin.

"Just watch me."

Chapter 13

She Could Eat Him for Breakfast, and He'd Thank Her

MELANIE STALKED into the club—the *dungeon*—poured into a black latex minidress, hidden under a long black wool coat. Thigh-high PVC boots flashing with every step, their five-inch heels clicking on the raw concrete floor. Her hair tucked up under the short black wig. Her eye makeup dark and elegant. Blood-red glossy lips. No doormats here, save for any she would trample.

The wheeled carry-on bag at her side held carefully chosen implements: a paddle, a flogger, rope from Home Depot—who knew the big-box store was a veritable treasure trove of budget-conscious torture devices? Some bottles of water, chocolate, and a blanket for "aftercare." Apparently it's good etiquette to pamper your submissives after you beat them up.

Speaking of which, there he was, kneeling patiently just past the check-in counter, on a carpet by the lockers, just as she had instructed. Hands resting on his thighs. As if meditating like a monk instead of waiting to be flogged on a cross.

His name: Ronan. The name he was using anyway, real or not. Melanie had stuck with Miss M for lack of better inspiration. It would do because she said so.

Ronan had emailed photos with his face blurred out, and they hadn't done him justice. Late 20s, gym-toned muscles, closely cropped dark hair. Above-average looks. Melanie already planned to leave a few bruises on those perfect muscles, souvenirs to remember her by.

He was fairly new to the scene himself, so they had agreed to go simple: emotional domination and light impact play. (Melanie had read up on negotiation and consent—no room for error when your business is on the line.) It amused her that Ronan was actually a med student. "First do no harm" apparently didn't apply to his ass.

Through emails and one phone chat, they had negotiated the scene. For him, no bruises not coverable by clothing; no calling him humiliating names likes "sissy"; no anal penetration. Her rules: no speaking to her unless spoken to. He must include "Miss" in every sentence. And no sex, although he was yummier than an ice cream sundae and she was starving. Potential creepy onlookers could get their sex-show fill somewhere else.

In fact, Melanie would have liked to do this whole thing in private. Sex on tap and no witnesses to any screw-ups. But Clay had strongly urged the club, with its dungeon monitors patrolling to oversee and assist in the event of an emergency. Dead clients couldn't give good referrals.

Melanie stood next to Ronan now near the dungeon's check-in counter, slipping her fingers through his hair and rubbing her boots against his freshly shaved cheek. A materials fetishist, this one: latex, leather, PVC. With the slimming effect of black latex, call it a win-win.

"Ronan." She stroked the top of his head. So strange, creating an intimacy with someone you'd never met. But the chemistry zinged between them. His eager face radiating openness and trust. She could eat him for breakfast, and he'd thank her.

Ronan remained silent.

"What a good boy you are, Ronan. On time and waiting so quietly." The boy glowed under her compliment, appreciation rising in the crotch of his black cotton pants. "Is there anything going on with you today I should know about? Injuries? Concerns?" Still petting his hair gently and rhythmically, but strangely, she felt like the cat.

Also feeling oddly maternal, considering her plans to leave him with bruise souvenirs. Not much younger than herself but such a boy, so tentative and insecure. She could smell his insecurity as strongly as his soap scented skin.

A gorgeous, intelligent med student with low self-esteem, Melanie pondered. *Needs some positive reinforcement—between floggings.* It seemed so obvious.

Ronan dropped his eyes docilely. "No, ma'am, no injuries or concerns. Thank you for asking."

Melanie winced and stopped stroking. "You are not to call me 'ma'am.'" Like some old lady in a grocery store, shuffling along in sensible shoes? "It's 'Miss.' Is that clear?" She pinched his arm hard for emphasis.

Ronan cringed but didn't protest the pinching. "Yes, Miss. I apologize."

"Good. Now stand up, take my coat, and hang it over there." She pointed to a horizontal rod holding a boutique's worth of black coats already.

Ronan held her coat like a queen's robe. What a catch—brains and muscles, obedient and well-spoken (or well-written at least, since she had limited his speech). So why the low self-esteem? Couldn't he see how desirable he was? Melanie shook her head. Some people were just blind to their assets.

"Where exactly, Miss?" Ronan's eyes flicked back and forth tentatively between Melanie and the coat rack.

She stared at the several empty hangers, wondering what on earth he meant. Did his self-blindness extend to real vision? Ahhh, right. "The sixth hanger from the right," she dictated. "And remember the exact spot so you can find it later in that sea of black. I don't want to wait while you dig for it." She held back a smile of pride. Oh yes, this authoritative stuff rolled off her tongue like honey.

"Yes, Miss." He hung up the coat carefully, settling the shoulders into place.

"Walk two feet behind me. If I stop, you stop. If I sit, you sit at my feet. Understood?"

"Yes, Miss." Geez, what's with the autopilot mode? If she had wanted a robot, she would have gone to Brookstone.

"Ronan." Melanie took his face between her hands and tilted it up—the boots gave her an inch on him and a mental edge. "From now on, I want you to use a different affirmative every time you answer me. You can choose which ones: 'Of course,' 'Absolutely,' 'Certainly,' or—if you're feeling less enthusiastic—'If it pleases you.' But I don't want to hear another plain 'Yes, Miss.' Is that understood?" Her hands a subtle vise on his cheeks.

A pause. "Without a doubt, Miss." Ronan clearly trying and failing to stifle a proud grin.

"Excellent!" Melanie rubbed his chin in approval. "We're going to get along just fine." And turned, her heels clicking again on the raw concrete.

"Most assuredly, Miss." His voice trailed her. She chuckled.

They rounded the corner, entering the dungeon proper. How different it looked from when she had attended those flogging and bondage 101 classes; the bright overheads now switched off and the folding chairs stowed. Lit for murky ambience instead with battery-powered candles and dark-shaded lamps. Dim spotlights beckoning guests to the benches, crosses, cages. Slings and padded tables and a sturdy wooden frame dotted with eyebolts. Melanie tried to take it all in nonchalantly. Never let 'em see you sweat.

She stalked over to an empty chair, just beyond the rail that marked the play area. Tucked the suitcase next to it and regally sat down, posture perfect. Ronan arranged himself on the floor at her feet. She needed the lay of the land without looking lost.

Two dungeon monitors wandered around, marked by bright orange armbands. Good. Other scenes in progress already, also good. Melanie didn't want to be the center of attention until she got a grip on things.

Although, hmmm, judging from the interested stares, attention might be hard to deflect. *Fake it till you make it*—if it worked for corporate power games, it could work for S&M power exchanges.

Ronan sat gracefully cross-legged on the floor, back straight. Yoga classes between med-school studies, no doubt. Good for him. Melanie rested a hand on his head, a subtle gesture of possession.

How silly some of the unfolding scenes looked! A corpulent naked man, flaccid penis locked up in a chastity cage, enduring being cropped by a skinny 60-ish woman in a corset. A girl in only fishnets and heels sucking off a man in full leathers, thanking him for every slap and kick. Other twosomes and threesomes— guys and girls, guys and guys, girls and girls—tied, contorted, in various states of giving and receiving pain or sex acts. A vaude- ville show for freaks.

Some of the clothes seemed downright ridiculous: pants with saggy old asses hanging out; corsets and lingerie on no one a Victoria's Secret casting agent would ever call; a handful of nurse and cop uniforms made of rubber or PVC. Melanie had never felt more fashionable.

But the faces, hello! Different story entirely. No silliness there, only very real emotions playing out like a Shakespearean drama: pain and pleasure and love. Such intensity—transcendence, even. One girl, twirling naked by her roped ankles from a wooden beam, her female partner wielding an enormous vibrator, looked as blissed out as a newlywed at a spa.

Melanie yearned to create a moment like that, a slice of time when everything bad disappeared. All the worries and regrets and uncertainties giving way to perfect order and satisfaction as she deemed fit. The queen of her realm—no, the goddess—even if she and Ronan were the realm's only dwellers. Who cared if it looked silly to an interloper?

Oh yes, Dan had been onto something. She got it now. And that's why they were a match made in hell: Each wanted to be the worshipped one. Their marriage wasn't big enough for two deities.

A couple vacated one of the X-shaped St. Andrew's crosses—apparently St. Andrew had felt unworthy to be crucified on a Jesus-style cross—and the girl wiped it down with cleaning supplies from a nearby table. Her back a map of bruises and slashes.

"Get up, Ronan. We're going over there." Melanie inclined her head toward the cross. "Take the suitcase. Stand in front of the cross with your back to me."

"Yes, M...I mean, um, certainly, Miss." Ronan shot her a look of apprehension and anticipation. His eyes sliding to her breasts. Pushed up like melons ready for plucking in the skintight dress's cutout.

Nice to know I've still got it, Melanie mused. *Eat your heart out, soccer moms. You can keep your pleated jeans and your color-coded day planners and your holier-than-thou organic vegan cookies. I'll take all the lustful stares.*

She left him standing by the cross for a minute, building the suspense. And mentally noting the location of the first-aid kit.

Let the games begin.

She walked over slowly and purposefully, each step of her boot heels deliberately placed. Time was hers for the taking. Everything now, hers for the taking. She gathered power with every step across the dungeon floor. By the time she reached the cross, Melanie felt 10 feet tall.

Ronan faced the wooden X with his hands clasped behind his back, head lowered.

Melanie made a "tsk" noise. "Ronan, is it chilly in here?"

A pause, considering. "No, Miss. Not chilly at all." Of course not. Space heaters stood evenly throughout the room. A trickle of sweat had pooled in Melanie's cleavage already, thanks to the nonbreathable latex dress. But she wanted to start this scene off on the right note.

"Then why are you wearing so much clothing?" She laid the suitcase flat on the floor, unzipping it, the black leather riding crop beckoning. She loved the feel of it in her hand, long and sturdy yet elegant too. No studying required, either—hard for even a beginning dominatrix to kill someone with a crop.

"Do you think your body is ugly?" Her voice low and seductive. Teasingly, she ran the crop over his neck and clothed back from behind. Outlining his muscles under the thin shirt. Her panties grew damp.

"Sometimes, Miss. I do work out but..."

"That's enough." She landed a sharp blow with the crop on his upper back. "Take off your shirt. Shoes and socks too." A naked torso had more appeal than naked feet, but the idea of him shoeless and vulnerable and her being fully clothed sent erotic charges through Melanie's veins.

Ronan quickly unbuttoned and removed his shirt. Folded it and placed it neatly next to the cross, still facing away. Next came the socks and shoes. Melanie inhaled sharply. "Ronan, you have a gooooorgeous body," she trilled. Lean but well-muscled. And smooth as a baby's bottom. God bless the metrosexuals for bringing waxing to the male masses.

He smiled weakly but said nothing. She cropped him again. "Say 'thank you' when you're given a compliment."

"Thank you, Miss." Melanie nodded curtly and placed each of his arms against each arm of the X.

But wait, there it was! How she could work him over *and* work up his self-esteem. "I want to hear you say it, Ronan. Say, 'I have a gorgeous body.'" She cropped him once just inside each shoulder blade, delighted with her own brilliance.

He bent his head down and flexed his fingers, hesitating. The muscle in his jaw twitched. Melanie whacked him with the crop again. "Say it," she dictated.

"I...I have a gorgeous body." Barely audible.

"Louder." Crop, crop.

"I have a gorgeous body." Still not even at conversation level.

"Louder!" She smacked his ass for emphasis with an open palm. Hard. Who did he think he was dealing with? He would obey or face the consequences.

"I have a gorgeous body!" Almost a shout.

"You cerrrrrtainly do." Purring now. Caressing his baby-smooth back, happily noting its newly pink shades. *She* had done that. Willfully. Unapologetically. Maybe Melanie would never apologize again. "And it pleases me very much. Now that we've established that, let's get started." She stifled the urge to kiss his neck. Damn, why had she prohibited sexual contact? She ran her hands over his bare skin. Next time.

The session only got better from there. Melanie fastened the cross's leather cuffs securely on his ankles and wrists. Took her sweet time warming him up, first light and then increasingly hard impact. Switching toys now and then, crop to flogger to paddle, building a crescendo of pain and pleasure. Stopping often to nuzzle his neck or ear, or take any caress she felt like. His body secured in bondage like a nicely wrapped present.

His face told her when the endorphins kicked in. A rush of adrenaline for her too, having him so completely at her command. Stepping into her power, owning it. Who knew that underneath the former doormat lay a tigress waiting to be unleashed?

Soon his cries of pain were almost indistinguishable from the moans of pleasure. And then, finally, his face took on a transported look. A goner in a good way. Her work here was done.

Melanie gently unfastened the cuffs, planting her feet firmly into the floor as he leaned into her. Led him to a loveseat covered in a bedsheet. Draped the throw blanket she had brought over him, that maternal instinct again. Wanting to baby him now that she had beaten him up.

She had planned to make him clean the cross, but how could she extradite him from his happy place? Did it herself instead. How many times had she resented cleaning, wishing a maid would do it? Now it felt like a labor of love.

Back on the loveseat, she put his head in her lap. Both of them marinating in the satisfaction. Nowhere to go; nothing to do but enjoy the moment. If Melanie could bottle this drug, she'd make a fortune.

"Ronan, I'm so proud of you." Finally easing back to reality. "You took it so well, like a real man. You made me very happy tonight." She gently massaged his scalp.

"Really?" His voice was dreamy, his eyes still far away.

"Really really," Melanie confirmed. "Very, very happy. You did very well."

"Thank you, Miss." Ronan turned his face up now, his eyes refocusing. "And may I say something else?" She nodded. "You're a natural. You said you were fairly new, but I wouldn't have been able to tell. And you're so beautiful! This was amazing. Really. Thank you."

"It was my pleasure." Melanie truly meant it. The thrill of the power, the relief that nothing had gone wrong, the sexual charge from his total hotness…hard to believe she had sought relief from alcohol when this better drug could be had. And no calories! In fact, she had probably burned a few. She pictured the 3 a.m. info-mercial: The Flogging Workout! Build upper-body strength while having the time of your life. Get two leather floggers now for only three payments of $39.95!!

She examined with pride the bruises surfacing on Ronan's body, each one a badge of honor. He would be reminded of her for a least a week—a gift that kept on giving. As she caressed them fondly, a single tear—of joy, Melanie was sure—escaped Ronan's eye. She wiped it tenderly away, then licked her fingertip.

She had never tasted anything so sweet.

As RONAN fetched her coat, a man Melanie had noticed watching her earlier approached. Humbly. She straightened her spine.

"I'm so sorry to bother you, Ma'am…" he began. Melanie cringed.

"Miss," she corrected. "Not Ma'am."

"I'm so sorry, Miss." The nondescript middle-aged man eyeballed the floor, shifting nervously. His arms and hands moving around like fish waiting to be speared. "I don't mean to bother you, but I was wondering…" Melanie waited patiently. Ronan moved closer. Possessively?

"Yes? What is it?" She fired the words out. She took in his paunch and graying hair. His hunching, his apologetic demeanor. The weaknesses pained her; she suppressed the urge to bark at him to stand up straight. But oh, wait…the vulnerability. It softened Melanie's heart. How hard it must have been for him to approach her. Had he been working up his courage for the past two hours?

"Yes?" she repeated, more kindly. "What do you want to say?"

His eyes flitted up at her gratefully and then back down again. "Miss, I was wondering if by any chance you would be interested in using me as you please? Maybe I could book a session?"

Book a session? He thought she was a pro! Ha, that was a good one. A few weeks of research and classes and only this just-completed scene under her belt. Martha Stewart was more a pro domme than she was.

But then…why not? The pros did exactly what she had just done—and what she had been doing to Clay more and more—only they got paid for it. "Seize the day," Piper would urge. And hadn't Piper just outlined a detailed plan for Melanie's going pro? Who would notice a few skipped steps? Move to the head of the class; do not pass Go. Collect $200.

"We can talk about it. Give me your name and email address."

She pulled out her cell phone and typed it in. "Good. I'm Miss M. I'll email you within the next three days." Enough time to figure out rates and rules.

"Thank you, Miss M." His face finally relaxed. "I appreciate it."

"You're welcome." Melanie watched him walk away, then turned to Ronan. "Interesting."

"I told you, you're a natural. You're going to be so busy, you won't have time for me anymore." He was practically pouting.

"Now, now, Ronan." She slipped into the coat he held out. "With that body, I will always make time for you." She stroked his cheek affectionately.

"Now take my suitcase to my car."

MELANIE UNZIPPED her boots and peeled off the latex dress. Eyed her naked body in the master closet's mirror. She had not lost five pounds or worked out at the gym since the morning, but everything seemed firmer, tighter. She stretched her arms up and out, a "V" for victory. The energy still bounced through her bones. Midnight, but who could sleep? She felt like she owned the world, wanted to stay up and count every cent.

Tomorrow morning she would pick up Sammy from Piper's. She would take him to his dentist appointment, work on his phonics, run errands, clean the bathroom. Tonight, she was still a goddess.

She recalled how Ronan had quivered under her touch, how she had broken through his everyday mask to reach the real, vulnerable, raw person inside. Did any greater power exist? *She* had done that; no one else. No help from anyone. Melanie had played him expertly like a fine musical instrument, drawing out the exact notes she wanted.

Dan had played *her* like that, drawn out her moans and cries as if pulling strings. His own personal sex toy. She had mistaken possessiveness for love. She wouldn't make that mistake ever again.

And how much better it was from the other side of the S&M coin anyway! Gratitude flooded her body now, ironically, for Dan's cruelty. Without it, she might never have found this much greater pleasure. This joy that curled around her heart and spread into her soul, courtesy of inflicting pain on someone else.

Melanie cupped her breasts, so beautiful now. No matter how many times Dan had lambasted her self-deprecation, had insisted she was gorgeous, she had never felt this radiant. She pinched her nipples, watching them stiffen. So responsive! She ran her hands over her naked hips. So smooth! Like she had bathed in a hundred milk baths. No five-star-spa treatment could compete with an S&M high.

Before she knew it, Melanie's fingers had found that warm, familiar place. That place so neglected by Dan toward the end. So neglected even by herself, until she met the indefatigable Clay Chumbley. Strange how a few positive encounters could change everything. She had found her true course, and it had nothing to do with being someone else's toy.

She leaned against the mirror. Her breath misted the reflection, blurring the lines. Her fingers pushing deep inside her, stroking in a hungry rhythm. She had no one to answer to but herself; she could come in 10 seconds if she wanted. Or an hour.

Grazing that sweet little bump at the top of her mound with a fingertip, drawing the wetness over it. Shivering with pleasure. So beautifully sensitive, that one small spot. She made her fingers flat and rubbed circle after circle over it, drawing out the pleasure. Only for her, this pleasure.

Recalling how Ronan had suffered for her on the rack. How she had repaid him in bliss. Only a goddess could have conjured that. "Goddess," she thought, stroking more urgently now. Feasting on the otherworldly deliciousness. "Goddess."

Her breath on the mirror now obscured Melanie's whole face, but how clear everything else seemed. Everything no longer needed—the worry, the self-doubt, the guilt—fell away as she scaled the heights of gratification. And it was the word itself that carried her over the top, rocking against her hand with unbridled force.

Goddess.

Chapter 14
The Pet of the Devil Himself

"GRANDE SKINNY mocha double-shot latte for Melanie," called the Starbucks barista. "And a café Americano for Piper."

"Can you get those?" Melanie glanced up from her cell phone. "I need to answer this text."

"Are you going to punish me if I don't?" Piper's voice teased in Melanie's ear. A smirk. Their three kids sat at the next table, snacking on organic milk and dried fruit.

"Haha, very funny. This is business." She was confirming the time and day with Paying Client No. 1, the middle-aged man who'd approached her in the dungeon a few days ago. Two hours at $150 an hour, with no sex on her part. Like taking candy from a baby.

The venue: her own house. Did Melanie like it? Not a bit. But she had checked out his references, including real pro dommes and a friend of Clay's, and all said nothing to worry about. The guy just apparently got off on doing perverted things in whitebread suburban houses. Not literally getting off in Melanie's case, of course, at least not during the session. What he did afterward, on his own time, was between him and the box of tissues.

"Here you go, your highness. Anything else I can get you? Some peeled grapes or perhaps…a nice footstool?" Piper set the personalized coffee down with an exaggerated flourish.

"You're really getting a kick out of this whole thing, I see," Melanie noted drily.

"Are you kidding? This is the most fun I've had since…" She glanced over at the kids. "Well, never mind since when. I can't wait to see your new outfits! As your best friend, I get borrowing privileges, you know. Howard would…" Her eyes slid to the kids again, obliviously turning their empty milk cartons into race cars, then back to Melanie. "Hmm, can I get you any *cream* for your coffee?"

Melanie snickered. Such a relief to have someone in on the secret, clearly enjoying the ride from the passenger seat. A confidante who never judged, who offered great advice and licked up the juicy details like they were whipped cream. She had never had a friend she could tell everything to before. But how careful they would have to be about no one else finding out—not just for the kids' sake but for their own reputations. People fear what they don't understand.

"What you can do for me is just what you've been doing already. Listening, watching Sammy. I can't tell you how much I appreciate all the babysitting." Melanie sipped her mocha latte. Delicious. How had she never had the guts to order one before?

"Oh, it's really no trouble. It's actually easier for me, because Sammy keeps Benjamin out of my hair. Besides, you can pay me back in scintillating stories."

"Deal." The two friends exchanged smiles.

"So you're all set for tomorrow night?" Piper scooped into her low-fat yogurt and granola.

"I think so. Except for cleaning the house. And upping the onsite accident portion of my homeowner's insurance." Bodily injury and property damage clauses—whoever invented liability insurance must've been a kinkster.

"You'll be fine." Piper waved away the concern with her spoon. "And you should make *him* clean the house."

"I like the way you think." Now *here* was a role model Melanie could finally get behind. Not her mother, so steely in her self-absorption and endless pursuit of perfection. Not her sister, whose husband and kids tracked her career marathon from the sidelines. Not her father and brother, enablers and escapists. But beautiful, down-to-earth, hysterical Piper, who balanced family and a personal-organizer career and sexual adventures with aplomb. Hanging up shelving systems into wall studs by day; boffing well-hung studs at night.

For the first time ever, Melanie really believed in the possibilities: a successful business of her own, as many clients as her cell phone could fit names. Sex on tap and on her terms. And of course, she already had her precious little boy. At least she'd hopped on the baby-making train before it left the station.

Melanie's life could be as a delicious as a skinny mocha latte. All she had to do was have the guts to order it up.

Nothing could stop her now.

"Well, there you are! So glad I got you. I had almost forgotten what your voice sounded like." A reprimand as a greeting. Trust Melanie's mother, Queen Victoria, to prick her only bubble of joy in ages.

Why did I even answer it? No good can come of this, Melanie lamented. *Still, she's my mother. Can't avoid her forever.*

"Hello, mother. How are you?" She leaned the Swiffer mop against the kitchen island. Client No. 1, coming tonight, shouldn't have to crawl over month-old sandwich crumbs. Not his first time here anyway.

"Better now that I know my offspring is still alive. I assume my grandson and your husband are too?"

"Yes, Sammy's fine. We're all fine." So much easier to lie. "We've just been really busy."

"Too busy for your child's only grandparents within driving distance?" Victoria shot to the point. "When are we going to get to see him again? And you too, of course."

Melanie sighed. Children should have good relationships with their grandparents; all the books said so. But if only this particular grandparent were warmer and fuzzier, like the ones pictured in the books. Bearing cookies and wrinkles, not pushing diets and harboring a Botox addiction.

Grandparents were supposed to be cheerful helpers. On-call babysitters who didn't consider it babysitting. Spoiling the kid with sugary treats and "Don't tell your mom" winks, not stuffing him with "character-building" activities.

Melanie wanted to protect Sammy from her mother, from the perfectionism aimed like a laser beam and cutting just as sharp. Once-a-month visits had been plenty, and Melanie had always stuck around for the duration. Ironic how her mama-bear protection instinct kicked in around her own mother.

"We'll come visit soon, Mom. But now is not a good time." *Because Dan has abandoned us. Because I'm nearly broke. Because my first paying S&M client is coming in a few hours.* "Sammy's really into his friends these days, could care less about grown-ups. And I think…" *I think you and Dad would keel over and die if you knew the truth.* "That it's important to foster his social development as much as possible that way, to…you know, encourage his independence." Would her mother smell the bullshit over the phone?

"Independence?! He's three years old, Melanie, not going off to college. Besides, one day with his grandparents isn't going to destroy his chances for social success." Melanie could just picture Victoria's expression: arched eyebrow, glint in the eye. Burned into Melanie's memory, that look.

She grabbed some cleanser, started scrubbing the counters vigorously. "Soon, OK, Mom? I promise. But really, it's just not a good time right now." *Because Sammy would spill the beans about Dan as fast as he could say "hello."* "So let's just drop it, OK?" She surprised herself with the forcefulness. And curtness.

A pause. "Well, if that's how you feel about it, *fine.*" Had that word ever so obviously meant the opposite? "You're his mother. But any good mother—and I'm not saying you're not a good one; don't get me wrong—but any good mother knows that children need extended family."

Melanie threw the sponge down on the counter and took three deep breaths. Holding back the scream: *Don't you dare tell me how to be a good mother. You could have used lessons yourself!* Very calmly, she replied: "Mom, my phone is almost out of juice. I'll call you soon and we'll set up a visit. Give Dad a hug for me. Bye." How satisfying to click off without even a cursory goodbye. To not take the back seat on one of her mother's power trips for the first time ever.

Melanie laid the phone on the counter. Picked up the sponge and cleanser again. Letting the anger and newfound power fuel her cleaning efforts. Client No. 1 would get a hit of it tonight too. Literally.

Oh, he had no idea what awaited him.

MELANIE STRUGGLED into her new lipstick-red latex catsuit, the baby powder puffing up in little clouds, settling back into the bedroom carpet. Her claw-like press-on nails, in a fiery matching red, threatening to pierce holes in the thin fabric. Donning fetish wear was its own form of torture.

Every blind in the house was shut tight against prying eyes, the heavy curtains pulled closed for good measure. No one would ever know—no one except Piper, babysitting Sammy and probably counting the hours until the juicy recap. Melanie felt like a teenager sneaking out in slutty clothes, except she was in her thirties and staying put.

"Down in Mexico" by The Coasters blasted through the wireless speaker, classic lap dance music. When the catsuit fit like a second skin and she had donned the wig, Melanie swiveled her hips lasciviously, eyeing herself in the full-length mirror. Who was this woman, this wild creature with her scarab-black bob and lips like blood? Every trace of the sorry old Melanie was gone, erased by a godless artist and replaced by the devil's spawn. A cat from hell.

Only for a split second did she question the wisdom of the night's undertaking. *What choice do I have?* she reminded herself. *I need the money. Besides, I want this. Forget about the money. I'd do it for free.* Still, she couldn't quite shake the feeling of prostitution. Even with his penetrating her off the menu, kink seemed like a feast of intimacy; you could penetrate a person more deeply than with mere sexual acts. You could touch their secrets.

Kind of like a psychologist, Melanie landed on. How many jobs involved intimacy and skill that only a trained pro could provide? Psychologist, massage therapist, bikini waxer....Call her just another a service provider—with a service you couldn't find in the Yellow Pages.

The doorbell jolted Melanie out of self-soothing mode. She froze—too early for Client No. 1. Her car in the driveway and the lights on meant no chance to fake nobody home. Dammit. The last thing she needed was some nosy neighbor sniffing out her dirty secret.

Insistent knocking at the downstairs door now. Melanie sighed and shimmied hurriedly out of the skin-tight catsuit, careful not to rip it. No sense wasting her nine lives on fabric with human flesh at future stake.

"Coming, coming!" Irritated. Not that the interrupter could hear down the stairs and through the solid front door anyway. She pulled on her jeans and a T-shirt, forgetting a bra in the rush. Ran down the stairs. *Nothing weird going on here; just a regular night at home knitting sweaters for homeless children in front of the TV.*

A peek through the curtain revealed a young pizza delivery guy. What the hell? Melanie opened the door, annoyed.

"Hi." His eyes immediately dropped to her breasts, bare under the thin white T-shirt. "Uh, that'll be $18.75."

"I didn't order a pizza," Melanie snapped. "You must have the wrong house." She glared at him, then thawed. Just a clueless teenager trying to earn some money, probably to play big spender for a girl. More kindly: "What address are you looking for?"

He handed her the order slip wordlessly, lifting his eyes to hers and away from her breasts with obvious difficulty. Embarrassed. She tilted the paper up to the porch light, outrageous nails gleaming. The boy blushed harder at the nails. Chewed nervously on his lip and shifted from one foot to the other.

"Two doors that way." Melanie handed him back the slip and pointed, the scarlet lacquer catching the porch light.

"Uh, OK. Really sorry to bother you." The boy cleared his throat. "You have a good night." He stepped away from the door, then turned. "Nice nails, by the way."

Melanie grinned at his gutsiness. All those tales of bored housewives luring in delivery guys for a romp. Ha. Most of the housewives she knew were too exhausted to boff their own husbands, let alone the pizza guy.

She briefly pondered blowing his mind entirely: *Come on in and let me show you my new toys.* But no. She had bigger fish to spank.

"Thanks. Have a good night yourself." *Maybe next time. Who knows what I'm capable of now?*

Back safely behind the shut door, Melanie realized a few future adjustments were in order; interruptions were distracting, but worse, they could blow her secret wide open. Tonight, though, she'd have to fly by the seat of her pants. While she was pulling Client No. 1's down for a paddling.

Anyway, you can't plan for everything, remember? Hasn't Dan's leaving made that perfectly clear? I planned the perfect life, and look where it got me.

But wait. *It got me just where I needed to be. My own person, living my own life. I had a plan, but fate's was better.*

The catsuit slid on more easily this time. Then makeup and six-inch red stilettos. Melanie surveyed the final result in the mirror, a long reed-like cane completing the picture. She swished the tail on the catsuit back and forth, slowly. The slick red latex hugged her curves. Yes, here stood the pet of the devil himself.

"Get on your knees." She started rehearsing her lines in the mirror, working on her stern face. Looking every inch the part. Client No. 1 would get his money's worth.

She struck the cane on an open palm. How lovely, the music of reed against skin.

"Melanie Hightower, you've come a long way, baby," she congratulated herself in the mirror. Her mirror self frowned back. Why hold on to Dan's last name? Dan had nothing to do with this— this was *her* show. A solo act.

"Melanie *Merriweather,* you've come a long way, baby." Her mirror self nodded approval. Melanie landed the cane on her palm again. Let out a long, low purr.

Being a hellcat beat being a doormat any day.

MELANIE MERRIWEATHER contemplated the naked ass draped over her dining room chair, stroking it lightly. Hmm, what to do? A spanking, perhaps—nice and reliable. Maybe a paddling, as a press-on nail going rogue in the crack simply wouldn't do. Really she wanted to whack the guy's butt with a frying pan, the ridiculously expensive one Dan had given her for Christmas. Alas, she had already hurled the pan into the outdoor trash bin, ignoring the bin sticker proclaiming GOES TO LANDFILL! RECYCLE IF POSSIBLE. A soda can had more recycling potential than her marriage to Dan now.

The client scratched his butt cheek. Melanie halted midstroke. "Did I say you could scratch?" Dropping each word like an ice chip into a crystal goblet. *Maybe I should tie his hands,* she thought. *Decisions, decisions.* He would pay for making her think so hard—and not just the $150 an hour.

But aha! He had just provided the perfect reason to punish him. Gotta love small favors. Melanie extracted a bamboo cane from the lineup on the polished mahogany dining table, site of so many lovingly prepared family meals, and swiftly struck his rear end. Tingles dancing along her arm. Yum. A good caning tasted even better than her legendary beef bourguignon.

"No, no you didn't. I'm s-s-sorry, Miss." The words a mumble, beads of sweat glistening along his spine. Melanie immediately opted for a set change away from the dining chairs. First rule of dominatrix club: no sweat, blood, or cum stains on the ivory damask upholstery.

Down came the cane on his derriere again. Then she scooped his shirt off the floor with it, a bored highway worker picking up trash. "Wipe yourself up," she ordered. "And if you stained my chair, you'll regret it. That chair cost more than you make in a week."

The client quickly slid off the chair onto all fours, a hand darting out for the dangling shirt. No unsightly splotches on the chair fabric, whew. But how dare he make her worry about upholstery stains! She skewered his naked back with the heel of her scarlet stiletto. Pushed down into the flabby white flesh until his chest was flat on the floor. His blotchy, sweaty face sinking into the swirls of plush carpeting. The carpeting, thankfully, was stain-resistant.

Near-disaster notwithstanding, pleasure bubbled up inside Melanie. Sure, the client's groveling was pathetic. His paunch, pitiable. But gratitude, maybe even tender affection, had entered the ring of her feelings too. The scene's script was writing itself, but she'd happily take the credit. It was hard enough just balancing on the carpet in stilettos.

"Sorry...what?" Another cane stroke. Another thick red line. Now this was accomplishment. Better than earning compliments on her bake-sale brownies or finding the perfect Jimmy Choos for a new dress. Better even than selling the most raffle tickets for her son Sammy's preschool fundraiser. This was power! She owned the control, no doubt about it. She was not someone you would give a *frying pan* to for Christmas, for fuck's sake. Not if you knew what was good for you. Moisture surged in the soft spot between her legs.

"I'm so sorry…Miss."

"Damn right you're sorry." She made her voice low and mean—sharp, to match the heels and nails. Suppressing the pleasure. "You're a sorry, pathetic, sniveling little boy. But you're not half as sorry as you're going to be when I'm finished with you. Lift your head up." Facial checks were important to read how much he could take. Heaven forbid he had a heart attack—her red latex catsuit was meant for private dominatrix sessions, not the ER.

His eyes darted to meet her gaze. She saw trepidation, excitement. Reverence too. *We have a winner!* Melanie bent over. Nuzzled his damp cheek—the one on his face—enjoying her own growing wetness. He had just made another perfect infraction. Infractions and wetness: sweeter than cake and ice cream.

Back went the cane in its precise spot on the table. Out came a smooth leather paddle. "Did I say"—*thwack*—"you could"—*thwack*—"look me in the eyes?" *Thwack thwack thwack.* Electricity crackled through her veins.

"No, Miss. I'm sorry, Miss." His ass glowed a fiery red now, riddled with lines and a purple blotch that would surely bruise. Legs quivering. Time for a break. *Can't have the clients going away unhappy,* Melanie thought. *Bruised, choked, beaten, sure. Unhappy, no.*

"For God's sake, stop blathering. 'Sorry' isn't good enough. I'm sick of hearing your 'sorry's." Dan had never said he was sorry, the bastard. Not when she cried about that stupid frying pan, her face as crumpled as the pink cashmere scarf blotting her tears. Not when he stood her up for their anniversary dinner, the waiter serving up pity and condescension with the chardonnay. Not when he cheated on her with that *waitress,* the one with breasts like unripe cantaloupes because she had never nursed a child the way Melanie had nursed Sammy—the son she *had borne* him, for fuck's sake. And not when he finally left her, taking that soup-slinging whore with him. Leaving only a terse note on the kitchen table and his dirty laundry still in the hamper.

"But don't you worry…" Melanie refocused on the present, shoving the hurtful memories back into the shadows. This was her moment now. "I'm going to give you some help not talking, and the last words I want to hear out of your mouth are 'thank you' for how nice I'm being, even though you don't deserve it." She ground a spiky stiletto heel into his doughy ass for emphasis.

"Th-thank you, Miss." A worshipful whisper, the sweetest music. Time for his reward. Melanie reached around his head and tucked a ball gag in his mouth, pulling the strap's buckle tight. Took her sweet time selecting a dildo from the brand-new rainbow assortment. Good things come to those who wait.

"Purrrrple silicone, purrrrfect," Melanie purred in her crimson catsuit. She dangled the extra-large dildo in front of his eyes, noting with satisfaction the anticipation and fear. At last she allowed him a glimpse of her Cheshire grin, as she reached for the lube.

Melanie would make him suffer, oh yes. Just as she had suffered.

"So how was it?" Piper's whole face was a question mark. She opened the front door before Melanie had even reached the top step.

"Mommyyyyyyy!" Sammy hurtled out the door with the force of a small cannon, flinging himself at her legs. Melanie plopped down on the spot and hugged him tightly.

"Ooh, I missed you, Samster." *While I was torturing a strange man in the dining room.* "Did you have a good time?" She rained kisses on his head, as if to make up for abandoning him aground while she spread her wild wings.

"*Awe*some!" Her son wriggled out of the hug. "Dey have a Wii. Ben teached me to bowl an' I eated dinosaur nuggets. Do we hafta go now?"

Melanie laughed. So much for feeling abandoned. "Fifteen minutes. I want to talk with Piper."

"Sixteen," he countered.

"All right, 16." She kissed him again. "You drive a hard bargain."

"Yay!" He darted back into the house.

Melanie followed Piper inside. "Did Sammy do OK? I hope he didn't drive you crazy."

"Are you kidding? You know it makes my life easier, having him here. And he's a total doll. Now, for the moment we've all been waiting for. *How was it?!* Tell me everything."

Once again Melanie silently thanked the universe for sending Piper her way. Confidante, babysitter, best friend. And maybe one day she'd tag along on one of Piper's sexcapades. If the seemingly bottomless sex well with Clay ever dried up.

They navigated the strewn toys and socks and games on their way to the aqua couch.

"Let's just say he won't be sitting pretty today." Melanie's mind flashed on Client No. 1 splayed on the floor, the dildo protruding from where nothing should protrude. His ass covered in cane welts and paddle bruises. All in a day's work.

Piper sighed. "You're not going to tell me, are you?" A pretty mock pout appeared on her angelic face. More quietly: "Here I am just a bored housewife looking for a titillating tale to keep me going through the dry spells, and you won't even throw me one tiny sordid crumb."

Melanie smiled appreciatively. Her new best friend was more likely to get drilled in orgies by strange men than be bored. There were way more wet spots than dry spells in Piper Lovejoy's life, thanks to the swinging.

"Domme-client privilege. My clients rely on my discretion."

"Oooh, look at you, talking like a pro! Well. I guess you *are* a pro now. And 'clients' plural. Does this mean you have more than one already?"

"Soon enough." Last night's session had gone so well, the client immediately asked for another session the very next week. And Clay, God bless his well-endowed, submissive self, couldn't seem to get enough of her mistressy ministrations. Big plans had been bouncing through Melanie's brain all morning. Marketing, PR, building a client base, a private dungeon space of her own....She would tap all of Clay's marketing expertise sometime when his ever-hard rod wasn't pounding her.

Oh, yes, the future held big things. Bigger even than Clay's hardworking cock.

Chapter 15

"You're Welcome to Do My Bidding Any Day"

EIGHT NEW voicemail messages? Melanie glanced at the number sleepily, hitting snooze on her cell phone alarm. *That's weird,* fluttered through the fog of her 8 a.m. brain. Clay had snuck in and out last night while Sammy slept, the perk of a huge house with good soundproofing, carpeted stairs, and sturdy bedroom locks. But she was paying for that perk in sluggishness and sore girl bits this morning.

Why would I have eight new voicemail messages since last night? Melanie forced herself to wake up and focus. And change the sheets before Sammy came in.

The first voicemail she wrote off as a wrong number:

"This is David Fisher with the SEC. Please call me as soon as you get this message."

The second, could that be a wrong number too?

"This is Courtney Nettle from *The New York Times*. Please call me before you call anyone else."

The third sent a chill up Melanie's spine.

"Oh my God, Melanie, is it true? It's Piper. We can't believe it! Are you OK? Please call me as soon as you get this."

Melanie's head spun as she scribbled the names on a notepad. Those three plus her brother, her sister, her parents, another reporter, and someone from the FBI. All of them wanting her to call right away. None of them telling her what the fuck was going on.

Instinctively, she pulled out the iPad and hit up Yahoo News to scan the headlines. And there it was.

Dan Hightower, founder and CEO of investment firm Hightower Ventures in Palo Alto, California, has been indicted today by a federal grand jury on 14 counts, including conspiracy, securities fraud, wire fraud, and obstruction of justice.

The indictment paints a detailed portrait of how Hightower allegedly bilked investors in what was essentially a giant Ponzi scheme. Allegedly duping them with false reports of higher-than-average returns, Hightower spent the funds on a lavish lifestyle that reportedly includes a $2.3 million home in Palo Alto, luxury cars, trips to five-star resorts around the world, and a private getaway on an island in the Bahamas.

Melanie gaped at the screen. No! Impossible. They didn't even have a house in the Bahamas. Or...did *Dan*? Her eyes swam over the words, floundering in the awful criminal allegations.

Hightower's whereabouts are currently unknown, but he is believed to have fled to Europe recently when the investigations began. If convicted on all counts and given the maximum sentences, Hightower would face prison time and multiple millions in fines, in addition to being forced to return all funds gained illegally. All of his known assets have currently been frozen, but investigators believe portions of those assets remain to be discovered...

Melanie dropped the iPad on the bed and flopped back onto the pillows, too stunned to move. Her brain reeled. All of Dan's money—all of *their* money—gotten illegally? *In a Ponzi scheme?!* Her Prada and Gucci paid for by the IRAs of little old ladies? Their family vacations funded by draining firefighters' pension funds? Melanie's stomach heaved. She bolted for the toilet, retching in dry heaves.

So nonsensical. And yet it all made perfect sense. Dan's secrecy, his lack of good friends, his refusal to be questioned or disagreed with about anything. The creepy spying on her right from the beginning. *No wonder he never wanted a child. Who'd want to bring up a kid in a world of fraud?* Even through the shock, Melanie knew in her heart that every word of the indictment was probably true.

She lay back on the tiled bathroom floor, its coolness calming her. As the situation fully sank in and her wits returned, Melanie realized that fate was actually doing her a favor, meting out justice with a swifter hand than her own.

She had known nothing, hadn't even a clue.

She was innocent.

Dan alone would suffer.

He would lose everything, including possibly his freedom. Whereas Melanie already had lost everything when he left, and gained her freedom in the process. And with the indictment—and the inevitable criminal convictions—no one would fault her for a failed marriage. With the frozen assets, no one would question her seeking financial help.

Melanie would stand among the victims of Dan's fraud, blameless and wronged, and the whole world would see it. She would come out as spotless as new-fallen snow, ready to start a fresh, new life, while Dan rotted in a dirty prison.

Enjoy your hell, you bastard. You made your bed, and you'll lie in it for the rest of your life. Calmly, triumphantly, Melanie picked up the notepad and phone, and called the SEC.

Dan would never, ever have the power to hurt her again.

MELANIE PUT the finishing touches on Sammy's cake with a flourish. Piping HAPPY 4TH BIRTHDAY onto a flag fluttering merrily near Thomas the Train's face. *How fast they grow,* she thought mistily. She could still remember Sammy's expression when he took his first steps, could still hear him forming his first words. Now he was crashing around the house firing off questions:

"Will I get lots of pwesents?"

"When I can open dem?"

"Is deh candy in deh piñata now?"

"When is Benjamin coming, Mommy?"

Sammy and Benjamin had become almost inseparable. Piper and her husband and kids felt like family—especially nice since you don't pay family for babysitting.

There's family you're born with, and family you choose. Where had she heard that? No matter. Melanie was glad to have that chosen family balancing out her birthright today. Dan's investigation, still grabbing news coverage after a month, had only reignited the fire of her mother's and sister's fault-finding. Whatever. Just let them try getting an arrow through her steely new heart.

When the news had broken a month ago, a maelstrom had hit. Raging victims banging on the door at all hours. A rock through the window. Melanie quickly picked the best lawyer of the pro bono dozen chasing the PR gold mine. Her on-camera statement expressed deepest sympathy for the victims, denied all knowledge of the fraud, and pledged full support in the investigation. Her tears flowing as pure and genuine as a country stream: She was a victim too, taken for a ride. Social media instantly cast the majority of its votes in Melanie's favor. Just another clueless, wronged wife. Take a number and get in line.

More important, cash was increasingly pouring in too. Melanie upped her Miss M disguise with dark brown contact lenses and heavier makeup along with the inky short wig to cover her long caramel hair; not even her own mother would have recognized her. A rental car and a dungeon space that charged by the hour completed the anonymity. None of the half dozen new clients had a clue about Melanie's real identity, only plenty of bruise souvenirs and lighter wallets.

The only sign of Dan still: a birthday card for Sammy with a $100 bill tucked inside. *From someone's pension fund? Sammy doesn't even understand money yet, you idiot. A phone call or video chat, now that would have meant something.* But of course fugitives don't Skype. No matter. Hiding out abroad or locked up in prison, Dan was out of their lives. Good riddance to a very bad man.

The postmark on the birthday card was too smudged to read. Melanie had glanced at it and tucked it away for the FBI anyway. Full cooperation.

She eased four candles into the cake and set it on the big dining room table, laid out now with mini sandwiches and fruit kabobs instead of canes and paddles. The big wheeled suitcase held her kinky toys these days, the easier to tote them around—and to keep them hidden at home.

The doorbell rang. Sammy sped over like a locomotive.

"Sammy! Remember, only Mommy opens the door." Extra caution seemed more crucial now than ever, despite the media vindication. Melanie surveyed the table one last time. Juice boxes, sparkling water, bowls of fresh veggies, and festive partyware rounded out the goodies. A perfectly set table in a perfect setting. Losing the house soon seemed inevitable—it would be sold along with everything in it, down to the last sterling fish fork, to give the defrauded some restitution. But right now, Melanie reveled in the perfection of her son's birthday prep. *Martha Stewart, eat your heart out. I'm a pro domme and a pro parent.*

"*Huh*-wee, Mommy! We can't keep deh guests *waiting*," Sammy yelled. Melanie smiled. How many times had she told him that very

243

thing? Her son was turning out to be good-hearted and attentive, very much unlike his dad. Thank goodness the apple had fallen far from *that* tree—no, thank Melanie for that.

Piper could barely be seen on the doorstep under the armfuls of games and toys: whiffle bats covering her face, ring toss parts circling her arms, Hyperdash, Twister, you name it.

"This should keep them all busy for about 20 minutes." She stepped into the entryway. "Wow, nice! You've got enough balloons here to fill Party City."

"Auntie Piper, Auntie Piper! It's my birf-day!" Sammy practically tackled her, as if he hadn't just seen her the day before. Everything tumbled out of Piper's arms inside the entryway. She bent down and ruffled his hair.

"I never would have guessed!" she played along. "So today you're, what"—pretending to study him—"11 years old?" As if they hadn't been discussing his fourth birthday every day for the past month.

Sammy cracked up. "Silly Auntie Piper. I'm four!"

"Four, huh? Well it's a good thing I brought you four presents then." Piper nodded to a big handled bag printed with toy cars.

"Piper, my goodness!" Melanie tried not to frown. "You'll spoil him." *And I couldn't afford four gifts for your kids' birthdays—not yet anyway.*

"Don't worry, they're little presents. Unlike this young man right here, who is looking a whole year more grown-up today." She beamed at him.

"Tell me about it." Melanie reached for the bag. "Sammy, why don't you go put the presents on the side table in the dining room? You can open one now, but the rest are for later. Parties are about people, not presents."

"Yay thanks, Mommy!" He grabbed the bag and ran out.

"I'm so glad you're here." Melanie hugged Piper warmly. "Lots of people had 'previous engagements,' of course. You really learn who your true friends are at a time like this." She dialed her voice down a notch: "Clay is coming too, but I'm not 100 percent sure it's a good idea."

"Why? It's not like he's going to trot out in a dog collar and drink from the hose, is he?" Piper's eyes twinkled mischievously. Trust Melanie's outrageous friend to bring the levity.

"No, we save the dog collar for special occasions." The joke was meant to hide the fact that Melanie had in fact collared and leashed Clay recently. Made him crawl around on all fours while she rode on his back, giggling. Why have a submissive boyfriend if you can't leash him like a puppy and ride him like a pony?

The doorbell rang again, kicking off a parade of parents and kids, including her own parents and her sister's contingent. Melanie had rehearsed her lines well for all the people she hadn't seen in person since the news broke: *Yes, I'll be fine; I'm more concerned about all the victims. No, no one knows where he is exactly yet. I've started doing part-time consulting to support Sammy. Have you tried the smoked-turkey wheels?*

Everyone bore presents along with awkward, sympathetic smiles, like at a postfuneral reception. Yes, Melanie had even considered canceling the party, but she would be damned if Sammy would suffer one unnecessary minute for the sins of his father. *So there's no bread. We can still eat cake.*

Besides, why let Dan's drama hold them back? Melanie had so many plans now, eager to boost business. Next up: a website and guerilla-style marketing. Maybe she'd even branch off into merchandising eventually. Mistress to the masses—how's that for a route to fame and fortune! The whole world would kiss her feet.

She saw BDSM everywhere these days. Her white-haired neighbor domming the hubby during yardwork. Teens sporting spiked leather collars. That supermarket girl apologizing all the time and rushing to find what everyone needed. People might not have the words for it, but they played the S&M game as surely as the dungeon dwellers. Even her own parents...

"My goodness, Melanie, look at all these balloons!" Her mother perfunctorily handed over a large, professionally wrapped gift box and a cheek peck. "Are you trying to stave off wagging tongues with helium?"

"Now Victoria, it looks very festive." Her dad leaned in for a kiss. "Melanie, you did a great job."

"Thanks, Dad. Sammy deserved a real party despite everything."

"I told you we would have rented out the club and paid for everything." Victoria eyeballed a guest's nearby plate. "Had it catered properly."

Shut up, Mom. Just shut up. Enough already! Melanie's new self had no patience for the old ways. She took a deep breath, counting to three. "Sammy wanted it here. I like it here. No one's complaining but you. Why don't you both head out back and get some sun while I check on the food?" She nodded briskly at her mother and walked to the dining room without waiting for a response.

Dan wasn't the only one who would never have the power to hurt her again.

"How's the birthday mom holding up?" Clay snuck up behind her, wrapping his arms around her waist.

Melanie turned, took a step back out of his arms. Enough drama with Dan's scandal. No way would she feed the rumor mill with even a hint of extramarital PDAs.

"Oh, Clay, I'm so happy! Everything's turning out even better than I expected." Melanie's eyes sparkled.

A little girl from Sammy's class skipped over. "I like your house. It's really pretty."

"Thank you, sweetie. I always thought having pretty things was important." Melanie took in the girl's fluffy dress with ruffled underskirt and bow. "But you know what?"

"What?" The girl's face so fresh and sweet. Melanie had once been that innocent.

"It's not as important as having people who really love you."

The girl shrugged. "I have lots of people who love me. My mom, my dad, my cat, all my friends…and when I grow up I'm gonna have lots of babies and they'll love me too." She twirled, watching the dress flare out in a perfect circle.

Melanie's stomach tightened. She had once wanted a big family. Sayonara to *that* dream. "You can do a lot more than just have babies, you know."

246

"I *know*." As in, *duhhhhh*. "I'm going to be a gymnast and a scientist and a hairstylist too."

Melanie laughed. "Sounds like a plan."

"OK, bye." And the pretty little partygoer skipped away, toward the backyard. Piper was setting up the games, luring the kids outside like a siren song.

"Hey, Clay." Melanie glanced around. No one within earshot, good. "Thank you for everything. Really. You've changed my life."

He leaned in, his mouth just brushing her ear. "So you'll be keeping me around a while? I've gotten rather fond of doing your bidding." He drew back again, grinning like a schoolboy on the first day of summer break.

"You're welcome to do my bidding any day." Melanie's eyes said what her body couldn't, not at her four-year-old's birthday party, not when no one but Piper knew that her marriage had definitely moved to splitsville. Not when human-pony riding was her new favorite sport. "By the way, if anyone asks, I'm a consultant. The hospitality industry."

His mouth again just glanced against her ear. "I find your catsuit *very* hospitable." Then, out loud, slyly: "Ah, I see there's a piñata out back. Care for a whack?"

"You know I do."

"Mommy, Mommy!" Sammy rushed over, trailed by three friends. "Can we do deh piñata now? Pleeeeeease?" Grabbing her hand.

Melanie glanced at the clock on her cell phone, noting several new voicemails from numbers she didn't recognize. New potential punching bags? Could be; a well-beaten client makes the best calling card. More likely reporters asking about Dan, though. Clueless that the juicier story of her double life lay right under their noses. What a thrill that gave her.

"Alrighty, piñata time it is," she answered. Sammy's eager face glowed up at her. Her sunshine. A wave of love and happiness almost knocked her over. The worst part of her life would soon pass. The sun had defeated the storm, shining down on a new and better world. A world in which Dan suffered, Melanie answered to no one, and sex and love flowed as freely as water.

She scooped Sammy off his feet. Razzed his tummy. Listening delightedly to his elated squeals. "Let's go!" she enthused. "When it breaks, you get to make a wish."

Once upon a time, Melanie did nothing but wish and wait and hope. Now, she realized, she would have more than she ever knew to wish for. She could finally spy truly exciting adventures on the near horizon.

No more waiting for anyone or anything to make those adventures happen.

At last, her life had begun.

Acknowledgments

KEITH KORMAN, you found the gold in the muck and championed this from the start, and I will be forever grateful. Oleksandra Godlevska, thank you for your lovely cover illustration that helped bring this book to life. David Delp, you always inspire me and are such a wonderful friend and supporter—I appreciate you! D.Z., thank you for the early read and the encour-agement and, of course, the forever friendship. Many thanks to each and every other early reader, reviewer, and supporter. Thank you to my parents for always supporting my career as a writer even while knowing nothing about what I write. C.V., thank you for always being in my corner and being a force for good in the world. And my darling L.H., thank you for being one of my greatest teachers and for bringing more joy to my life than I ever could have imagined.

Thank You

Your support as a reader makes writing a joy. Without you, I'd likely be fighting loneliness while typing away all day by myself in pajamas. With you, writing feels more like a reward than work. If you like this book, please do consider leaving a nice review on Goodreads, Amazon, or somewhere else, and letting your friends know. Thank you!